A DEMON'S TALE

A DEMON'S TALE

The Lies We Believe

MICHELLE PENTIFALLO

© 2026 Michelle Pentifallo
All rights reserved.

Cover Art: Louise Lobo
Interior Art Beginning Each Chapter:
Hope Marie Vallentine Chapters 1, 3, 5, 6, 9, 10, 11, 12
Meyre Assis Augusto Chapters 2, 4, 7, 8, 13
Amanda Dinan Chapters 14, 15, 16

No part of this book may be reproduced, distributed, or transmitted in any form or by any means—electronic or mechanical—including photocopying, recording, or any information storage and retrieval system—without the prior written permission of the author, except for brief quotations used in reviews or scholarly works.

This book is a work of fiction. Names, characters, places, and events are either the product of the author's imagination or used fictitiously. Any resemblance to actual persons, living or dead, or actual events is purely coincidental.

For bulk orders, contact the publisher:
New Life Publishing House
admin@newlifepublishinghouse.life

ISBN: Print 978-1-961787-16-2
ISBN: Digital 978-1-961787-17-9
LCCN 2026902991

First edition, 2026

Contents

Introduction	ii
Chapter One: Words That Hurt	1
Chapter Two: Soul Stealing	38
Chapter Three: Family Roots	60
Chapter Four: Feeding Frenzy	83
Chapter Five: Out of Time	111
Chapter Six: The Voice of Lust	125
Chapter Seven: Let's Get Down to Business	142
Chapter Eight: Whose Life Is It Anyway?	158
Chapter Nine: Control Center	194
Chapter Ten: No Place to Go	209
Chapter Eleven: Death's Door	225
Chapter Twelve: Confused	240
Chapter Thirteen: No Life to Live	261
Chapter Fourteen: Ray of Light	270
Chapter Fifteen: No Way Out	294
Chapter Sixteen: Rusty Bumper Final Death	308

Introduction

A Demon's Tale: A Book About Life and Who Is in Your Driver's Seat

Please take a moment to ask yourself if you have ever felt out of control of your life and truly believed it was all your fault. What if you are wrong? What if, in fact, you are not in the driver's seat, but someone else is in charge, and you have no idea? It is not someone you can see or hear audibly, but a voice you hear in your head that sounds just like you. In the flickering neon sprawl of New Terra's megacities, where neural implants pulse with encrypted thoughts, this voice slithers through the static, alien, yet familiar. It may tell you something so off the wall you feel like you are a stranger in your own mind, but somehow, after listening to it long enough, it begins to sound, and even act, just like you. It is a different version of you, but somehow, you are no longer in your own driver's seat.

In some way, you have given over complete control, and someone else is driving as fast as they can in your truck, the truck of your life, with mistakes and mishaps along the way, yet packaged as your ideas. You mistakenly think you are in control, driving 110 miles an hour down the highway with no place to go and no end in sight. You sense the never-ending trail of lies and deceit, not remembering how it started, but recalling that faint voice in your head so long ago that it no longer sounds like a stranger. It began, perhaps, as a glitch in the neural net wired to optimize your mind, but now it is a lifelong friend that doesn't even consult you anymore for your own decisions. In fact, you don't even want this truck anymore.

You are ready to get out of this vehicle and move on, but you can't see a way out.

Let this book help you open the door and get out, or allow someone to help you open the door, so you can get off this highway and out of this life to a new and improved you, someone ready to drive your own thoughts and actions once again. In a world where algorithms predict your desires and shadows whisper your choices, this book is your guide to breaking free. This edgy series of stories will take you down paths of different people with life choices seemingly made for them, that have led them to places of no return. Or so it seems. They know there is a better life somewhere, but they just aren't sure it's for them. They are lost and need hope for a better future. This redemptive story is a narrative to help even the most lost person find their way again. There is a way out of the passenger's seat, so to speak, and the goal of this book is that you, the reader, will find a glimpse of yourself and no longer feel alone. The desire, quite frankly, is that you will see that the beginning of your end didn't even come from yourself; it came from a demon's tale, a shadow in the system that can be overcome with courage and clarity.

LET THE STORY BEGIN

As the sun shone through the trees onto her face, she could feel a sense of relief. There she was, standing tall and raising her head to the sun, feeling the victory of so many years. In the fractured biosphere of New Terra, where synthetic forests pulsed with data vines, her triumph glowed brighter than the holo-displays that once clouded her mind. So many generations before her had battled the same demons that had haunted them, haunted her, and now, at last, they were gone. It took years of focus, hard work, and trust that He would take her to a new place. A place where she could be at peace. A place where she would no longer be looking over her shoulder or feeling the presence of darkness behind her, staring at her. No longer did the neural whispers—the coded demons of the Nexus taunt her thoughts, steering her life's truck into chaos. This was a new place, with trees, limbs, moss, and vines all around her, their bioluminescent glow a testament to her reclaimed freedom. No longer was she afraid that the vines would entangle her and take her down. Victory was hers. She had won. She had won for generations to come, and now it was her duty to reach those with the same fate, to show them the path to seize their own driver's seat. In the distance, she hears, "Hey, Sam!" And she turns to see her friend, a figure emerging from the shimmering undergrowth, "Hey, Tia!"

1
WORDS THAT HURT

I have her exactly where I want her: crumpled on the floor, tears streaming down her face. This is easier than I ever imagined. I am Fear, and Samantha is mine.

Words That Hurt

When she was born, I watched from the shadows as followers of the Father of Light prayed over her, dedicating her to Him. I thought my assignment would end there, that I'd be sent elsewhere. But humans are so predictable. It took mere weeks for her parents to unravel their blessings. I still hear the echo of her father's voice, heavy with disdain: "She's just like your mother, Jo Anne. She never stops crying." Days earlier, they'd wept tears of joy, speaking life over their daughter. Now, dissatisfaction had opened the door for me.

Samantha. That's her name. How fragile her father was, giving up so quickly. I've lingered with some humans their entire lives, watching them die, still bound to me. But these two? They surrendered their child to my influence in weeks. Humans receive blessings from the heavens, yet they're never satisfied. It's almost too easy.

I waited outside their home at 18356 Destiny Road, patient as ever. The insults soon flowed like a river. "Well, George, she has your insomnia. Now both of you will keep me awake. I can't even feed her because she nurses constantly. She won't take a bottle." Jo Anne's words were an invitation, and the door swung wide for me to enter.

I settled in, knowing my full-time assignment from the Father of Darkness was imminent. My excitement grew as I crafted lies they'd believe without question. I'm convincing like that. I reveled in the plots I'd weave to tear them apart, my arsenal of destruction ready.

"Where do you think you're going, Jo Anne?" George snapped. "You don't need coffee with a friend. All you do is sit around and complain, just like your dad. This baby has only made you worse." They played into my hands, and that day, I claimed their home as mine.

Nearly eighteen years later, little has changed. I recall when Samantha took her first steps. Her parents cheered, their faces alight with pride. But hours later, George drowned himself in rum, my special blend, laced with hate and rage. That night, as Samantha toddled past the table, he knocked her down. Her head struck the wall, and her screams pierced the air. Jo Anne rushed to console her, but George just walked away.

Now, Samantha sobs on her bed, a symphony to my ears. She turns eighteen next week, and then I can intensify my grip. Humans are foolish, casting out their young at eighteen, unaware of the influence they relinquish. If they knew, they might fight harder. But with Samantha Sammy, as they call her, it hardly matters. Her parents stopped caring five years ago when she started lying. The first time she was caught, Jo Anne was devastated, and George's anger erupted. Anger, my oldest ally, always delivers.

They ambushed her after school, yelling the moment she walked through the door. "What are you, an idiot, Sam? Did you think we wouldn't find out you were lying?" Jo Anne's voice was a crescendo, and I pulled up a chair to savor the chaos. I leaned close to George, hissing, "Tell her she's one of your biggest disappointments."

He stiffened, then spat, "You are one of my biggest disappointments."

Samantha's eyes widened, tears spilling over. I laughed, delighted. Jo Anne didn't need my prompting. Her words came like fire: "You've been trouble since the day you were born." A new curse settled over Samantha, a shroud only I could see. More of my kind would join me soon. The more we are, the weaker she becomes. As she fled to her room, I relished the moment this began, eager for the pain that awaited her, pain she couldn't yet fathom.

How did I end up here? Samantha's thoughts pull me back to the present. She's on a ledge, figuratively and perhaps literally, her journal open before her. *A Harvard graduate, with everything at my fingertips, and I've lost it all. My addiction stole the life I wanted. How did I let this happen? It's my fault, and there's nowhere to go but down.*

I chuckle, a low, sinister sound. She thinks she hears me, her head tilting slightly. That laugh, she's heard it before. When she wrapped her car around a pole in college, writhing in pain, she heard it. Last year, in bed with Huron, she heard it again, mistaking it for the TV. It's me, always me, lurking in her darkest moments.

Am I going crazy? She writes, her pen trembling. *I'm so tired. Maybe if I sleep, I won't feel the urge to jump. But what's the point?*

She senses me watching. "What the hell, dude! Who said you could read my journal?" she snaps at Kevin, her friend lounging nearby.

"I didn't see anything, Sam. Relax," he says, raising his hands.

"Yeah, sure. You can't keep your mouth shut, Kevin."

"It's no big deal. I didn't read it."

"It's private! I've kept journals since I was a teenager, and *no one* reads them!"

"Jeez, Sam, chill. I didn't see anything."

"You better not be lying."

"I'm not. Can we go to Charlie's now? There's this new bartender I'm eyeing."

"Eww, Kevin, TMI," she laughs, her tension easing. Her secret, her desire to end it all, remains hidden. *If anyone knew, they'd treat me like a pariah*, she thinks. *When I do it, I won't hesitate, pills, a bridge, no chance for rescue.*

They sit on the grass outside her dorm, the sun warming the butterfly tattoo on her shoulder. She closes her eyes, remembering her father tossing her into the air as a child, the sun blinding her. *He always caught me. I wish he'd catch me now. But who catches a loser?* Her father's last words echo: "No one wants to hang out with a loser like you. Get out and don't come back."

She was eighteen, days from graduation. She stayed with a neighbor that night, her mother already gone. Jo

Anne had packed her bags months earlier, saying, "I can't take it anymore, Sammy. I'll see you at graduation." She never showed. Samantha doesn't know if she's alive.

Kevin's stare pulls her back. "Ready to go, diva? I'm on a mission."

"Fine," she giggles. "You don't like my ripped yoga pants and tank top?"

"Not for Charlie's, girl. Go change."

"I'll meet you in the parking lot in thirty. I'm driving, so I'm not drinking. I've got class tomorrow."

"Boring. Have a drink with me."

"I'll think about it." She gathers her journal and heads to her room, passing a girl crying on her bed. *New kid,* she thinks, unwilling to get involved. *I've got my own mess.*

Inside her room, her bed is neatly made, adorned in navy blue and yellow. Flowers sit on the nightstand beside a lamp and a photo of her grandparents. The shade is drawn, dimming the afternoon light. *Will it always be like this?*

Her roommate, Amber, greets her. "Hey, Sam! Heading to Charlie's with Kevin?"

"Yeah. You coming?"

"Maybe later." Amber slips out, her voice trailing, "See you!" before Samantha can respond.

In the closet, Samantha grabs a sundress and sandals. Glancing in the mirror, she sees her frown. *They're right. I'm a loser.* She pulls her hair into a messy bun, adds mascara, lip gloss, and matching earrings. It'll do.

I watch, my voice a whisper. "She's in college now, away from home, time to turn up the heat. Let's follow her, Insecurity. That crying girl down the hall can wait."

"Fine," Insecurity grumbles. "I wanted to watch her fall apart."

"No time. Samantha's ours now."

I push the blinds aside and peer down at the parking lot. Kevin's there, chatting with Brie Hodges. *What a piece of work.* I shove my journal into the locking drawer, turn the key, and toss it into my bag. Flicking off the light, I pull the door shut, lock it, and head downstairs.

"There's my girl!" Kevin's voice booms as he wraps his arms around my waist. "Missed you, Sam!"

"Whatever." I push him away, glancing at Brie. "Hey, Brie." My tone is flat, barely polite. "You ready, Kev?"

"Born ready, love. Let's roll. Catch you at Charlie's, Brie!"

Is she seriously coming? I bite my tongue, but the thought burns.

"See you later, Kevin," Brie says, her voice gratingly whiny.

As Kevin slides into the car and shuts the door, I can't hold back. "Why the hell did you invite Brie?"

"Chill, she's fun," he says, unfazed.

"She's dating John."

"And you're still into him."

"Shut up."

"Oh, come on, Sam. You *look* at him. What's the deal?"

"It doesn't matter."

"Spill it!"

I sigh. "Fine. I met John in my freshman year. We studied together, and I thought it was going somewhere. That's it."

"More, mi amore!" Kevin's grin is relentless.

"There's nothing else."

"Sam, come on!"

"It doesn't matter, Kev."

"It does," he insists, his voice hitting that high-pitched, I-won't-drop-it tone.

"Alright! He asked me out one night. We had an amazing time. Then Brie showed up a few months later, and that was it."

"No way, girl. You're holding out. Spill the tea. I'm your bestie, why haven't you told me this?"

"It's a sore spot," I mutter.

"Who else are you gonna tell? Your journal?"

"Low blow, Kevin!"

"Sorry, sorry. Just tell me."

I hesitate, then relent. "He texted me the day after our date, said he had a great time. I felt the same. We planned another date for next week. We talked on the phone, saw each other at school it was going great. He picked me up and took me to this incredible restaurant. After we walked in the park, talked, and he kissed me. It was perfect. We were sitting on a bench when he got a call from his mom. His face went pale. 'I have to go,' he said. 'My dad had a heart attack.' He drove me home, apologized for not walking me to the door, and kissed me softly." My mind drifts back to that moment, his sad eyes locked on mine. "'I'm so sorry, Samantha,' he said. 'I had a great time. I'll see you soon.' That was it."

"You're kidding!" Kevin's eyes widen. "That's it?"

"What do you want? There's nothing more."

"He came back and ghosted you?"

"He was gone the rest of the year. No calls, no texts."

"That's the saddest thing I've ever heard, Sam."

"Yeah, well, that's what happens when you're a loser." The word slips out, raw and unguarded. *Shit, I said it out loud.*

"Sam, stop. You're not a loser." Kevin's voice is firm, but he doesn't know the half of it.

I, Fear, chuckle from the shadows. "Slam dunk, Insecurity! Diverting, John crushed her, and now she despises Brie. Bonus points!"

Insecurity grins sheepishly. "Thanks, Fear."

"Add it to the Fuck-with-Samantha list," I say. "Planting those thoughts that John would never accept her? Genius."

"I threw in some extra doubt," Insecurity adds, a spark of pride in its voice.

"I'd say I couldn't do better, but we both know I can." Our laughter fills the air, unheard by the humans.

Samantha's voice cuts through my glee. "I saw him at the library one day. I was at a table, raised my hand to wave, but then I saw him grab Brie's hand. He kissed her forehead, pulled her close, and they walked to the history section. I'm not sure if he saw me, but I grabbed my stuff and bolted. I felt humiliated."

"Why?" Kevin asks.

"He didn't even say hi. I must've screwed up on our date, and he lied to me."

"You don't know that, Sam."

"Don't I? We had this amazing date, and he never called. Not even a text. What the hell?"

"Whoa, girl, you don't usually talk like that."

"Well, I do now."

"Let me do some recon, find out what happened."

"No way, Kevin!"

"Why not?"

"It's done. He's with Brie. It's over."

"You don't know that."

"Kevin, drop it. If he wanted to talk, he's had time. I saw him at Panera once. He smiled and kept walking."

"What a jerk!"

"No, I'm just not what he wants."

"That's ridiculous," Kevin says, shaking his head.

The red neon glow of "Charlie's" interrupts us. I pull into the parking lot, and the conversation dies.

"Hey, Kevin!" someone shouts from a table across the room as we step inside.

"Hey, bitches! Your VIP has arrived!" Kevin hollers back. I roll my eyes, scanning the bar. My heart stops. John. We were just talking about him, and there he is, alone. Where's Brie? We left her on campus. A whisper slithers into my ear: "Go talk to him." I whip around, but it's just the door behind me. Turning back, I catch John's gaze, or maybe he's looking through me.

"Samantha," he slurs, barely audible. "How are you doing?" He stands, wobbling toward me.

"Now the party starts," I, Fear, hiss. "Brie's not here, and Samantha hasn't seen John in months. Insecurity, grab Doubt and Anger. We need backup."

"On it," Insecurity says. "They're probably at the dorms. We'll be back fast."

"Hold the fort," I reply, lingering in the shadows.

"Hey, John." My voice trembles, my whole body shaking. "Good to see you."

"Been a while," he says.

"Yeah, a year and a half, I'd say." Sarcasm drips from my words.

"I'm sorry about that."

"Oh, really?" My anger flares. "You're sorry?"

"You gotta forgive me, Samantha. I didn't mean to ignore you."

"Didn't mean to? How do you accidentally ghost someone? That's bullshit." I turn toward the exit, my heart pounding.

He grabs my arm, pulling me back. "Don't go, please," he pleads, desperation in his voice. I struggle, then freeze, caught by the same soft, sad eyes from that night in his car. I stay, staring into them.

"Thank you," he says softly. "Can we talk?"

"Now? You've been drinking, John. How's this gonna go well?"

"Please," he insists, his grip firm but earnest. Those eyes, I can't resist them.

"Fine. But put that drink down and get a coffee. I'm not dealing with your drunk ass saying something stupid."

"Sam, can I call you that?"

"Everyone does."

"I won't say anything I don't mean. I've been rehearsing this since the night you left my car."

My mind reels. Is this good? Bad? Is he lying? "Come with me," he says, taking my hand. We head to a corner table, leaving his glass on the bar. He orders a coffee from the waitress, Lacey, whose name tag reads. He seems too familiar with her, and a pang of doubt hits me.

"Sure, John. I'll bring it right over, plus some water. You want something, sweetie?" Lacey's kind eyes meet mine.

"Dirty martini, extra olives," I say, my voice steady despite the storm inside. I need something strong to get through this, not some soft drink. I keep my composure, hiding how much John's presence unnerves me. He pulls out my chair, gesturing for me to sit, then drags his chair close. His head drops into his hands, and I fight the urge to stroke his hair, aware of prying eyes. Slowly, he lifts his gaze, tugging at his hair as he wipes a tear from his cheek. He's a wreck. My anger fades, replaced by a pang of empathy.

"What's wrong?" I ask softly, unsure if I want the answer but needing closure to move on. I haven't dated since he left, and I'm clearly not over him. Let him live his fairy tale with Bitchface. I just need to let go.

"I don't know where to start, Sam." His words tumble out frantically, like he's racing to unburden himself. "That night I left you, I didn't know what I'd find at home. I lost myself. I got there, and my dad was dead on the floor. My mom was curled up in the closet, too broken to call 911. The EMTs arrived, but it was too late. My mom fell apart, and I couldn't get back to school. When I finally saw daylight again, I knew you'd be furious. I was a coward…" He trails off, looking away, wiping more tears he thinks I don't see.

"Here's your coffee, two waters, and your martini, sweetie," Lacey says, her voice tinged with concern.

"Put it on my tab," John says firmly, cutting off my attempt to protest.

"I'll bring another in a few," Lacey replies, heading back to the bar.

John sips his coffee, collecting himself. "So, how are you?" he asks, his tone suddenly gentle, almost dismissive of his earlier frenzy.

"I'm okay, I guess." I want to scream, 'I'm great, asshole!' but I can't. His sadness stops me from adding to his pain.

"You look fabulous, by the way," he says, catching me off guard.

"Would Brie be thrilled to hear that?" My voice rises, sharp with resentment.

"Who cares what she thinks?" he snaps. "She's great, don't get me wrong, but she's not…" His words hang, unfinished. He shakes his head. "Anyway, I did most of my classes online until I could function again. Brie was in my first in-person class, sitting next to me. She was kind, and I was lonely. That's it."

I take a long sip of my martini, the sting of olives grounding me. That's your story? I want to shout, but the words stick. Standing, I say, "I need to go."

"Don't." He grabs my arm, tighter than before, his eyes pleading. "Please."

"I'm just going to the ladies' room, John. I'll be back." My tone is harsher than intended. He releases me, and I saunter, though I want to sprint.

In the restroom, I lock myself in a stall, tears blurring my vision. Sobs wrack my body, and I can't breathe. Get it together, Samantha. A familiar voice hisses, "See, you're a loser. You can't even hold it together. He doesn't want you."

"Shut up!" I yell.

"I didn't say anything," a quiet voice from the next stall replies.

"Sorry, talking to myself," I mutter.

"I get it, honey. I do it too. You okay?" she asks, concerned.

"Yeah. Guys, you know."

"Tell me about it."

I, Fear, growl. "I don't like John explaining himself. Sam's softening. Anger, stir something up."

"On it," Insecurity says, darting off.

I wipe my eyes, steady my breathing, and step out. The mirror shows no trace of tears, but my heart's a traitor. Pull it together. I return to the table, only to find

Brie in my seat, yelling, her hands flailing. "Samantha again? You never stop talking about her, John! I'm done!" She grabs my martini, hurls it at him, olives scattering across his lap, and turns to me. "He's all yours!" she screams, storming out, her hot pink pumps clicking furiously.

I freeze, wanting to yell, What the hell? But she's gone. John wipes his face, laughing uncontrollably.

"What was that?" I ask, stunned.

"Nothing. Just Brie throwing a fit, as usual."

"Didn't go well, huh?"

"Nah, it never does when I mention you." Our eyes lock, and my stomach drops. He grabs my hand, pulling me to my chair. "Please, sit. Talk to me."

"Shouldn't you go after her?"

"Probably, but we were over before we started." He exhales sharply. "I tried to move on, Sam. I couldn't. I loved you then. I love you now."

The room spins. He didn't just say that. My heart races, but doubt bites. "This is how you show it? You're an idiot!" I wrench free and bolt for the door, hearing him chase me. I reach my car, fumbling with my keys, but he catches me, pulling me into his arms. His lips find mine before I can protest. I push back, but who am I kidding? I've waited for this. I melt into the kiss, unsure how long it'll last but craving every second.

He pulls back, staring at me. I snap to my senses. "You wait until now? You're a coward." I shove him aside, open my car door, and slam it shut. Starting the engine, my heart fractures. What am I doing? I want to stay, but fear of another betrayal drives me away. I make it to a gas station, nearly out of fuel. As I shut off the car, tears flood out.

"I don't want to cry for him!" I scream. "I've shed enough tears. This is insane!" But the tears won't stop, and my internal battle changes nothing. He needs to hear me. I refuel, pay, and head back to Charlie's, determined. John's not in the lot, so I park and walk inside.

"Hey, love! Where'd you go?" Kevin shouts from the bar. I wave, focused on one thing: finding John.

"You looking for John?" someone asks.

"Yes!"

"He just left."

I turn and race out, knowing his secret spot. He took me there once, upset about his mom. I speed toward the airport parking garage, ignoring a stop sign, my heart pounding. Climbing the winding ramp, I see him at the top, leaning against the cement barrier, watching planes take off. I park, slam my door, and march toward him.

"I hoped you'd come," he whispers, his bloodshot eyes meeting mine. He's been crying too.

I open my mouth to unleash my anger, but instead, I ask, "Are you okay?"

"You're such a loser," Fear's voice sneers in the wind. I ignore it. I won't hurt him as he hurt me—that would make me no better.

"I'm not okay, Samantha," John says. "I was wrong. I was a coward, like you said. Those words haunt me every day. I should've fought for you. I've loved you since we met. It was instant, like I knew you were the one. But I let my life pull me away." He looks down, ashamed, unable to meet my gaze.

I want to agree, to lash out, but my heart won't let me. I've dreamed of these words, and despite my fear, I love him too. "I don't know what to say, John. Maybe tonight's not the time. Let's go home and talk tomorrow. I can drive you; you shouldn't be driving like this."

"Sam, I'm sober now. When the love of your life drives away, and you don't know if she'll return, you wake up fast."

"You just called me the love of your life?" I stare, stare; his tear-filled eyes locked on mine.

"Yes," he whispers, his voice breaking.

My heart sinks, my mind doubting. I stand frozen, watching tears stream down his face. Finally, I reach up, cupping his cheeks. "Took you long enough to admit it," I say, a sincere smile breaking through. I wipe his tears, my voice soft. "What are we gonna do with you?"

He exhales, pulling me into an embrace, not just a hug, but a promise: I won't let you go. And I believe him.

Sunlight spills through the slats of my window shade, painting stripes across my bed. I want to sink back into sleep, but the sun won't let me. Blinking, I realize it's well past morning. The room is empty, my roommate gone. I grab my phone: 1:16 p.m. "Shit!" I yell. "I slept all day!" I missed both my classes. Frustration bubbles, but last night's events flood back, and a grin spreads across my face. I squeal, joy overtaking anger.

Four unread texts await: Grandma, Kevin, John, and a jeans ad. My mind replays last night, and my smile widens. I reach for John's message, but Fear's voice hisses, You're a loser. He was pranking you. I shake it off, but the doubt lingers. What's the worst that can happen? He says he didn't mean it, and I'm back to being lonely as hell. I open Grandma's text instead.

HI DARLING. I MISS YOU. LOOK FORWARD TO SEEING YOU TONIGHT.

"Damn it," I mutter. I forgot I'm supposed to visit Grandma tonight and need to grab dessert. Next, Kevin's texts:

WHAT THE FUCK HAPPENED LAST NIGHT? I WANT THE DISH, GIRL! CALL ME!

An hour later: GIRL, WHERE ARE YOU?

Thirty minutes after that: ARE YOU OK?

I type, I'm fine. Just woke up and hit send. The message delivers, and I hesitate before opening John's, squinting as I read: I KNOW OUR LIVES WILL CHANGE FOREVER AFTER LAST NIGHT. WHEN CAN I SEE YOU?

My eyes widen, and I squeal again. He wants to see me! Fear's voice tries to creep in, but my heart drowns it out. I've waited too long for this. I WOULD LIKE THAT, I reply. His response is instant: PHEW! I THOUGHT YOU WEREN'T GOING TO WANT TO SEE ME.

Unbelievable. He really wants me. WHEN IS GOOD FOR YOU? I send.

HOW ABOUT NOW?

UM, I'M IN MY PJs.

PERFECT! LUNCH?

OK. SANDWICH BARN IN AN HOUR.

MAKE IT 45 MIN. I CAN'T WAIT THAT LONG.

DEAL.

I catapult out of bed, showering in ten minutes flat. Toweling off, I grab black yoga pants, a pink tank top, and a matching bra and panties. I slip on socks and tennis shoes, pull my hair into a messy bun, and wipe steam from the mirror of steam. You look different today, Samantha Lee. Your life is changing. I smile, slip on my favorite earrings, and check myself in the full-length mirror. My roommate, Amber, stands in the doorway as I open it.

"Hey, Sam! Where are you off to, looking all cute?" she asks.

"I'm going to see John!" I call, breezing past her.

She stares, confused. I shrug and practically skip down the hall. "See you later!"

I rush to my car, but the engine won't turn over. What? The overhead light glares, left on all night. Dead battery. I'm so stupid. My glee sours to frustration. Way to sabotage the day, Samantha. I slam my hands against the steering wheel, screaming, "You're such a loser!"

A knock on the passenger window startles me. John's sheepish grin greets me. I step out, peering over the car roof. "Having trouble?" he asks, flashing a warm smile. "And for the record, you're not a loser."

"What are you doing here?"

"Couldn't wait to see you."

"How'd you know where I live?"

"I know more than you think, Sam." He holds out a Starbucks cup. "One grande caramel macchiato, two pumps, coconut milk."

I raise an eyebrow. "How'd you know that?"

"As I said, I know more than you think."

"Are you stalking me, John Francis Tate?"

"Maybe a little, Samantha Lee White." He grins, and I can't help but laugh.

"Right now, I'm okay with that. I like it." This is precisely what I needed.

"So, what's up with your car?"

"Dead battery. Light's on."

"Let me take a look."

"Nah, later," I say, as he pulls me close, kissing my forehead, breathing me in. "I missed that smell."

"What smell?"

"The smell of you."

I giggle. "You're ridiculous. I don't have a smell."

"Oh, you do." He kisses me gently, then steps back. "I'd better behave. Don't want to scare you off on our first day together." His words float like a soft breeze.

"Let's go to the zoo," he suggests. "We can talk and have fun."

"Love that. I have a yearly pass I go at least once a month." Does he know that, too? I push the thought aside. He guides me to his car, a sleek black 2017 Mercedes-Benz C300 with silver rims. "Nice car, John."

"Thanks. I came into some money after my dad died. Life insurance. Horrible way to get it, but Mom insisted I buy something to lift my spirits." He stops, shifting gears. "You hungry?" He opens my door, kissing the top of my head before closing it.

"I could eat." He slides into the driver's seat, the engine purring to life. "So, where to?" he asks, rubbing his hands together boyishly.

"I thought we said Sandwich Barn?"

"Oh, right. Got caught up." He flashes a smile, grabbing my hand as we pull out. His phone pings repeatedly.

"Should you check that?"

"Nah, it's just Brie being difficult." I want to agree, but his harshness feels off.

"You'll need to talk to her. She's been your girlfriend for a while. It's only fair."

"Doesn't matter what I say. She overreacts, and I'm left looking like the jerk. I'm done with her."

"I get it, but you don't want to repeat past mistakes."

"Sam, my only mistake was leaving you. That's what I need to fix. I never loved Brie; she knew that."

"She did?"

"Yeah. I told her I was broken, that I couldn't give her what she wanted. She wouldn't listen, kept saying I'd love her someday." I feel a twinge for Brie, but today's about me, my new beginning.

"Let's not talk about her," John says, reading my mind. He grabs his phone to silence it, but I catch a glimpse: I'LL FUCKING CUT HER THROAT. The screen goes black. No way she means me. This isn't my fault. Fear grips me, but John's kiss, deep, determined, erases it. His hand cradles my head, pulling me close. The kiss lingers, satisfying. When I open my eyes, he's still there, the man I've dreamed of since he left. Fear fades, replaced by thoughts of him. He rests his forehead against mine.

"Hey, Insecurity, Doubt, do your job!" Fear snarls.

"She's not afraid anymore," Insecurity snaps. "That's on you, Fear."

"Fuck you!" Fear retorts. "They're forgiving each other. The Lord of Darkness won't like this. We have plans for Samantha, and this ruins everything!"

"I missed you so much," John whispers, his voice raw. I break the tension, opening my door. He's at my side instantly, grabbing my hand as the car locks with a beep. At the Sandwich Barn, I know exactly what I want. John doesn't hesitate either.

"Number 1 with chips and a drink," he says.

"Number 4 with potato salad and a drink," I add.

"Ma'am, mayonnaise on yours?" the cashier, a young girl with a Southern drawl, asks.

"Yes, and mustard," John answers for me, spot-on again. It's unnerving how well he knows me, but I'm too happy to care. I don't want to lose him again. As he tosses our trash, I notice a scratch down his neck. I start to ask, but Kevin walks in, stealing my focus.

"Girl! I was worried about you!" Kevin's voice booms as he spots me at the Sandwich Barn. He extends a hand to John, who grins and shakes it. "Let me meet the guy my girl's always staring at. I don't know the whole story, but man, she was a mess."

I shoot Kevin a death glare, mimicking a throat-slashing gesture behind John's back and mouthing, Shut up. He pivots fast, hugging me tightly and whispering, "Sorry, girl, it slipped." Stepping back, he looks at John. "She's a keeper. Be good to her." He winks and heads to the counter. "Love you, Sam. Catch you later."

"Yep, Kev, later," I call, moving toward the door.

"Nice to meet you," John says, flashing a smile as he grabs my hand and leads me out.

At the zoo's ticket booth, a sign catches my eye: NEW ARRIVAL: GERTIE THE GIRAFFE.
I squeal, clapping in delight.

"What?" John asks, startled.

"Gertie's here! I've been waiting for her!" His smile widens, and he scoops me into a bear hug, lifting me off the ground.

"I love that about you."

"What?"

"How you see the world with such wonder."

"I'm not a child," I snap, bristling.

"I'm sorry," he says, panic in his voice. "I didn't mean it like that. I meant your innocence, like you find joy in the little things."

"It's okay, John." Is this the same man I fell for? Doubt flickers, but I push it aside. I flash my zoo pass, John pays for his ticket, and we head straight for Gertie.

"Sam, I'm really sorry," he says again.

"Don't worry about it," I respond as he pulls me close, kissing me, his arms wrapping around me. His eyes are serious when I meet his gaze.

"Please don't be mad."

"I'm not. It's all good," I say, my tone calming. He exhales, shouting, "Let's see Gertie!" I bounce with excitement, and we follow the signs to the giraffe enclosure. At the feeding station, John buys two bags of food without hesitation.

"Here, my love," he says, handing them to me. "Have fun." I grin and approach Gertie. She lowers her head, her tongue gently taking the food from my hand.

"Oh, John, she's gorgeous."

"Not as gorgeous as you." I giggle, touching his face, reassuring him my feelings haven't faded. He closes his eyes, leaning into my hand. As I turn back, Gertie's tongue swipes my face.

"Eww!" I yelp. John bursts into laughter.

"Think that's funny, huh?"

"Absolutely." He says, laughing. I smirk, feeding Gertie the last of the food. At the washing station, I scrub off the slobber, drying and drying my face. When I look up, terror contorts John's face.

"What?"

"About time someone did their job," Fear hisses. "Violence is here, and he'll handle this."

"I'm so sorry, Sam," John says. I follow his gaze and see Brie charging toward us. John steps in front of me, pulling me behind him, his stance resolute.

Michelle Pentifallo

"I'll fucking kill her, John!" Brie screams. Before she can reach me, he grabs her wrists, spinning her around and pinning her arms. She shrieks, thrashing. John glances back, nodding for me to get help. As I turn, Brie's free leg hooks mine, and I trip, crashing face-first into the wooden fence.

Fear's laughter slithers into my mind, coiling around my thoughts. A shadow flickers at the edge of my vision. My breath catches.

I come to, John's eyes, locked on mine. It feels like hours have passed, but it's only minutes. An officer's voice cuts through the haze. "Ma'am, I need you to calm down.

What's your name?" Brie's screams echo, amplifying the pain radiating from my head.

"You okay?" John whispers.

"I think so." Dizziness hits as I try to stand. Nausea churns, and before I can speak, I vomit, splattering John's shirt. My head spins violently. As I collapse, he catches me, holding me tight.

"John!" I try to shout, but my voice fails, and more vomit comes, soaking me. This is disgusting. I hurl again, desperate to hide my vulnerability, but John's grip is unyielding.

"Stop moving, Sam," he whispers. "You're making it harder for me to carry you. I know you're embarrassed, but don't be. Just hold on. I'm getting you help."

Sirens wail, promising relief. I want to walk, but I'm too weak. A man's voice demands that John hand me over. I try to resist, but the new arms are stronger. Pain surges through my head and stomach, and my body convulses. Voices blur.

"Put her in the back, on her side," someone orders.

"I'm coming with you," John insists. The ambulance door slams, and we're moving. I try to open my eyes, but pain sears through me, forcing them shut.

"Is she going to be okay?" John's voice trembles. No one responds, and I want to snap at their rudeness, to reassure him I'm fine, but I can't. My breathing steadies, the vomiting stops, but my head throbs relentlessly. If I could just tell them I'm okay...

"You can't even have a normal date," Fear's voice sneers, mimicking my own. "Typical." I force my eyes open a sliver, catching a dark figure beside me, grinning wickedly. It's him, the voice I've heard my whole life. Terror grips me. John's shocked expression meets mine, but before he can speak, darkness swallows me, and the voices fade.

This is surreal. I hear everything: beeps, voices, the hum of machines, but I can't speak or see. I try to talk, hearing my own voice in my head, but no one responds. A woman says to John, "It's okay, it's only been a week. She'll wake up."

A week? I scream internally. Have I been here a week? "John!" I shout, but he doesn't hear. His shoes tap as he leaves the room. I feel the IV in my arm, the breathing machine's rhythm. I'm in a hospital, my thoughts foggy as I piece together what happened. We were at the zoo, feeding Gertie. We were heading to the monkeys when… I fell. Hard. Now I'm trapped in this bed, unable to move or speak, but I hear everything. How do I tell John I'm okay? Exhaustion pulls at me. I'll rest now. We'll talk later.

"Hey, Kevin," I say, my voice heavy as I step into Samantha's hospital room.

"Hey, John! How's she doing?" Kevin's concern is palpable.

"She still hasn't woken up."

"I'm so sorry." He steps forward, arms open. I hesitate, knowing he's just a friend, but I let him pull me into a hug. My head rests on his shoulder, and tears spill before I can stop them. Kevin tightens his embrace.

"I just got her back," I choke out, my voice muffled. My tears turn to sobs, my breath ragged. I nearly collapse, but Kevin steadies me.

"Let it out, John. It's okay. I love her too; she's my best friend. She's gonna be okay."

I try to pull away, an apology on my lips, but he holds firm. "Just cry. You need this."

Wiping my face, I avoid the gazes of passing nurses. Crying's normal in a hospital; no one bats an eye. I meet Kevin's eyes. "Thank you. I needed that," I manage, my voice breaking.

"Don't get all gushy, John. I might take it the wrong way," he teases, giggling.

"You're not my type, Kev," I shoot back, a faint laugh escaping.

"Oh, don't worry, sassy, you ain't mine either." Our laughter fades quickly, the weight of Samantha's condition anchoring us. My face falls, and I glance toward her bed.

"I should check on her."

"John, she's out. She doesn't know what's happening. You need to eat. When was the last time you ate?"

"I don't know."

"Exactly. What good are you to her if you're starving when she wakes up? She'll rip into you; she gets all fired up." Kevin snaps his fingers, twirling with a giggle, and I realize how much I need his lightness right now.

"Fine, something quick," I concede.

As we head to the cafeteria, guilt gnaws at me. What if she wakes and I'm not there? Kevin's confidence feels hollow. I saw her hit that fence, blood, vomit, chaos. The only time I was this scared was finding my mom in that closet after Dad died.

"Hey, John!" Kevin's voice pulls me back. "You with us, man?"

"Sorry, got lost in my head."

"Dark place, dude. Get outta there. She'll be fine."

"How do you know?"

"I know Sam. She's a fighter. I was with her after you left, and if that didn't break her, this won't."

"What do you mean?"

"Nothing. I shouldn't have said that." Kevin's face tightens.

"No, what?"

"Forget it, John."

"It was that bad?"

"I didn't mean to shit, I forgot who I was talking to. I don't wanna betray her trust."

"She was that bad?" I press.

"Man, I barely recognized her. But it's okay now. You're here, she'll wake up, and everything'll be right." Kevin saunters into the cafeteria, tugging my arm. I want to dig deeper, but exhaustion and hunger win. My stomach growls, urging me forward.

"Look, John, this is called food. Try some," Kevin quips.

"Smartass," I mutter, heading to the cooler. "I'll grab an egg sandwich."

"That's it? That won't hold you."

"It's all I can manage." My tone's sharper than intended. My phone vibrates—a number I don't know. I answer instinctively.

"Hello, this is John."

"Hi, John, Detective Velez. I need a minute. You available?"

"I'm at the hospital with my girlfriend."

"I can come there if that works."

"Yeah, I'm grabbing food. Her room's 2212, ICU."

"I'm sorry to hear that. I'll be there in thirty."

"Thanks." I hang up, biting into the sandwich. It's the best damn egg sandwich I've ever tasted, and my face must show it.

"Good, huh?" Kevin grins.

Words That Hurt

"Best I've had." I offer an apologetic smile for my earlier snap, and he nods, understanding. He's been a rock, despite how I hurt Sam. He deserves my respect. He taps my arm playfully.

"Told you, not my type," he says, and we laugh, the tension easing. His friendship's a lifeline, and I'm grateful.

The elevator doors open on the second floor. Two officers wait outside Sam's room.

"Mr. Tate?" the taller one asks.

"Yes."

"We need a moment to discuss the incident."

"I understand." I glance at Kevin, then close Sam's door gently. I've read she might hear us, and I don't want her upset. The dark-haired officer gives me an odd look but turns away. Who cares what he thinks? I mutter.

"On the day in question, you and Samantha White were at the zoo, feeding the giraffe. Then what happened?" he asks.

"My ex-girlfriend, Brianna Thompson Brie, came at us."

"What happened next?"

"She was yelling she'd kill Sam. I restrained her, told Sam to get help. As Sam ran, Brie tripped her. Sam hit a fence pole and passed out."

"How long was she unconscious?"

"Felt like forever, maybe ten minutes. Guards arrived, and I stayed with her."

"Then what?"

"Someone called 911. Sam tried to stand, got dizzy, and started vomiting. She grabbed her head and said it hurt. I carried her to the ambulance. She kept throwing up, said she was dizzy, then passed out. She hasn't woken since."

"Did Ms. Thompson trip Ms. White intentionally?"

"Absolutely. Brie yanked free and stuck out her leg. Sam was running when it launched her into the fence. I thought she was dead."

"Anything else to add?"

"Brie hated Sam. She said I'd regret getting back with her."

"Thank you, Mr. Tate. We may follow up."

"Whatever helps." I turn, desperate to be with Sam. Inside, Kevin's holding her hand, talking softly. He really loves her. If he weren't gay, I'd be jealous. I chuckle faintly.

"How'd it go?" Kevin asks, looking up.

"Fine. They asked about the zoo."

"I hope you told them Brie's why my best friend's hurt!"

"I gave them everything. It happened so fast. I can't believe it was right in front of me." I drop my head into my hands, tears threatening. "This is my fault," I whisper.

"What?" Kevin leans closer.

"This is my fault," I say louder.

"Don't you dare say that, John. This isn't your fault."

I come to as Kevin's voice cuts through the haze. "John, it's not your fault. Don't think that!"

Why can't I speak? Frustration claws at me. It's not your fault! I scream inside, but my voice is trapped. Damn it!

"What'd you say, Kev?" John asks.

"That wasn't me. That was Sam!"

"What?!" John's at my side in an instant, his voice trembling with hope. "Sam, what'd you say? It's just a mumble. Oh my God, Kevin, get the nurse!" He grabs my hand. "I'm here, Sam. It's gonna be okay. I love you. I'm so sorry." I manage a faint squeeze, my heart racing to reach him.

The nurse rushes in, standing across from John. "What'd she say?" she asks, her tone flat.

"We can't make it out. She mumbled and squeezed my hand," John says, breathless.

"That's really good," the nurse replies. "Samantha, can you hear me?" Her voice booms, as if I'm deaf.

I can hear you! I want to shout.

"Did you hear that?" John exclaims.

"Yes, it's faint, but she's trying to communicate. I'll get the doctor. He's in surgery, so it'll be a bit, but he'll come soon. I'll be back to check her IV." She leaves, and Kevin and John sigh with relief.

"I knew she'd come back," Kevin says, his dramatic flair a familiar comfort. John pulls a chair close, his exhaustion evident.

"Hey, Sam, we're here," he says softly. "Kevin and I have been here every day. You've been in the hospital for a few days, but you'll be fine."

I'm fine! I can hear you! I try to squeeze harder, to open my eyes, to move anything to reach them, but my body betrays me.

"What else did the officer say?" Kevin asks.

"He wanted more details. I told them Brie threatened to kill Sam if we got back together."

"What?!"

"I didn't take her seriously. I thought it was just talk. Look at her now." John's voice breaks. "This is my fault." Fear's voice slithers in. Yep, it's your fault.

No! I scream silently.

"John, this is not your fault," Kevin insists.

"Isn't it? I let Brie into our lives because I was too cowardly to fight for Sam. I took the easy road with someone who made me feel safe. What kind of man leaves his girlfriend, doesn't call, then shows up with another girl? It's my fault."

You're wrong! I want to yell.

"Let's talk later," John says. "I read she might hear us. We don't wanna upset her."

"Okay. John, go shower and sleep. I'll stay with her."

"I can't. What if she wakes and I'm not here? I've already failed her too many times."

"She's out, John. Look at her."

I'm not! I rage internally.

"I smell like garbage," John admits.

"Yeah, I can smell you from here," Kevin teases, laughing.

"Really?"

"Nah, I'm messing with you. Go. A little time won't hurt."

Go clean up, John. I love you. He can't hear me. Don't flirt with my man! I giggle to myself, warmed by their bond.

"Text me if anything changes," John says. "I'll set your number as a favorite, so it gets through 'do not disturb.'"

"Woo, I'm a favorite!" Kevin quips.

"Don't get excited. I don't have many." John hesitates at the door, his steps heavy. At the nurse's station, he says, "I'm going home to shower and sleep. If Samantha in 2212 wakes up, call me."

"Of course," the nurse replies. "Any other family to contact?"

"No, she has us." John's voice cracks. I left her once. I won't again. The elevator dings, pulling him from his thoughts. He fumbles for his valet ticket, hands the attendant a five, and slides into his car.

"Have a great day, sir," the valet says.

Great day? John scoffs. My girlfriend almost died because of my ex, whom I dated after abandoning Sam. Anger surges, radiating from his chest. "You're a fucking loser!" he screams, pounding the wheel.

Hours later, John's alarm jolts him awake. Two texts from Kevin: SHE IS WAKING UP and WHERE ARE YOU BRO? Panic seizes him. I missed it. He swaps shorts for jeans, sniffs a T-shirt to ensure it's clean, and types, I'M ON MY WAY. Grabbing keys and wallet, he sprints to his car, guilt gnawing, no time for a breakdown.

"She opened her eyes. What the fuck, Violence?" Fear snarls, unheard by the humans. "I thought you had this!"

"I can't control her will," Violence retorts. "She's strong."

"Useless. Find Anger and Resentment; they're a few halls down, messing with a grieving family. I need them now. We can't hear her thoughts unless she speaks. I need backup!"

John drives on autopilot, his heart pulling him to Sam. At the hospital, he tosses his keys to the valet. "Sorry!" he yells, bolting for the elevator. A man inside grumbles, "You don't gotta push the button that many times."

"My girlfriend just woke up after days in a coma," John says. "I need to see her."

"I get it. My wife just had a baby, and we almost lost them both."

"Damn, that's rough. Glad they're okay." John steps off, glancing back. "Good luck, man."

"You too," the man calls.

John races past the nurse's station. "Mr. Tate!" a nurse shouts. He ignores her. "Mr. Tate!"

"I need to see Samantha!" he snaps, turning.

"She's sleeping."

"Tired of sleeping or still in a coma?"

"Coma. She opened her eyes briefly, then slipped back." John's legs buckle, and he collapses. The nurse rushes to him. "Are you okay?"

"Yeah," he mutters, embarrassed, pulling himself up with a chair. "Just lost my footing."

"Maybe you should sit," the nurse suggests.

"I need to see Samantha."

"The doctor's waiting to speak with you."

"Tell him to come to her room."

"Yes, I can do that."

John enters, finding Kevin by Sam's side. "I'm so sorry," Kevin says, tears in his eyes. "She opened her eyes, and I was so excited. I should've told you she went back to sleep. I was a mess."

John pulls him into a hug. "You've been strong for her, Kev. I've been selfish, only thinking of my pain." He was here when I wasn't. "Go home, shower, sleep."

"I don't want to. What if she wakes again?"

"I'm not leaving, Kev."

"I believe you." Kevin hesitates, then sighs. "Okay, I'll go. I need to call my mom and boss."

"Life goes on. We still have to do the daily grind."

"It's hard. When I was struggling, Sam never left me. I feel like I'm betraying her."

No, Kevin, go home, love, I think, unheard.

"If anyone betrayed her, it's me," John says. "I won that award. Don't worry."

Words That Hurt

John, stop. I've forgiven you, I want to say.

"Thanks for the hug," Kevin says, smiling. "Still not my type." He heads out.

Hi, John. I love you. The room falls quiet, save for the machines and my pounding heart. John's at my side, kissing my forehead, his scent mingling with mine. "I love you," he whispers, tears in his voice.

I love you too. I'm trying to open my eyes. It hurts. I need rest, but I fight to stay present.

"You're so beautiful," John says, stroking my hair. "When you wake, we're going on a trip anywhere you want, my treat. I'll show the world what you mean to me."

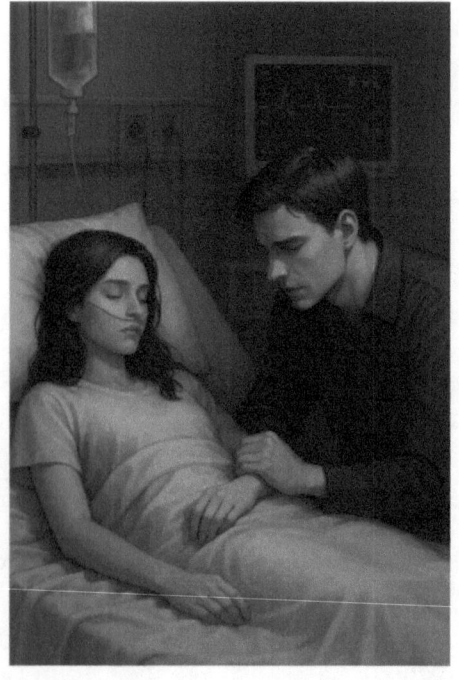

The TV interrupts: "Brianna Thompson was arrested today on charges of attempted murder. The incident hospitalizing Samantha White may escalate to manslaughter, but authorities can't release more." Brie's image flashes, handcuffed, shoved into a cruiser. John's face hardens. "Fucking bitch tried to steal my Sam!"

"Mr. Tate, you can't talk like that here," a voice says from the doorway.

"Sorry, I thought I was in my head," John mutters. Fear's voice creeps in: Good, John. Hate her. She's a monster you brought into Sam's life.

What if Sam wakes and hates me? John thinks, panic rising. "Sam, are you trying to open your eyes?" Her blinks quicken. "Can you hear me?"

Yes, I can. I strain to respond.

"I'm here, Sam."

I know. I've always known.

Her eyes flash with panic. "What is it, Sam?" Her hands claw at her throat.

"Don't pull the tube," John says. "You'll hurt yourself." Nurses rush in as Sam's eyes darken, staring past him. I see you behind John. Get out! I think I glimpsed a shadowy figure.

"Ms. White, can you hear me? Blink if you can," a nurse says.

I blink hard. Yes, I hear you.

"Stay calm," the nurse urges loudly. "Don't touch the tubes. We'll take care of you."

Hurry. I need to tell John not to listen to them. John texts Kevin: SHE'S COMING BACK TO US. But her dark gaze haunts him. She's angry. She looked past me, as if she hated me. He steps back, giving the nurses space.

"What an epic fail," Fear screams, unheard. "She wakes up loving him? The Lord of Darkness will reassign me! Doubt, get to work on John. I've got to fix this!"

SIX MONTHS LATER

"Hey, gorgeous," John whispers. "Wake up, it's almost ten."

"Ten?!" I bolt upright. "Shit! I've got a dress fitting in an hour, and the florist for next week's flowers!"

"Sam, you've got time," John soothes.

"No, I don't!"

"What can I do?"

"Coffee, to-go cup, one sugar, some cream, please, my love."

"Done, beautiful. Kiss me first."

"Easy." Our lips meet, and I can't wait to make him mine forever. I head to the shower, ready for my day and my new life.

"Now they're getting married?" the Lord of Darkness growls. "After her rehab, John proposed? Fear, you failed."

"I tried, my Lord," Fear stammers. "She's too strong-willed."

"Excuses! She's not worth our time. Your new assignment is Nadia. Don't fail again."

"Perhaps later, when they have kids, we can stir things up," Fear ventures.

"Out of my sight!" the Lord roars.

ONE YEAR LATER

"Hey, Sam!" John calls.
"What?"
"The baby's crying."
"I'll get her."

"Good. I can't handle the crying."

"Hey, Selfishness," the Lord of Darkness summons. "Fear, mentioned John, said something. Check it out. Stir up a fight, make space in their home."

A door creaks open. Selfishness steps toward me, eyes gleaming. "Why are you here?" I demand.

"I sense you're upset, Samantha," Selfishness purrs.

"I told you to leave long ago. The Lord of Light guides me now."

"He can't stop your words."

"I didn't say anything."

"But John did. It hurt you."

"Listen, Selfishness," I snap. "I'm fine. John's tired, he didn't mean it. Get out, or I'll call the name that'll tear you apart." Selfishness hesitates, then retreats, the door closing.

I kiss John's cheek as I pass. "Don't worry, love. It gets better."

"I'm sorry, Sam," he says. "I shouldn't have said that."

Heading out for my morning run, I slip my AirPods in, and music pulses through my Apple Watch. A year ago, I felt like a loser, lost in darkness. The Rusty Bumper changed everything, a haven that taught me to silence those voices. This isn't the end; it's my beginning, a life of freedom. As the music swells, a faint, familiar voice echoes in the distance, but I run on, leaving it behind.

2

SOUL STEALING

America, they say, is the land of the brave. But courage feels like a distant dream for me. Ten years in this country, and I still don't belong. Today, a man's gaze stripped me bare, leaving me feeling exposed and violated. My father's words echo in my mind: "Sweetie, your beauty will get you everything you need." But is that true? I'm tired of hearing it. It feels like a betrayal of who I am. I'm more than my looks; I'm smart, brimming with dreams and ideas no one seems to care about.

In this foster home, my third in a month, I'm invisible yet overly seen. The foster mother calls me worthless, while her husband, Noel, fixates on my body. I tug my shirt up, desperate to shield myself from his leering eyes. Once, he slapped my backside, grinning, "Hey, babe." It left me shaken, unsafe in a place meant to be a refuge. I want to run, to escape this suffocating space.

Retreating to my room, I seek solace in sleep. The distant hum of the TV in their bedroom fades as I slip under the covers, unnoticed. But peace eludes me. A nightmare jolts me awake, the moon's faint light casting eerie shadows. In my dream, Noel's predatory eyes haunt me, his burly figure lurking in every corner. I can't escape his gaze, not even in sleep. Once, I dreamt he inhaled the scent of my hair, his face twisted in obsession. My body trembled, and the memory lingers, making me feel watched even when alone. What's wrong with me? Why does this shadow cling to me?

My only memories of peace come from my mother. Her Armenian lullaby, "Peace comes to the light at heart," soothed me as a child. I ache for her voice now. In Armenia, poverty was our only inheritance, and when her landlord discovered me, he took me as payment against her will. Years later, we fled to America, chasing a job opportunity that turned out to be a lie. At six, I watched my mother struggle, taking odd jobs despite the language barrier. One day, she left me with someone she trusted, and I never saw her again. Orphaned, I landed in an orphanage, and now this foster home is a dump where my looks and willpower are all I have.

Soul Stealing

Passing a mirror, I catch my reflection, and self-doubt claws at me. A cruel inner voice sneers, "You're ugly. That big nose, those crooked teeth, you think you're pretty? Think again." Turning the corner to the kitchen, I freeze. Noel stands there, cigarette smoke curling around his predatory eyes. That looks like it's the same one from my nightmares, undressing me with every glance.

"Excuse me," I murmur, praying he'll let me pass. Did I hear Barbara, the foster mother, slam the door earlier, shouting, "See you later"? If she's gone, I'm trapped. If I retreat to my room, he'll follow. My mind races for an escape.

Noel reaches out, grazing my face. "You sure have pretty eyes."

"Thank you," I mumble, eyes fixed on the floor.

"Look at me," he snarls, his whiskey-soaked breath hitting me like a wall.

His hands claw at my chest. I jerk back, but he's stronger. Just then, a car pulls up to my salvation. Barbara bursts through the door, her glare accusing me. "What the hell are you doing, little girl? Making a move on my man?"

My voice catches, unable to explain. Her rage explodes. "Get out of my house, you little bitch! NOW!"

"What about my stuff?" I whisper.

"That crap? I'll send it to the center tomorrow. Get the fuck out!"

Tears stream down my face as I grab my purse, phone, and pills inside and flee down the alley, heart pounding.

"Hey, Nadia, you okay?" George's voice pulls me back to the present.

"Just remembering something from a few years ago," I say, brushing it off.

"What happened?"

I lift my bangs, revealing a scar. "Got hit by a car. Was in the hospital for months."

"Whoa, I never noticed that."

"Yeah, I hide it well." I force a smile, joining George's familiar banter. "So, about that job you mentioned yesterday, what's the pay? Does he want me to start at 8:00 tomorrow night? I'm at The Coffee Perk until 5:00, and it's an hour's drive to the Candy Stick."

Soul Stealing

"How the hell should I know?" George laughs. "He just asked if I knew anyone who strips. Said some big shot from Florida's coming, likes orgies and stuff."

"What? I never agreed to that. I just need cash to get out of this town."

"Hey, I live in this town," he teases.

"You're used to it, George. I'm dreaming of New York, a modeling career."

"Well, this guy owns the joint, and he's from New York. Maybe he'll notice you," he chuckles.

"Shut up." I shove him playfully, my only true friend in Montana. "Forget it. I'll find another way."

"Nadia, I already told him you'd show. He's not a nice guy. I owe him a favor, and if you bail, he'll come for me."

"You left that part out," I snap.

"You said you'd do it. Simple."

"I'm nervous, George. It's been years." After escaping Jim in Idaho, a so-called father figure who lured me into stripping, I swore I'd never return to that life. He profited off me until I walked away at 18. "I'm clean now. I don't want to go back."

"It's one night, Nadia. I didn't say you're his new dancer. Maybe this Florida guy will sweep you off to New York."

I laugh, meeting his eyes. "Impossible. I'm a lesbian."

His jaw drops. "No way. I had no idea."

"Really? I thought you knew."

"Nope. You never talk about that stuff."

"It wasn't relevant. But don't try hooking me up."

He leans in, voice low. "Keep that quiet around here. This town's not ready for it."

"It's the 21st century, George."

"Not here. Seriously, lower your voice."

I roll my eyes. "Whatever. Tell that to Anita at The Coffee Perk. She's been giving me looks."

"She's not into you, George," I say with a smirk, my voice brimming with playful confidence. "Anita's got her eyes on me."

George scoffs, holding the door open as I step outside. "That's what you think. We'll see."

"I'll call you tomorrow to let you know how it went," I say, heading for my car. "But George, if these guys are creeps, I'm coming for you."

"Nah, it's easy money. Talk tomorrow." He waves, climbing into his car and driving off. I grin to myself, amused at how easily he bought my lie about being a lesbian. I'm a damn good liar when I need to be.

The day blurred by, leaving me no time to brace for tonight. My stomach churns as the GPS announces, "Five miles to your destination." I grip the wheel, fighting the urge to vomit. Why am I doing this again? Two years to escape that hellhole, two more to get clean, yet here I am, driving toward the Candy Stick. I crave freedom, a new life in New York where my modeling dreams can take root. That's my destiny, but it demands money I don't have.

"Turn left in one mile," the GPS drones. I could turn around. I don't owe George anything except that he was there, every day, helping me stay clean. Damn it.

The hot pink neon sign of the Candy Stick looms ahead, tacky and unapologetic. I roll my eyes as I park. Candy Stick? Really? As I step out, a venomous whisper cuts through the air: "I knew you'd come back, you whore." I whip around, heart racing, but no one's there. Shaking it off, I grab my coat and bag and head for the entrance.

Soul Stealing

A woman greets me in the open bar area, her southern drawl warm and unexpected in Montana. "You must be Nadia. George described you perfectly. The guys are gonna love you." Her blonde curls are pinned back, and her kind eyes, framed by wrinkles, suggest she's about sixty-five. Her figure hints at a past in this very role.

"Hi," I say, shy but curious.

"Come on, girl, I don't bite," she says, her smile reassuring, like a promise of safety.

"How'd you know it was me?"

"You're the only five-eleven gal with auburn hair around here."

I laugh, touching my hair. "Can't hide this, can I?"

"Why would you? It's gorgeous."

"Thank you," I say, warmed by her sincerity.

"I'm Carrie, by the way."

"Nice to meet you, Carrie."

"Likewise, Nadia. Let's get you to the girls' room. You're the first one here."

"I wasn't sure how long the drive would take, so I left early."

"No worries, child. The others will show up soon." She glances at me as we walk. "I love your accent," I add.

Carrie rolls her eyes playfully. "You're the only one. I'm from Alabama, and my mama always said, 'An Alabama girl is known no matter how far she roams.' Everyone teases me about it."

"I didn't mean it like that," I say, worried I've offended her.

"Oh, I know, don't fret. Here's the girls' room." The space is spacious, clean, and professional, nothing like the dives I've known. "Put your stuff in a locker and pick any dressing table. First come, first served."

Carrie notices my surprise. "Yeah, the owner runs a tight ship. Caters to rich folks, caviar on the menu and all. He keeps me around to look after you girls and tidy the bar. I danced back in the day, so I know the ropes."

"Thanks, Carrie. This place is… different." I wonder why George called the owner a bad guy. Maybe he just crossed him.

"If you need anything, I'll be setting up the bar. Just holler, Red. Is it okay to call you that?"

"Absolutely," I say, smiling. "Not the first time I've been called that."

"See you later, Red." The door closes softly, leaving me alone.

Soul Stealing

This isn't Pussy Cats. The air feels cleaner, the vibe professional. I hang my costume, a white T-shirt with cut-out shoulders, a garter, stockings, and gold heels on the rack and sit at a dressing table. Staring into the mirror, I lock eyes with myself. "Don't do anything stupid, Nadia," I say aloud.

"Girl, I tell myself that every day," a voice chirps behind me. I spin around to see a petite woman with black hair and striking green eyes, maybe five-foot-three.

"Hi, I'm Sonya," she says brightly.

"Nadia. Nice to meet you." I shake her outstretched hand, puzzled by her warmth.

"Not used to a high-end club, huh?" she says, reading my expression.

"How'd you guess?"

"Your face says your last place wasn't like this. Were the girls rough?"

"Yeah," I admit, surprised she gets it.

"Here, we're pros. Clean, too. The owner drug-tests monthly; if you fail, you're out. No fighting either, or you're gone that night."

I'm stunned. This is nothing like my past experiences.

"Where are you from?" Sonya asks.

"Bainville, about an hour away. But I've been all over."

"Small town. What brings you here?"

"Need cash to move to New York. I want to model."

"You're pretty enough for it," she says, winking. My stomach flutters. Her look feels more than friendly. Did I lie to George? I used to date women, but that's a story for another day.

The door swings open, and another girl strides in. "Hey, Sonya!"

"Leyah! Meet Nadia," Sonya calls.

Leyah, all smiles, bypasses my handshake for a hug. "Wow, you're tall. Love your hair." She claims a locker next to mine. "You got here early, smart move. This place fills up fast."

More girls pour in, their chatter and perfume filling the room. "Who's the new girl?" one asks.

"Nadia," Sonya announces.

"She's tall," another says. "Love your hair."

The warmth is disorienting but comforting. For the first time in ages, I feel at home.

"Hey, I'm Bianca," a new voice says.

"Nadia. Nice to meet you."

"You're doing a duo with me tonight," Bianca says. "New girls don't go solo until we know you're up to par."

"Sounds good," I say, relieved.

"What's your costume?" We check my outfit, and she grins. "Perfect. I'm in black, let's do good girl vs. bad girl."

"Love it," I say, excitement creeping in.

"When'd you last dance?" she asks.

"Five years ago."

"Let's hit the stage and plan your routine. We'll keep it simple for your first night."

"My first night?" I echo, nerves flaring.

"Yeah," she says, unfazed. "Your first night."

"This is a one-time gig," I tell Bianca firmly. "I'm just here for the Florida high roller George mentioned, maybe some locals."

Bianca giggles, locking eyes with me. "Girl, you'll be back. Trust me." My skeptical look doesn't faze her. She grabs my hand, pulling me toward the stage. "Let's do this."

Behind the curtain, my heart pounds. The announcer's voice sultry, commanding voice fills the air. "I should've practiced more," I mutter, but it's too late.

"Welcome to the stage, Red and Violet!" The curtain sweeps open as the crowd cheers. Bianca squeezes my hand, mouthing, Come on! I step into the spotlight, facing a sea of suited men with stacks of cash on their tables. My nerves spike. In the corner, a man sits, flanked by a group of men and a woman on each side. Who is he? I wonder, but there's no time to dwell. Bianca launches into our routine, and I follow, fighting to keep up.

The crowd's gaze feels like an audition, intense and unyielding. I nearly trip but recover smoothly, finishing with grace. As we bow, the room erupts, standing and cheering like we've delivered the performance of a lifetime.

"Wow!" I exclaim, adrenaline surging as we head to the dressing room. "That was incredible!"

Bianca grins. "Told you. And that was your first go."

Sonya brushes past, heading for the stage. "Wish me luck!" she calls.

"Luck!" I shout, still buzzing. The room hums with voices and footsteps, but for the first time, I feel... safe.

"Don't change," Bianca says. "They like us in costume. Grab some food." She gestures to a buffet loaded with fruit, vegetables, salads, crackers, and water.

"Is this normal?" I ask, eyeing the spread.

"Yep. Eat up, you'll need the energy for a full night."

"A full night?" My stomach twists. "What does that mean?"

She catches my panic. "Not like that. We don't sleep with them."

Relief washes over me. I grab a plate, picking out snacks and a water, and sit beside Bianca. She loads her plate and joins me.

"Nadia, there's no hidden agenda here," she says. "This place is legit. The owner checks in twice a month, and there's a manager daily. Customers pay $500 just to get in, $4,000 for a private booth, plus whatever they tip us. Some girls do extra in the back, but it's their choice, and they're paid well. I don't, and I don't judge. After the final act, we all go on stage for a lineup, then wait here for our names to be called. Clients pay upfront for services, and you get 60%. As the new girl, you could make $3,000 tonight."

"Three thousand?" I gasp. "That's life-changing."

"Bet it is," she says. "Enough to get you to New York."

"Exactly." I pause. "You said the owner's from New York?"

"Yep." She smirks. "We'll see if you leave."

We eat in silence, the room's energy swirling around us. Time slips away until a calm voice cuts through. "Nadia."

I look up to see Carrie. "Someone wants to speak with you. Follow me."

"I thought we would go back on stage together," I say, trailing her, the scent of roses from the other girls lingering.

"Usually, yes, but this is a regular, and he's impatient." She leads me to a cozy office adorned with family photos and children's pictures. "Sit, Nadia."

"Am I in trouble?" My voice trembles.

"No, honey, not at all. Why would you think that?"

"I'm the only one here."

"It's your first night, and we've got a special request. Rare for a newbie. I didn't want to spook you, so let's talk."

I exhale. "Okay. What's the request?"

Carrie leans in, her drawl soothing. "A gentleman, Mr. Smith, we'll call him, is taken with you. He's a regular, always respectful, usually just watches from the back, and leaves. He's had one private session in three years, and it wasn't sexual. We're aboveboard here, Red, I promise."

"I get it," I say, projecting confidence while my insides churn.

"He wants a private session all night and to take you to his home."

"What?" I blurt, heart racing.

"I know, I know," Carrie says, taking my hands. "Trust me, we don't allow creeps. These are wealthy men, millionaires, some of them. You'd have a guard with you, either in the car or inside, your choice. You'll get a secure phone, and you can leave anytime if you're uncomfortable."

I hesitate. "I don't know."

"Hear me out. He pays upfront $5,000 just to go, plus $2,000 more when you return the phone and guard tomorrow. You keep it all, even if you leave early."

"Seven thousand dollars?" I squeak, stunned. "That's insane."

"He's got the money, Nadia. You'll be safe. I've never seen him this eager in three years. He's usually so composed."

"Why me?"

"He called you the most beautiful woman he's ever seen."

"That sounds like a line," I scoff.

"His words, Red. Any questions?"

"Yeah. Does he get to touch me?"

"Only if you allow it."

"Do I have to sleep with him?"

"Absolutely not. We don't push that."

"Can I change first?"

"He'd prefer it."

"Can I talk to him before deciding?"

"Of course, sweetie. It's your call."

"Okay, I'll talk to him, then decide. Should I change now?"

"I'd suggest it," Carrie says, her smile warm. "Come back here after, and I'll take you to a private room to meet him."

Soul Stealing

"Got it. Twenty minutes."

"He'll wait. I've never seen him like this."

I head to my locker, mind spinning. Should I bolt out the back door and forget the money? What if he's dangerous? My head's about to explode when Sonya touches my arm.

"Hey, I heard about Tom," she says.

"Who?"

"The guy Carrie's talking about."

"Everyone knows already?"

"Yeah, it's big news. He's only asked for one girl in three years, and she broke his heart. Got into drugs, lost herself. Tom's a good guy, respectful, tips us even when he doesn't ask for anything. Lola's friends with him, says he's solid."

"Who's Lola?" I ask, curiosity piqued.

Sonya points across the room to a petite woman with long blonde hair, barely 5'1", and maybe 110 pounds. She motions for Lola to join us.

"No!" I protest. "I don't want to talk to her if she's into him."

Sonya laughs. "Relax, Nadia. Lola's gay. It's not like that."

"Oh," I say, caught off guard. I hadn't sensed that vibe here, unlike the judgmental environments of my past.

"Hey, Sonya, what's up?" Lola calls, approaching with a radiant smile.

"Lola, meet Nadia, aka Red. Tom's totally into her. Isn't that wild?"

Lola beams at me, her warmth disarming. "Don't worry, Nadia. He's a great guy. I'm up on stage now, but let's chat later. Nice to meet you!" She hurries off, her energy lingering.

"See? He's solid," Sonya says.

I exhale deeply. "Okay, I'll talk to him." I open my locker, change into my regular clothes, and head to the mirror to touch up my hair and lipstick. The girl at the next dressing table glances over.

"You're really beautiful, you know," she says softly.

"Thanks," I reply, offering a shy smile before heading to Carrie's office. My nerves flare, nails bitten to stubs. If my mom could see me now, she'd be heartbroken. Thank God she's in heaven, spared this sight.

Carrie looks up as I enter, relief washing over her. "Girl, I thought you'd bailed!"

"I almost did," I admit. "But Sonya vouched for him."

"Tom's been coming here for years. All the girls know him. Sonya was probably as shocked as I am that he's asking for you."

"She seemed it. I just hope this is legit."

That cruel voice creeps in again: She's a liar and a whore, just like you. I shake it off, no time to dwell on its venom.

"No reason to deceive you, sweet lady," Carrie says, resting a hand on my back. She guides me down a hall to a door with tempered glass, opening it to reveal a stunning room adorned with flowers, pearls, and soft pinks and teals, nothing like the gritty strip clubs I've known.

"Hello, Tom," Carrie says, gesturing to a tall man with a striking physique. "This is Red."

"Pleased to meet you," he says, standing and approaching slowly. His presence is commanding yet hesitant.

"Hello," I reply, extending my hand.

"I'll leave you two to talk," Carrie says, meeting my eyes with reassurance before slipping out.

"Would you like a drink?" Tom asks, his voice surprisingly shy for his stature.

"Coffee would be nice."

"No problem." He gestures to a bar stocked with every refreshment imaginable. "Take a seat, if you'd like."

"Thanks." I settled into a chair near the couch he'd been on.

"Cream or sugar, Red?"

"Call me Nadia, please."

"Only if you call me Alex," he says with a nervous smile. "That's my real name. They use Tom here for privacy. My board would lose it if they knew I was here. Sorry, too much information. I'm nervous."

"Two sugars, one cream," I say, hiding my own jitters.

"Got it." His hands tremble as he pours, spilling sugar on the bar. He's a mess, I think, surprised. I expected to be the nervous one. He stirs the coffee and hands it to me.

"Thank you."

"My pleasure." His eyes hold mine, a look that says, I see you. It's unfamiliar, intense. I look away, clearing my throat.

"So, Alex, what do you do?" I ask, sipping my coffee.

"I'm in investments. Started at 18, working my way up in my father's company to earn the board's respect."

"The same board you're dodging now?" I tease.

He chuckles. "Not dodging, just… discreet. They might not get it."

"I get it. I sling coffee all day. Not sure my customers would respect me if they saw me here."

"Why not? You're a beautiful woman leveraging your assets for revenue. It's what I do daily." His words catch me off guard, and I laugh, nearly spitting my coffee.

"That's not the same!" I gasp, still laughing. His grin widens, and our laughter fills the room. His dirty blond curls frame bright blue eyes that seem to pierce my soul. I grab a napkin to dab my chin, and he jumps up.

"Need something?" he asks, eager.

"Just a napkin."

"Don't hesitate to ask for anything. This is about serving you."

"Excuse me?" I raise an eyebrow, confused.

"I pay to give you what you want, Nadia. You don't have to do anything you're not comfortable with."

"Carrie mentioned that. I'm just… wary about going to your house."

"I get it. I'm not a creep. This place is great, but it's not private. I prefer comfort."

"How far is your place?"

"Three hours by car, but I have a private jet. It's a quick flight."

"A jet?" I blink. "Carrie didn't mention that. I have work in the morning."

His face falls. "I'm sorry, I didn't mean to upset you."

"No, it's okay. I just didn't expect that."

"I thought the money might help," he says softly, pulling $1,000 from his pocket. "This is yours just to talk here, no strings attached."

"You don't have to pay me to talk," I say, surprised by his earnestness.

"I just want to talk," he insists, voice steady but cautious. Something about him feels off, not threatening, but different.

"Give me a second." I stand, heading for the door.

"Are you leaving?" he asks, rising quickly.

"No, just grabbing my phone."

"You don't have to do that, Nadia," Alex says softly. "I'll have someone get your phone. I'm here to serve you."

I hope my shock isn't obvious. No one's cared for me like this since Mom died. Alex steps to the door, whispering to someone in the hall. He returns, settling back on the couch.

"Where were we?" he asks, his voice steady, easing the tension.

"Taking a jet to your house, I think." I manage a smile, and he mirrors it.

"Carrie mentioned you'd have a guard and can leave anytime," he says. "I can fly you back, or a car can take you straight home. Whatever you want."

"And I'll have a secure phone if I need to reach anyone."

"I know," Alex nods. The door opens, and an arm passes my phone to him. He hands it to me, pausing. "Anything else?"

"I'm good. I ate in the dressing room." I open my phone and text my boss: Sorry, I'm not feeling well and won't be in tomorrow. I hesitate, then hit send.

EIGHT MONTHS LATER

Alex's gaze pierces me, raw and unfamiliar. Is this what love looks like? My foster parents were too consumed by their own chaos to see me, their fleeting pride lost long before Pussy Cats. But Alex's blue eyes shimmer with an intensity that feels like love, a warmth I've never known. It's overwhelming, urging me to run not from him, but from the foreign ache of being truly seen.

"What?" I ask, almost defiant. "Something on my face?"

"No," he says, voice soft. "I just love looking at you."

"Why?"

"You're beautiful, inside and out."

You don't know all of me, I think, but I force a smile. He leans in, kissing me, his trembling hands tucking my hair behind my ear.

"I love you," he whispers. "Marry me."

My body locks up, panic surging. Love? Marriage? How can I?

"That's a yes, right?" he teases, pulling me closer.

"Um…" I push against his chest, breaking free. "Isn't that a bit arrogant?"

"Maybe," he admits, grinning. "But I've never loved anyone like you, Nadia. I want to marry you now."

"Alex, I'm a mess. You don't know everything about me. I can't give you the 'married with kids' life. I don't want kids, I'd only mess them up, as my parents did me!" My voice rises, sharper than intended.

His eyes soften. "Come here." He wraps me in his arms as tears spill, unstoppable. I sink into his chest, sobbing. After what feels like forever, he lifts my face, kissing me gently.

"Nadia, I love all of you. I'm not leaving. I want you as my wife to spend my life with you."

"But, Alex…" I protest.

"No buts. You're my soulmate. If you need time, I'll wait, but I can't live without you."

He releases me, sinking onto the couch, and leaves the room quietly. Damn it, Nadia, I think. You've ruined it. He's done. But then he returns, holding something small. My heart races. What's that?

Soul Stealing

Alex kneels, head bowed. "Nadia, my love, I knew you were the one the moment I saw you. I don't care where we met, only that we did."

"But"

"Please, let me finish," he says, voice quivering. "I've never felt this way. You're my forever. Please, marry me." He looks up, eyes locked on mine.

Shock and warmth collide in me. "Alex, I don't know what to say."

"Just say yes."

"What if I mess it up? What if I'm not enough?"

He leans in, kissing me softly, holding my gaze. "I love you, Nadia," he whispers, tears brimming. "Marry me. I can't live without you."

His words sink deep, silencing the doubts for a moment. "Yes," I whisper, barely audible, fear lingering. What if the voices are right?

His face lights up, the happiest I've seen him. He pulls me into his arms, whispering against my neck, "I'll be an amazing husband, Nadia. You'll see."

"I know," I say, voice steady despite my worry. "It's not you I'm scared of. You're the best, Alex."

He slips a dazzling ring onto my finger

"Wow, that's huge!" I laugh, breaking the tension.

"Only the best for you."

I wrap my arms around his neck, smiling, but a quiet fear lingers. I hope I'm enough.

It almost feels like a dream, but I'd just have to live it and see where it takes me.

Michelle Pentifallo

3

FAMILY ROOTS

My head throbs, the cold cement floor biting into my skin. Waves crash faintly outside, wind howling, pierced by a girl's scream. My stomach twists. Where am I? I haven't seen my family in a year. Who would I even call for help? I'm alone, adrift. Would Dave and Natalie search for me? How would they know where to look?

Days blur into darkness. When I open my eyes, foreign voices murmur outside my door, unfamiliar, unintelligible. My wrists and ankles are bound, silver shackles chaining me to a low platform on the cement floor. My head feels like lead, ears ringing from relentless music that's been pounding for days. Hunger gnaws; exhaustion clings despite endless sleep. A memory flickers: a man approaching as I climbed into a taxi. "Hi, I'm Glen. Who are you?" he said, then nothing. A needle's sting, searing pain, and darkness swallowed me. Was it a dream? I drift back into sleep, the voices outside my only tether.

I wake to sunlight seeping through blacked-out windows, a man's angry shouts, Russian, maybe, assaulting my ears. I can't understand, but his rage is clear. He yanks

Family Roots

me upright by my chains. My legs buckle, but fear keeps me standing. This man, later revealed as Anton, frees my hands only to toss me a barely bread sandwich. I devour it, choking without water. My desperate glance at him prompts more yelling, this time at his partner, Vadim, who rushes in with a half-full, murky glass. I gulp, nearly vomiting, but force it down, survival overriding disgust. Those cruel voices whisper again: Whore. Look at her right where she belongs.

Shaking off the taunts, I'm met with Anton's slap across my face, his obscenities inches from me. I swallow the urge to fight back, instinct honed from years of survival. At five, my dad sneered at my school outfit: "Only sluts dress like that. You're just like your mother." She left after my birth, leaving him bitter and me to bear his scorn.

Anton's punch to my ribs snaps me back, pain doubling me over. As I brace for another, a woman's voice cuts through, sharp and accented but in English: "Knock it off, you idiot, before you damage the merchandise. I told you to handle the other girls. Get out before I chain you to a bed!" Hope flares she'll save me. But I'm wrong.

I open my eyes to a striking woman, maybe six feet tall to my five-foot frame, with piercing blue eyes and pale skin, dressed in black like a soldier. Anton's tone shifts, childlike, as he mumbles an apology, calling her Nisha. As he exits, I glimpse a door across the hall, later known as the waiting room.

Nisha grabs my hair, yanking me close. "You're mine, little one," she hisses. "Run, and I'll kill you." My knees weaken; she tightens her grip to keep me upright. "Don't damage my merchandise," she warns, "or I'll give you to the homeless." Her threat sinks deep, fear unlike any I've known gripping me.

This isn't a nightmare; it's worse, with no escape. She releases me, and I collapse, my head striking the cuffs on the floor. "Cuff her, you idiot," she snaps at a man watching. As Anton's breath grazes my neck, his hands clamp the cuffs on my wrists. He licks my ear, muttering something vile, and a needle pierces my arm. "Nighty night," he chuckles as darkness claims me.

I stir to a light touch trailing my thigh, fleetingly mistaking it for Frank's. Reality crashes in; it's not him. A rough voice growls, "I think I like this one." This one? Are there others? He grips my inner thigh, forcing my legs apart. Rage flares, my glare meeting his, forgetting my chains. Anton's slap stings my face. "Don't pull away, girl," the man sneers. "I'm your new owner, little one."

My eyes dart around a crowded room, other girls chained like me, men in suits inspecting us like livestock. Horror fills me, and he laughs, mocking my shock. "Didn't know, little one? This is purchasing day."

"Purchasing day," I whisper, earning another slap, but his hand intercepts it. I cry out, and he looks startled that I have a voice.

"Don't touch her," Anton mutters, his confidence gone.

"I want her, you stupid fucker," the man snaps. "The sooner she learns my hand is god, the better. Get Nisha here now! I'm catching a flight to New York." His authority silences the room, and I know to stay quiet.

Anton leaves, and I never see him again. Nisha returns, marking the start of my new, enslaved life.

Tears blur my vision as I face my audience, their eyes fixed on me, gripped by my story from years ago. Only recently have I found the strength to speak of my enslavement. Thank God for those who saved me.

"Need a minute?" the Pastor asks gently.

"No, I'm okay," I say, voice shaky. "Just a glass of water, please."

A bottle appears instantly. I grimace as the cold water stings my throat, still scarred from past injuries. My four listeners' faces shift from concern to fear, unable to grasp my pain. No one can, unless they've lived it.

A door creaks behind me, and I flinch, turning instinctively. Relief floods me at Dodge Andrews' familiar, wrinkled smile, my rescuer, the father I never had. "Hey, Dodge!" I call, warmth spreading. My thoughts return to my story. "I was about to tell them about Jude," I say, gesturing to him.

"Oh..." Dodge's voice catches, a tone I know well. Jude's death, the one he doesn't regret, though they're trying to pin it on me. "Don't let me stop you," he says, taking a seat behind my audience. I feel safe, despite Officer Jones looming in the back.

"Lucy, please continue," says the tall man in charge, his blonde hair and green eyes paired with a confident yet judgmental tone.

Before I can object, Nisha reappears. "Hey, Jude," she says calmly. "How can I help you today?"

"I want this one."

"She's new," Nisha replies. "We haven't had time to groom or train her yet, Jude."

"I don't care," Jude snaps. "She's the one. I've been searching for this exact match. I'll train her myself. Just clean her up, she smells like trash."

Nisha looms over me. "You know my reputation, Jude. I deliver quality. I'll do it, but you'll sign a waiver. Without training, I can't guarantee she won't act out."

Jude's laugh is cold, his voice deep. "When have I ever let anyone get the better of me, Nisha?"

"Fine, have it your way."

"What's her name?"

"How the fuck should I know?" Nisha kicks my side, pain flaring. "What's your name, little whore?"

"Hey, don't mess with my merchandise," Jude says, half-joking. "What's your fucking name?"

"Lucy," I whisper, clutching my ribs.

"There you go, Jude. It's fucking Lucy. Happy?"

"Get her last name," Jude orders. "I need to research her. Don't want anyone sniffing around my office."

Family Roots

"Come on, Jude. You know we vet them thoroughly. We don't just grab random girls off the street."

Panic surges. Have they been watching me? How long? I'd just moved, knew no one, and hadn't started my job. I was heading to an interview when Glen drugged me. My mind races, grasping for answers.

A woman enters with keys to free me, as Jude and Nisha discuss payment. "Three hundred thousand, no less," I hear as they exit. My wrists scream as the shackles fall, my legs collapsing under me. The woman's scarred face offers a pitying half-smile, but her eyes say she's powerless. Was she once chained here, too?

She leads me to another room, the scent of beauty products sparking fleeting hope. She gestures to a soft lounge chair, asking me to undress. Nearby, a tub brims with bubbles, champagne on a stand. An elderly Russian woman, Helga, beckons me in with a thick accent.

"Let me know when she's done, Helga," the scarred woman says, leaving.

A navy-blue dress and flesh-tone heels hang on the wall. "This is what he wants you to wear," Helga says, her face blank.

"'He?"

"Jude."

Tears spill, and I wrap my arms around myself, sobbing. "Please, I don't want to go."

"You have no choice," Helga says curtly, washing my back.

"Hey, Lucy," Lisa interrupts gently, her voice pulling me back to the present. "It feels like you're reliving this, not just telling it."

"I'm sorry," I say instinctively.

"No need to apologize," Lisa replies, her eyes kind. "You've nothing to be sorry for."

"I've never had a voice before," I admit. "I don't know how else to be."

"You're not upsetting us," Lisa assures. "We're honored to hear your story."

"Please continue," Pastor David urges softly.

I nod, slipping back into the memory. Dressed in the silk gown, I'm led to Jude, whiskey and cigar smoke thick in the air. "I hate that smell," I blurt, stronger than intended. His eyes fix on my breasts, the thin fabric hiding nothing. I'm exposed, vulnerable. He rises, approaching slowly. The door clicks shut behind me, and I flinch as he touches my face.

"Some bruising," he murmurs seductively. "That'll fade. You'll obey me, little Lucy." His hands grope my

Family Roots

chest, sliding down my stomach, lifting my dress. With no underwear, I'm defenseless. Instinct screams to pull away, but fear of his violence roots me. I let him touch me, mortified by my lack of choice.

I pause, meeting Lisa's shocked gaze. "Is this too much? I'm sorry, I thought you wanted the full story."

"No, please go on," the woman in pink insists, voice heavy with empathy. "This is horrific. We feel for you."

I raise a hand to Dodge, signaling him to sit as he starts toward us. His protective presence steadies me.

Jude takes my hand, leading me down a long hallway. I glimpse an office desk, cabinets, and a window revealing endless water. Nisha peers out. "See you later, Jude. Pleasure doing business." That's the last I saw of her, though Jude returned to her for new "staff."

The blinding sunlight outside nearly topples me after days in darkness. Jude catches me, carrying me to a helicopter. He places headphones on me, and I hear the pilot, Jasper, ask, "Ready, sir?"

"Yes, Jasper, head home."

Exhaustion overtakes me, and I sleep, half-hoping I won't wake. The helicopter lands, jarring me awake. A sprawling mansion looms, surrounded by acres of woods and an island's isolation. No one will find me here.

"This is your new home, Lucy," Jude says calmly, his gaze unnervingly kind. "I hope you'll be happy."

Happy? I'm a prisoner. But I manage, "Thank you."

A man, Walter, opens my door, shielding me from the rotor's wind. "Hello, Miss. I'm at your service." His knowing smile suggests I'm not the first. I follow him, Jude, close behind, into the mansion. A British woman, Sophia, peels potatoes. "I'm at your service, Ma'am," she says.

"Thank you," I murmur. Jude clears his throat. "Are you hungry?"

"Yes," I admit. "I haven't eaten properly in weeks."

"Sophia will make anything you like." He guides me to a breakfast nook, sunlight streaming through a bay window. The warmth on my neck feels like a fleeting gift.

"Something to drink?" Walter asks, avoiding my eyes.

"Water, please." He offers three kinds, smiling.

"Any is fine," I say. "Better than where I was."

The room stills, Walter and Sophia tensing, bracing for Jude's reaction.

Jude's voice catches, low and sharp. "We don't talk about that in this house. If you do, there'll be consequences you won't like." His dark eyes pierce mine.

"I'm so sorry," I whisper, barely audible. His face softens.

"No worries, first warning." First warning? More to come? Why didn't Walter warn me? I hope he'll clue me in later, so I can escape this place.

"The blue bottle, please, Walter," I say, voice steadier.

Sophia turns. "A sandwich, Miss?"

"That'd be wonderful, thank you," I reply, mustering enthusiasm.

"What kind?"

"Anything," I start, but Jude's glare and Walter's subtle nod stop me.

"Be assertive, Lucy," Jude interrupts. "Tell her what you want. This isn't a prison."

"Turkey and cheese, with mayonnaise, please," I say slowly, tears falling. I don't wipe them, hiding my fear.

"Certainly, Miss," Sophia says boldly. "What shall I call you?" Her confidence mirrors our shared captivity.

Family Roots

"Lucy," I reply, matching her tone. I devour the sandwich and water. Jude's hands rest on my shoulders, his breath warm in my ear. "Time to head upstairs."

His eyes betray his intent, undeniable, familiar. He grabs my hand, leading me to a marble stairway. Each step feels endless, my fate sealed, with no one to save me.

He opens a door to a sparse room bed, a dresser, and a small bathroom with a shower and sink. "This is our room to create our children," Jude says firmly. Confusion floods me, but he dismisses it. "I'll return shortly. Play some music. The iPad by the bed syncs to the speakers." He heads to the bathroom, shedding clothes. His physique is striking, but I focus on the iPad. Music? For rape?

The shower starts, and he calls playfully, "Pick something instrumental, classical."

I select Classical Relaxation Radio on Pandora. Violins and piano fill the room, unfamiliar to me. I fidget, unsure what's next.

"In the top drawer, there are clothes," Jude says over the water. "Choose something." I grab a soft, light-grey nightgown, slipping it on, still unwashed from my makeover hours ago, feeling like years.

"You're tired," Jude says, emerging, aftershave wafting. "This won't take long, then I'll take you to your sleeping room." Sleeping room? I sit on the bed, music swaying, bracing for my fate. He'll take my body, not by choice. Screaming won't help; only fellow captives would hear. I'll retreat inward.

"Stand up, Lucy," Jude commands calmly. "I want to see you." I rise, nearly falling. He catches me, his eyes holding doubt, not anger. I look away, pulling back slightly, fearing his contempt.

"You okay?" he asks, concerned.

"I'm fine, sorry," I say, panicking. "Just dizzy." He presses his fingers to my lips, silencing me.

"It's okay, Lucy. Our first time," he says gently. "You're nervous." My shock is evident. "I'm not a monster," he insists. "In your world, this isn't normal, but it's all I know. My father taught me, his father before him. We buy what we want. You'll understand one day, and I'll teach our son the same."

Son? I can't look at him, hiding my plan to escape. "Oh," I murmur.

He lifts my nightgown off. "Good choice," he whispers. "It hugs you nicely." He removes my panties, ignoring my flinch, kissing my thigh and waist as he rises. Instead of the bed, he carries me to a tub, warm water waiting. When did he fill this? He joins me, washing my body, kissing me. "Lucy, if you let me, I'll care for you. You're lucky I bought you."

I stare, incredulous, bracing for a hit. None comes.

"Don't look at me like that," he says sternly. "Open your eyes." I gaze out the window, wondering what's beyond the trees. "Other men make their women sleep with many for money. I want you only with me. Your job is to have my children." Children? I've never wanted kids. "I've let go of women who couldn't, and they're with those men now. I'm shrewd, Lucy. I'll give you a life you wouldn't have, but you can't leave or share your story. My family knows I bought you—they won't care. My mother bought, birthed me, and loves my father. I want that."

"What?" I blurt.

He raises his voice. "You're mine. Don't talk back, or you'll be punished."

"His punishments were harsh," I say into the microphone, voice raspy.

"Lucy?" Dodge steps forward. "You okay? It sounded like you were there."

Tears stream unnoticed, my audience concerned. "I'm fine," I say, wiping my face. "It still haunts me, his punishments."

"Maybe take a moment," Dodge suggests, worry clear.

"No, I'm good," I insist.

That first night, Jude forced himself on me. It became daily, except during business trips, when he'd return even more demanding. He stopped only when I was pregnant, resuming after each birth.

After our first child, Breezha, he started again at six weeks, ignoring my pain. He wanted as many children as possible, especially a son. When Brandon, our second, was born early, Jude was ecstatic about his firstborn son. I hoped he'd slow down, but six weeks later, he resumed. I prayed for a quick pregnancy with our third for relief. Two years separated Breezha and Brandon.

Six months after Brandon, I was pregnant again, relieved. Jude avoided sex during pregnancy, claiming he didn't want to harm the babies. He believed I wanted to be his, like his mother. Meeting her, she beamed about her first pregnancy, showing no signs of abuse, happy with Jude's father.

Sometimes, I wanted to love Jude and his family, and maybe I did, briefly. I had everything money could buy, beautiful children, and a family that adored me. But I couldn't accept my enslavement. Each time I softened, regret surged. I'd lost my freedom for his happiness.

One day, pregnant with our fifth child, Treavor, our second son, and I lay by the pool. Jude, in a sharp black suit and silver tie, looked handsome. His gaze mirrored

Brandon's love, fleeting but real. He kissed my belly, then my lips. "I know this is a boy," he whispered. Instantly, I realized his affection was tied to the child, and hate flared. Looking back, I believe he loved me, in his twisted way, shaped by his family's beliefs. I don't excuse him, but how could he see it as wrong?

"Excuse me, Lucy," Nancy says, her blue eyes questioning, pulling me back.

"Yes, Nancy," I reply kindly, shaking off the memory.

Nancy's voice trembles as she speaks. "Can I ask a question?"

"Isn't that why I'm here?" I reply gently, offering a warm smile to ease her nerves.

"Well, yes, but I didn't want to interrupt your thoughts," she says, hesitating.

Family Roots

"Go ahead, my dear," I encourage, my eyes conveying reassurance.

Then she dives in, her words tumbling out. "When was the last time you saw your children? Do you love them? Do you miss being with them?"

Her questions hit like a punch. A wave of consternation surges through me, a feeling I haven't faced in years. "That doesn't matter," I say sharply, my voice tighter than I intend. "We're not talking about that." My face must betray my emotions because Nancy looks away, and silence blankets the room.

I glance at Lisa, the head of the human trafficking rescue center, whose expression mirrors my discomfort. Her role is worlds apart from Nancy's, a news reporter with an agenda that seeks headlines, not healing. I remind myself to stay composed, to focus on why I'm here: to share my story, to help others survive.

Dodge, my steadfast ally, rises, his presence commanding the room. "That's enough for today. Come on, Lucy." Before I can respond, he strides toward me, Officer Jones at his side, cuffs dangling in his hands. I stand, turn, and feel the cold metal click around my wrists. As we head toward my cell, I fight the weight of injustice.

The accusation that I killed Jude is absurd. His family's wealth and influence have left me defenseless. Dodge confessed to finding me in an alley, barely alive, with Jude's fist raised above me. But because I grabbed Dodge's gun, its cold steel imprinted with my fingerprints, I became the suspect, not him. His prints should've been on it, too. What a broken system. The jury's verdict was swift and merciless, but I hold onto hope that sharing my truth will inspire someone else to keep fighting.

As Officer Jones guides me through the stark halls to the general population lockup, tears well up. Nancy's question about my children stings like a fresh wound. Who does she think she is? My children were taken from me; they belong to them. I was merely a vessel. Rage simmers, but I force myself to lie down on the thin mattress, the cell door's clang echoing in my mind.

"Wake up, cellmate 7589. Your guests are back," Officer Jones's voice cuts through my groggy haze. I blink awake, the cage around me a stark reminder of my reality. This feels worse than my life with Jude. At least there, I had a decent meal and a real bed.

"Can I at least brush my teeth first?" I snap, irritation flaring.

"Fine. I'll wait here," Jones replies dismissively, standing by as I navigate the lack of privacy. Everything here is exposed, a stark contrast to the secrecy of my life with Jude.

I shake off the memories, quickly pee, wash my hands, and brush my teeth. "Okay, I'm ready," I mutter, and Jones cuffs me again. As we walk down the long hall, voices echo, some cheering, others taunting. I keep my head down, knowing attention only breeds trouble. Good behavior and a thorough investigation might be my ticket out, but hope feels fragile.

Entering the room, I see familiar faces, including Dodge's warm smile. Relief washes over me. He believes in me. Jones removes the cuffs, and I notice a bagel and coffee waiting. "Good morning, everyone," I say into the microphone, my voice steadier than I feel. The group responds with warm greetings.

Nancy raises her hand, and I brace myself. "Yes?" I say cautiously.

Family Roots

"I want to apologize for yesterday. I was out of line," she says sincerely.

"No worries, Nancy," I reply, softening. "I'll only mention my children in the past tense. As for the events that led me here, ask anything you'd like." My voice carries a quiet strength, a reminder of my purpose.

Lisa raises her hand, her tone gentle but probing. "Yesterday, you mentioned your fifth child, Treavor. Was that the baby who didn't make it? I know of ten children, but none named Treavor."

"Yes," I say, tears spilling over. "I was punished brutally for that." The words escape before I can stop them, raw and heavy. Silence grips the room. I grab my bagel, glancing at Dodge, who begins pacing, drawing attention to give me a moment to breathe.

As a few approved guests enter, I steady myself. "Thank you for your patience," I say, my voice surprisingly clear. "Let's keep going, shall we?"

I remember my first time leaving the house, beyond giving birth. Each year, for my birthday, I was allowed one trip anywhere but my hometown or places where I might see family or friends. That first year, I forgot about a cousin in San Diego. When Jude spotted my face on a wanted poster in a diner, we fled on a plane back to the island. That night was brutal, but earlier, I'd been thrilled, stepping into a helicopter, knowing I'd be somewhere new in hours. For the first five years, I was drugged or blindfolded when leaving, unable to pinpoint our location.

By the time Jude trusted me, we had four children. He believed I was devoted, but I was a prisoner, no matter his words. In Colorado, a stretch limousine greeted us. "Where do you want to go, my love?" Jude asked, his voice deceptively warm.

"Can we tour the Coors Light Brewery?" I asked, hopeful.

"Really, Lucy?" he sneered, his disgust palpable. "Haven't you learned to be more refined?" His look branded me as lesser, a reminder that our worlds would never align.

Another year, he took me to France for my birthday. After ten years together, I heard a familiar voice in a café, Becky, my high school friend.

"Hey," I said, fear and confusion colliding.

"How have you been, Lucy? How are your parents?" she asked, concerned.

I recovered quickly. "They're great. I saw them last week. My brother Tom's married now, doing his thing," I lied, my old accent slipping through.

"Let's have dinner tonight! What's your number?" Becky said excitedly.

Jude's glare was lethal, but I rattled off a fake number. His tension eased, but as soon as Becky left, he grabbed my head, pulling me close as if to kiss me. "I'll kill you if she finds us," he hissed. We left the café, packed, and he demanded we return home.

"No, please!" I begged. "Can't we go to Toulouse? She won't be there."

"How do you know that?" he roared.

"She's not that kind of person. She'll stay in Paris; she can't afford Toulouse. Please, Jude, it's my birthday." I hadn't seen her since high school, but I couldn't bear returning to the island.

He relented, calling the pilot. "Get the chopper. We're headed to Toulouse," he barked. I exhaled, relieved, but knew punishment awaited. At the hotel, his grip on my wrist cut off circulation. Once in our room, the blows began on arms, legs, never my stomach. "You know I don't like this, Lucy," he shouted, hurling me across the room. "If you can't bear my children because of this, I'll kill you!"

He tied me to a chair and left for the bar. Hours later, he stumbled back, drunk, and untied me, laying me gently in bed. "I love you," he mumbled, his head on my chest. The next morning, he barely remembered, blaming me for his blackout rage.

The pastor interrupts. "Would you say he was a narcissist, Lucy?"

"Yes," I reply, the truth stark. Jude was the definition of it: controlling, paranoid, and incapable of fault. We stayed a few more days, but he never lingered away from home. His children, never truly mine, were his obsession.

Years later, in the Dominican Republic, I was surprisingly happy. It was after our seventh child, Seth, Jude's favorite. Unlike Brandon, whom he called a mama's boy, Seth was his mirror, groomed for domination, taught to see everything as property.

But I'm here now, sharing my story. Each word is a step toward freedom, a beacon for others to keep fighting, never to give up.

"Brandon won't be groomed like Seth," Jude would whisper to me in private, his voice laced with disdain. Unlike Seth, his favorite, Brandon was too soft in his eyes, a mama's boy. The only time I dared to escape was on Brandon's eighteenth birthday. He was at Harvard, and the ache to see him consumed me. I'd arranged with the pilot, Tom, to fly me there in the morning and return by evening. By then, I'd earned enough trust that Tom knew I wouldn't flee; it would've cost him his life. I planned to be back before Jude returned from his business trip the next day. But as I boarded the helicopter, a call crackled through: Jude needed to be picked up at the airport. My heart plummeted. I wouldn't see my son.

Back in my room, tears streamed down my face when Jude arrived. "What's wrong, Lucy? Didn't you know I was coming home? I told Walter," he said, his voice dripping with false compassion.

"I'm not upset about that, Jude," I snapped, my tone sharper than I intended.

His eyes narrowed. "Well, what then?" he demanded, as if he were the center of my universe.

"Today's Brandon's birthday. I wanted to see him," I said, choking on tears.

"You know the rules, Lucy. You only travel on your birthday," he replied coldly, as if I hadn't endured nineteen years of his control.

"What if I skip my trip this year and go for Brandon's instead?" I pleaded, grasping for mercy.

"Absolutely not," he barked. "I don't bend my rules for your whims!" He stormed out, leaving me crumpled on the floor, sobbing.

Jude grew suspicious, noting the helicopter's readiness that day. To deflect his wrath, I forced myself to play the part. "Hey, Jude," I said, swallowing my revulsion, "it's ten days from my period. You know what that means." The thought of bearing another of his children made my skin crawl, but it bought time for Brandon and me, though not for Tom. He vanished days later, a casualty of Jude's paranoia.

Sure enough, I conceived, and Sarah, our last daughter, was born nine months later. After her, only boys followed. I suffered four miscarriages and one stillbirth,

Family Roots

Treavor's death, which left me with ten living children. Jude never relented, demanding more until I fell gravely ill.

Lisa interrupts, her voice soft but curious. "Sick? I didn't know about that."

"Yes," I reply. "Jude hid it from his family. An ectopic pregnancy cost me one of my tubes, and he didn't want them to know. A 'blemished' wife could be cast out, and by then, he claimed to love me. He didn't want to unsettle our children."

Nancy interjects, her tone sharp. "You keep switching between 'his' and 'ours.'"

"You're right," I admit, my voice steadying. "They were ours, but Jude insisted they were his. I hope you grasp the weight of my story. I was bought plucked from a literal meat market for $300,000. He forced me to marry him, to submit to him whenever he demanded." My voice rises, raw with years of suppressed rage. My breath quickens, emotions overtaking me.

Nancy's face softens, regret in her eyes. "I'm sorry," I say quickly, meaning it. "I didn't intend to lash out."

Dodge stands, his glare silencing the media. "Don't print that, or you're out," he warns. The room stills.

I exhale slowly, grounding myself. "This may sound like a twisted fantasy to you, but it was my reality. Speaking now could cost me my life, but I'll keep fighting until I'm free or until I die. I owe it to my children and myself to rewrite this script."

Cameras flash as I force a smile, my heart heavy with dwindling hope. "That's enough for today," I say, exhaustion feigned to mask my pain. "I'm tired." My glance at Dodge signals the end.

Officer Jones approaches with cuffs. Even behind bars, I'm free not until they believe me, not until my children know the truth, not until Jude's name is just a shadow in my past, not until I'm exonerated. Each step forward is like debugging a broken system, and I won't stop until the code runs clean.

Family Roots

4

FEEDING FRENZY

The plate of food before me feels like a challenge. The fork weighs heavily in my hand, as if it's daring me to give in. I swallow hard and plunge it into the steak, my mind racing. What will this bite do to me? Will it tip the scale?

Feeding Frenzy

I could eat it and slip into the bathroom to purge, erasing the calories. It's been a while since I've done that since the chocolate cake. Each bite of that cake felt like a spotlight, eyes around me judging: Why would she eat the whole piece? Doesn't she know how she looks? My doctor disagrees, insisting I need to gain ten pounds. Ten pounds? The thought repulses me. I loathe food; its sight alone churns my stomach. I eat only to survive. Last week, when Mom called to check on me, I lied. "Have you eaten today?" she asked. "Yes," I said, though it had been two days. I'm fine, I told myself.

Months of therapy and self-reflection have shifted my perspective. My battle with food pales against the tidal wave of emotions crashing over me now. The word cancer haunts me, a specter threatening to steal my father forever. I push it aside to finish my plate, but the fear lingers.

There was a time I barely thought of him, convinced he cared nothing for me. But that feels like another life. He didn't even know I nearly died. I couldn't tell him. That chapter of my story feels like someone else's script I couldn't write. Alcohol and drugs stole him, a truth I didn't fully grasp until the whispers of temptation reached me.

Those whispers began when I was young, but food drowned them out. I'd watch adults at parties laughing, drinking, eating, living carefree. "One day, this can be you," the voice promised. I didn't understand then. But at a friend's urging, I mixed a drink from the basement bar, spiked with every liquor I could find. I grabbed some pot, too. That night, I thought I was stepping into adulthood. Instead, I stumbled down a path of temptation, losing my virginity in that same house.

The voices grew louder at night, invading my solitude. With Dad away on business, I'd hear Mom crying in her room. "Your father doesn't love you," the whispers taunted. "He's gone, and your mother's a mess. Who'll protect you?" Our home was a fortress of lies, its walls thick with deception. Fights erupted constantly, words cutting deep into my core.

Years after Dad left, Mom's boyfriend stared me down and called me a whore. I swear I heard cheers, as if a crowd surrounded us. Impossible, yet the sting was real. That man, a stranger to me, thought he could define me. His words, like those of others before him, carved wounds that took years to heal. But they pale against today's pain.

"Hey, Patrice," Dee says, opening my door. "How are you today?"

Feeding Frenzy

I can't answer. Instead, I hand her the letter trembling in my hand.

"What's this?" she asks.

"Just read it." Her eyes widen as she scans the page.

"I'm so sorry, Patrice," she says I had no idea."

"Neither did I," I reply, guilt tinging my voice.

"What are you going to do?"

"I don't know. I have to get out of here first."

"When's that?"

"My therapy ends in three weeks, but I'm not a prisoner. I can leave anytime. I just don't want to go until I'm ready. I can't relapse. I'm only now realizing food wasn't my problem, my dad was."

Dee nods, empathy in her eyes. "I see how that's confusing." Over these months, she's become my confidante, closer than anyone I've known.

"Just because your dad's cancer is stage 4 doesn't mean he's dying tomorrow," she says. "Take care of yourself first. Visit him in three weeks and sort it out then."

"But what if he needs me now?" I ask, fear creeping in.

"He'll be fine. It didn't start yesterday if it's stage 4 already."

"I guess," I say, uncertain. "I'm in a better place now. I don't want to jeopardize that." The day I realized my resentment toward food stemmed from my father's absence, everything shifted. I also saw how Mom's obsession with appearances, her criticism over five pounds, shaped me. That internalized shame led me here. I need more healing before facing him."

"Honey pie, leaving now could derail your recovery," Dee warns. "Stay. Don't leave your code half-debugged."

I nod, her words anchoring me. I'm redrawing my pictures stroke by stroke. Each bite, each truth, is a step toward freedom, a chance to rebuild, not just survive, but to thrive.

"Thank you, Dee, for being my anchor," I say, gratitude warming my voice. "I don't know where I'd be without you."

"Oh, please," Dee teases, her eyes sparkling. "You'd find another friend, maybe not as fabulous as me, but…" Our laughter fills the room, a balm for the bittersweet moment.

"Hey, Wanda!" I call out, spotting the familiar face of the center's staff.

"Patrice, you're glowing today," Wanda says, her smile wide.

"That's because I'm going home," I reply, shaking my head in disbelief. "These three weeks flew by."

"Good for you, young lady," Wanda says warmly. "It's time to start living."

"Exactly what I plan to do," I say, my resolve firm.

"If you ever need us, we're here," she adds.

"I hope I won't, but I'll keep in touch," I promise, turning to grab my bags.

Dee stands before me, tears streaming down her face. "Oh, girl, don't do this," I say gently. "We'll see each other soon."

"I know," she sniffles. "But things will change."

"They will, but we'll always be friends. Text me when you're out next week, and if I'm not in Colorado, I'll come get you."

"Deal," she says, pulling me into a hug so tight it steals my breath. As we part, we wipe our tears, forcing smiles.

Feeding Frenzy

"No goodbyes," I say firmly. "Just see you later."

"Agreed," Dee whispers.

Stepping into the morning mist, the air feels crisp and pure, or maybe it's me who feels cleansed. My time at A New Me was grueling, but it taught me the truth: food, alcohol, and toxic relationships weren't my problem. I was. Now, the new me is ready to run my updated code. I stride to my blue 2004 Ford Fusion, click the locks, toss my bag in the backseat, and slide into the driver's seat. The engine hums to life, and I pull away, uncertain of my first stop. Mom's house? My place? McDonald's? I laugh at the thought, then hear a whisper: Only disgusting people eat there. I shake it off, reminding myself that lies stem from darkness, and I've chosen light.

My car seems to steer itself, landing me at Mom's. As I step out, she bursts onto the porch, arms wide, screaming, "My baby!" The swing at her sacred spot for heart-to-hearts waits for us.

"Hi, Mom," I say, sheepish under her booming voice. She envelops me in a hug, reluctant to let go, then pulls back to study me.

"You look amazing, Patrice," she says, eyes misty. "I missed you so much."

"I missed you too," I reply, sinking into her embrace.

"Coffee? Something to eat?" she offers, then catches herself. "Sorry, love, I didn't mean to mention food." Mom's effortless relationship with food, eating freely, never gaining a pound, always felt unattainable. Her beauty set a standard I couldn't match.

"It's fine, Mom," I assure her. "I've spent months dissecting food. I'd love a croissant and coffee if you have it." A whisper creeps in: A carb overload. "Shut up," I mutter, silencing it.

"What was that, Patsy?" she asks, concerned.

"I'd really love that yummy croissant and coffee," I say, smiling.

We settle in the kitchen, then head to the porch swing, our sanctuary of conversation. Hours pass, fueled by coffee and fruit, until I summon the words. "Dad has cancer. I'm going to Colorado."

"I know," Mom says, tears welling.

"You do?" I ask, startled.

"He wrote to me too," she says. "I hoped you'd go see him. You need to rebuild that connection, Pats."

"What if he doesn't want me there?" I whisper, fear of rejection surfacing. "What if I feel unloved again?"

"Don't go there, sweetie," she says firmly. "Your dad loves you, he's just terrible at showing it. When are you leaving?"

"In a week. I need to head home now, though."

She gives me that look You just got here but softens. "If you need me, I'm here. I'll be thinking of you, love."

"I'll call when I get there," I promise, returning her hug. She holds me tight, then lets me go when I pull away.

Stepping off the plane in Colorado, I long for Mom's porch swing. When I told her about Dad's cancer, her empathy ran deep. Though divorced for years, my parents still carry a quiet torch for each other. "It'll be okay, love bug," she'd said, wiping my tears. "I'll be right here." I know she'll be waiting, arms open, when I return.

I steel myself. I can't let Dad see my pain; he has enough to bear. I head to baggage claim, planning to rent a car and drive straight to the hospital. Over the intercom, my name echoes, summoning me to the car rental counter. I drag my bags to find Nina, a warm woman with a bright smile, behind the counter.

"Hi, Nina. I'm Patrice Warren," I say. "You called me?"

"I'm sorry, Ms. Warren, but we're out of your chosen car. We have upgrades available, only two left—so I wanted to reach you quickly. I can upgrade you at no extra cost, but I'll need it back a day early. Can you manage that?"

"Absolutely," I agree.

"Perfect," Nina says, her fingers flying over the keyboard.

A voice behind me freezes my blood. "Patrice, is that you?"

I turn to face Ted, my worst nightmare. "Oh, hi," I say flatly.

"You look amazing!" he says, his eyes tracing my body.

"Thanks," I mutter.

"I mean it, you're hot!"

"Yep, thanks," I repeat, my tone clipped.

Nina interjects, sensing my unease. "Here you go, Ms. Warren. You're all set. Sign here, and you're good to go."

"Thank you, Nina," I say, grabbing the keys. I turn, but Ted looms closer.

"Let's get a drink. I'll carry your bags," he offers, his smile predatory.

"No, I'm good. I need to get going," I say, stepping back.

"Come on, just one drink. Catch up," he presses, his eyes saying more than his words.

"Nah, I really can't," I insist.

"Patrice, I don't see you every day, one drink," he demands, drawing stares from passersby.

The pressure builds, and a whisper creeps in: He just wants your body. Another hisses, Sex is love. "No," I say aloud. "Shut up!"

"You know, Ted, I have to go," I declare, grabbing my bags and striding away.

"Did you tell me to shut up?" he calls after me.

"Yep!" I shout back, my pace quickening.

"Whatever, Patrice," he mutters, his voice fading.

A smile breaks across my face. Months of hard work repainted the pictures in my heart have paid off. I'm stronger now. The airport doors slide open, and a breeze tousles my hair. Before me, mountains rise against a vivid blue sky. I scan the lot for my rental, expecting modest, but spot a sleek BMW sports car. No way. I click the key fob, and the lights flash, locks chirping. Thank you, Nina. I toss my bags in the trunk, slide into the driver's seat, and pull away, a new sense of self propelling me forward.

The twenty-minute drive to the hospital felt like two. This road, literal and metaphorical, is mine to navigate. Like redrawing a design in my heart and mind, hoping to make something ugly beautiful again.

The hospital doors slide open, and I hurry to the reception desk, unfamiliar with the sterile maze. A man looks up, his eyes kind. "Hi, I'm here to see Mike Warren," I say.

"And you are?" he asks.

"His daughter, Patrice Warren."

"Driver's license, please." I hand it over, and he makes a copy before returning it. "He's on the third floor, room 302. Take the B elevator, press the button for the B wing, and they'll buzz you in."

"Thank you, Earl," I say, flashing a smile as I head toward the elevator.

Feeding Frenzy

My thoughts race. It's been eight years since I last saw Dad. He was always larger than life, strong, unyielding. But cancer changes people. What will he look like now? Before I spiral, the elevator doors open. I press '3' and pause as the doors close, steeling myself. When they reopen, I step into the hallway, my heart pounding. I press the buzzer for the B wing.

"Can I help you?" a voice crackles over the intercom.

"Yes, I'm here for Mike Warren. I'm his daughter, Patrice Warren."

A loud buzz startles me, and the door unlocks. I glance at the signs, Rooms 300-320 to the right, and head toward 302. Pausing outside, I smooth my hair and shirt, a reflex from Dad's old critiques. Brush your hair, Patsy. You look like a bum. I shake off the memory and step inside.

"Hi, Dad," I say, my voice barely above a whisper. Surprise flickers across his face, a mix of regret and awe.

"Patrice, I didn't know you were coming," he says, his voice frail but warm.

"I wanted to surprise you," I reply, forcing a smile. "Figured you weren't going anywhere, so I wouldn't have to hunt you down."

His grin lights up the room, but it's not the face I remember. His cheeks are hollow, his frame skeletal where muscle once stood. "This is a great surprise," he says, his smile softening the shock.

"You look…" I falter, searching for words. "Um, well…"

"I know, it's a shock," he interrupts, chuckling. "Scares me every time I see a mirror."

His laughter cuts through the tension, and I exhale. "Good, because I wasn't sure if 'Hi, Dad, you look like hell' was okay," I tease, giggling. His laugh, louder than mine, eases me further.

"No need to sugarcoat it," he says. "I know I look rough. I'm dying anyway."

The words hit hard, and fear flashes across my face before I can hide it. He notices but doesn't press. "How was your trip?" he asks, shifting gears. "You come in today?"

"Straight from the airport," I say.

"I didn't mean to upend your life," he says, his tone tentative. "Just thought you should know what's going on."

"It's okay," I reply, dodging the truth about my months in recovery. "I just wrapped a project at work, so the timing's good." A small lie, but I don't want to burden him. My smile seems to reassure him.

"I'd offer you a drink, but all they've got is juice and junk," he jokes.

Feeding Frenzy

"I'm good," I say. "I stopped drinking over a year ago."

"Didn't know that," he says, surprised.

"It wasn't a good fit for me," I shrug.

"I get it. Didn't do me any favors either," he says, his voice darkening. "Liver cancer's eating me alive now. It's spreading everywhere. Nasty stuff."

"I bet," I say, unsure how to respond but wanting to stay connected.

"Let's not dwell on it," he says, his resolve startling me. "It's a losing battle. What's up with you?"

"Not much," I say, grasping for something neutral. "Working on a new clothing line. A couple of retailers might pick it up this fall."

"You've always been talented, Patsy," he says, pride in his voice. The nickname stings. I haven't been Patsy in years, except to Mom. My grimace betrays me.

"Sorry," he says quickly. "Forgot you're a big shot now, not 'Patsy' anymore." His jab lands, and I bristle.

"'Patsy' doesn't cut it when I'm pitching to top buyers nationwide," I retort, my own dig slipping out. Regret clouds his face, and I feel the old dance of our fractured bond. His cancer looms, a stark reminder of time running out. I push the thought away, and dwelling on it now feels like betraying the moment.

A nurse enters, breaking the tension. "Hi, Mr. Warren, how're we feeling today? I'm Lucile, your night nurse." She glances at me, smiling. "And who's this?"

"My daughter, Patuh, Patrice," Dad corrects himself.

"Nice to meet you, Patrice," Lucile says, checking the IV bag. "You've got about thirty minutes left on this. Then we can get some pain meds."

"Good," Dad says, wincing. "My side's killing me."

"We'll fix that," Lucile says, winking. "I've got some pull with the doc. I'll see if we can speed it up." She leaves, her warmth lingering.

"I didn't know you were in pain," I say, guilt creeping in. "I'm sorry."

"Not your fault," he says. "All mine. Nobody forced me to down a liter of vodka every night. That was my masterpiece."

His words hit hard. I remember him drinking beer on weekends when I was a kid, but hard liquor during the divorce? I hadn't realized how bad it got. My own struggles with my eating disorder started then, but I'm not ready to share that. He wouldn't understand.

"How's your girlfriend?" I ask, changing the subject. "Connie, right?"

"Yeah, Connie," he says. "She bailed when I got diagnosed. Loved to party, didn't want to slow down for me. I tried quitting at first, but when it hit Stage 2, I thought, screw it, I'm done. Might as well go out faster."

"I'm sorry," I say, anger lacing my voice.

"Not your fault," he repeats. "I was alone. Didn't seem to matter."

The weight of his words sinks in. He was alone, and I didn't know. "How's Mom?" he asks, softening.

"She's great," I say.

"And number four? What's his name?" he smirks, teasing.

"Rude," I shoot back. "Don? He's good for her." My jab lands, and he winces not just from pain, I suspect.

"Let's hold off on the heavy stuff," I say, noticing his discomfort. "I'll check into my hotel and come back tomorrow."

"Why a hotel?" he asks, his breath shallow.

"Didn't know what else to do," I say. "I'm surprising you, remember?"

"Stay at my house," he insists. "No need to pay for a hotel."

"You sure?" I hesitate.

"Nobody's there, Patrice," he says, gesturing to a closet. "Keys are in the drawer. I'll write down the address. It's five minutes away."

Dad always had a knack for money, navigating the stock market like a coder cracking algorithms. His home, I know, will outshine any hotel. He sent money to Mom and me long after I turned eighteen, even after she remarried. It was his way of making amends.

"Okay," I agree. "That'll save me some cash."

"I'd love for you to stay there," he says. "I'll cover the hotel cancellation."

"You don't have to," I protest.

"I insist," he says. "You came all this way. It's the least I can do."

The tension between us eases, like a stroke of the lines for a dress I have to design. I grab the keys and step to his bedside, hugging him gently and kissing his forehead. "I missed you, Pats," he whispers.

"I missed you too, Dad," I say, taking the paper with his address. His handwriting looks foreign, just like he does. Tears threaten, but I hold them back for him, for me, for what we're trying to rebuild. Wanda's voice echoes in my mind: Love yourself first, and show others how to love you. I smile, wave goodbye, and head out, ready to optimize this fragile connection, one step at a time.

Dad's house doesn't disappoint; it's stunning. Every detail is pristine, from the sleek crown molding to the brushed silver cabinet handles. The kitchen island, complete with built-in ovens and a farm sink, screams luxury. No hint of the chaos he caused lies within these walls. To an outsider, my stories of his cruelty would sound like fiction. During the divorce, Mom's revelations about his behavior shocked their friends. Some branded her a liar, cutting ties, while Dad's charm and generosity won others over. I remember their best friends leaving one night, Mom sobbing because they sided with him. They later saw the truth, but the damage was done. Mom couldn't forgive. She was left with two friends; Dad kept the rest.

The fallout hit me hard. Some of my friends lived in our neighborhood, but Mom, fearing Dad's influence, moved us away. I switched schools, leaving my world behind. Dad didn't seem to care. He sneaked women into the house, thinking I wouldn't notice. I kept his secrets, shielding Mom from more pain.

I wander down the hall, taking in the old photos of me. A side bedroom with an attached bathroom, larger than my apartment's master suite, will be my stay. The master bedroom is a spectacle: a walk-in closet fit for a celebrity, with a corner holding women's clothes and shoes, Connie's, no doubt. In the lavish bathroom, I pick up Dad's cologne, its familiar scent stirring memories. Who still wears this? My fingers brush a towel, hung from his last shower here. How long has it been?

A chime from the alarm snaps me out of my thoughts, signaling someone's arrival. I close the bedroom door and hurry to the mudroom. "Hello?" I call out. Silence. "Hello!" Fear grips me, but a faint "hello" echoes from the kitchen. Helga appears, and relief washes over me.

"Helga! I can't believe you're still here!" I exclaim.

Feeding Frenzy

"Patsy!" she cries, rushing to me and wrapping her arms around my waist. She cups my face, planting a kiss on my cheek. "I missed you so much. Look at you, a woman now!"

I twirl playfully, and she stops, tears in her eyes. "You're so beautiful," she says.

"Don't cry, Helga," I say softly.

"I'm fine," she insists, smiling. "Just thrilled to see you. Your dad missed you. He brags about you constantly: 'Patsy's a designer,' 'She sold her first line,' 'She won best new designer.' On and on."

Her words stun me. "He loved me?" The thought feels foreign.

"What did you think, girl? That he stopped caring?" Helga says, surprised. "Come on, you know that's not true."

"Do I?" I murmur, doubt lingering.

"Let's not dig up old wounds," she says, shifting gears. "You hungry? Want me to whip something up?"

"Actually, I'm starving," I admit.

"How about mac and cheese?" she teases, laughing. "Oh, wait, you're a big shot now. Probably too fancy for that."

"No way," I say, grinning. "Yours is the best. I haven't had it in years."

She catches the flicker in my eyes but doesn't pry. "Alright, mac and cheese it is. Catch me up, it's been too long." I hesitate, then let the words flow, spilling my story to the one person who knows me without judgment. I skirt around A New Me; she wouldn't understand. Helga's been with Dad since Mom left, a constant through his storms. She's seen things she'd rather forget, I'm sure. Dad once told her, "I can't live without you, Helga," and I bet he pays her well to manage his life, cooking, cleaning, errands. What will she do when he's gone? Knowing him, he's left her something substantial. She's earned it, putting up with his mess.

Minutes later, a steaming bowl of mac and cheese sits before me. "Bon appétit, Pats," Helga says, her warmth enveloping me. I dig in, savoring the creamy comfort, but a whisper creeps in: Why eat something so fattening? You'll ruin everything. Another hisses, You just lost that weight, don't gain it back. My chewing slows, fear flashing across my face.

"What's wrong, love? Doesn't it taste good?" Helga asks, concerned.

"No, it's perfect," I say, forcing a smile. "Just remembered something I need to do." I grip the fork, summoning my new voice: You are loved. You are beautiful. Food is fuel, not failure. The dark whispers fade, powerless now. Months ago, I silenced those lies, trading the lord of darkness for the Lord of Light. These echoes are just glitches of my old design, and I'm drawn to them.

"So, Helga, how long has Dad been this sick?" I ask, steering the conversation.

"About three years ago, he started declining," she says, her voice heavy. "The last four months have been brutal. He hates hospitals, but sometimes it's easier than home care. He gets rude with the staff, and they quit. At the hospital, they have to stick it out." She scowls, sighing.

"Still mouthing off, huh?" I say.

"To everyone but me," Helga says, smirking. "Years ago, I gave him a piece of my mind. He's been respectful since. Knows I'll walk if he crosses me."

"Good for you," I laugh. "You're the only one who can handle him. His main squeeze."

"Damn straight," she chuckles. "But you're his true love, Pats. Enough about him, tell me about you. Where've you been?"

I pause, then let the truth slip. "I was in rehab," I say softly. "For an eating disorder."

Helga's eyes widen. "Pats, I had no idea."

"I don't talk about it," I say. "Dad never allowed weakness. He wanted a son, so he pushed me to be perfect. I succeeded except with food. It got bad. I was down to 85 pounds when I checked myself in."

"Dear Lord, that's too thin," she says, shocked.

"My friends noticed, and I got scared," I continue. "I had to rewrite my life. It was tough, but I'm here, alive."

"I had no clue," Helga says, guilt in her voice. "You were always small as a teen."

"It started at 15," I explain. "At a party, some guy called me fat when I rejected him. His words stuck. I thought everyone, family, and friends were lying about how I looked. I started working out obsessively and cutting my food intake. It spiraled. I'd eat and purge, then go days with just water, coffee, and vodka to sleep. Designing let me hide it 'too busy to eat', but when the work stopped, the truth hit. I didn't see what others saw in the mirror. I saw a girl who couldn't overeat." A girl desperate for love, I think, but don't say.

"I'm so sorry I didn't notice," Helga says.

"Not your fault," I reassure her. "I wasn't around much."

"What triggered it at 15?" she asks.

"That guy's comment was the spark," I say. "Then, my boyfriend a few years back said I was too thin, so I gained a bit to please him. He left me for a model I worked with, and I crashed. Stopped eating entirely. But I'm past that now." I shove a big bite of mac and cheese in my mouth, puffing my cheeks playfully.

"I'm so glad you're okay, Pats," Helga says, her eyes soft. "Your dad would be devastated if he knew."

"He'd do nothing," I say, my voice muffled by food.

"Girl, you know he loves you," she insists.

"Do I?" I challenge, but let it drop. "I'm gonna shower and unpack. Don't go playing Cupid while I'm gone."

"Cupid?" she laughs. "I'm just having Brad, the neighbor, check the garbage disposal."

"Uh-huh," I tease, eyeing her. "I don't need a guy to be happy!"

"Don't forget your bags," she calls as I head down the hall. I double back, grab them, and dash to the bedroom, grinning.

I'm reframing my thoughts. Each bite, each truth, is a commitment to a stronger version of me, one that runs clean, free of old ideals.

Feeding Frenzy

The bedroom is a dream, painted in my favorite colors. Did Dad design this for me? A photo of us on the dresser, next to the ballerina figurine he gave me when I was five, answers my whispered question. I open a drawer, pajamas, tags still on. Another reveals socks, then shirts, and shorts, all neatly folded. A full wardrobe? How did he know I was coming? I glide to the bedside dresser, finding books, pens, markers, and a journal beneath an adjustable light. Strange, how did he guess? The closet doors swing open, revealing dresses, pants, and rows of shoes, all brand-new. Above the bed, my first place drawing from age thirteen is framed. Opposite, a full-length mirror flanks a slim dresser topped with jewelry, its drawers holding undergarments. This room feels like a home I was meant to claim. Why didn't he tell me?

Helga peeks in, her smile mischievous. "He buys you things constantly but never sends them. I thought I'd organize them for you. There's more in the spare room, loads of stuff."

"Why doesn't he send them?" I ask, bewildered.

"Who can figure him out, Pats?" Helga shrugs. "He's your dad."

"This is hundreds of dollars' worth," I say, stunned, spotting a Tiffany box with two-carat diamond earrings in the dresser.

Michelle Pentifallo

"He loves buying for you," she says. "But he's scared you'll reject them or him. He always asks, 'Will she like this?' I say yes, but he holds back. Buying stuff, sending money, that's how he shows love. It's all he knows."

"That's wild," I murmur, holding the earrings. "These are too much, just sitting here."

"I tell him you'd love them," Helga says. "But he's terrified of your rejection."

"I don't know what to say," I admit.

"Maybe say thank you next time you see him," she suggests, shutting the door. "Take a shower, you stink!" she yells, laughing down the hall.

I sniff my armpit, yep, she's right. I set my bags at the foot of the bed, realizing I barely need them with this setup, and head to the bathroom. The hamper's empty, the vanity brimming with perfumes. Drawers reveal makeup, face creams, and an organizer with cotton balls, Q-tips, and wipes. Everything's thought out. Why now? I strip, catching my reflection. "You look good, girl," I say, smiling. "You've come a long way." No dark whispers haunt me now. I trace my hand over my stomach, tousle my hair, and grin. "You got this, Patrice." Turning on the shower, I belt out, "Yesterday, love was such an easy game to play, now I need a place to hide away, oh, yesterday came suddenly…"

Morning arrives swiftly. I dress and head to the living room, soaking in the sunrise through the bay window.

"You look fabulous," Helga says from behind me.

"It's so beautiful here," I say, turning.

"Your dad only picks the best," she replies.

"I'm heading to the hospital," I say. "Want to come?"

"Oh, child, I don't do hospitals," Helga says, chuckling. "Your dad and I have a deal: I keep his secrets, and he doesn't drag me there. He's in every other month now. I know he hates it, but I'm not dealing with his nonsense. Works for us."

"Fair enough," I laugh. "Need anything while I'm out?"

"Nah," she says, handing me keys from a rack. "Go through the garage. These are yours."

"Mine?" I stare, shocked.

In the garage, a candy-apple red 1969 Chevy Camaro SS with white racing stripes gleams. My dream car. "What?!" I squeal. "This is mine?"

"Yes, girl," Helga laughs. "It's yours."

"No way!" I run my hand along its frame, inhaling the scent of new leather and restored parts. The original radio and controls are pristine. "I can't believe it."

"Enjoy!" Helga calls, hitting the garage door opener.

Michelle Pentifallo

I slide in, turn the key, and ease out, my mind reeling. When did he get this? Why didn't he tell me? Joy surges as I tap the accelerator, the engine purring. I cruise the neighborhood, mindful of the early hour, then hit the main road for a quick burst of speed. *Get back, Patrice,* I chide myself. *You haven't eaten.* I return, whip up pancakes, apply makeup, and slip on the diamond earrings.

"See you later, Helga!" I call, heading out.

"Later, Pats," she replies, warming my heart.

At the hospital, I bypass the valet, nobody's touching my Camaro, and park. Earl, the receptionist, greets me with a grin. "Patrice Warren," I say, and he directs me to elevator B, third floor, room 302. I flash a smile and head down the hall, peeking into Dad's room.

"Hey, loser, what's up?" I say, grinning. "I got all your gifts. What's with that, Dad?"

"Watch your mouth, child," he says, coughing deeply, pain flickering across his face.

Feeding Frenzy

"Excuse me, Prince Harry," I tease. "Forgot you're a gentleman." My laugh bubbles up.

"Funny little girl," he retorts, smirking.

"Seriously, Dad, it's too much," I say.

"I can't take money with me when I die, Patsy," he says softly. "Might as well spend it on those I love."

Confusion clouds my face, and he sees it. "It's that serious now," he admits. "I'm here every other month. The meds aren't working anymore. It's getting close."

"I'm sorry," I say, the words slipping out.

"Me too, Pats," he says, his eyes heavy with unspoken regrets. I let it pass.

"Wanna play Yahtzee?" I ask, lightening the mood.

"How about Spades?" he counters, a glint in his eye, reaching for cards in the drawer.

"Prepared, huh, Mr. Warren?" I tease.

"Always, Ms. Warren," he replies.

"I'm gonna whip you," I say, pulling a chair to the table.

He shuffles, and I cut the deck, a memory flashing: us in the kitchen with Mom, laughing over Spades when I was young. I miss that. Dad's concern snaps me back. "You okay, Pats?"

"Just thinking," I say, fanning my cards

"Seeing anyone, Patrice?" he asks, formal now.

"Nope, Father," I mock. "Not currently."

"Got your eye on anyone?"

"Dad, I'm not discussing my love life with you," I say, rolling my eyes.

"Who said love life?" he protests, sticking out his tongue. "You're ruining the game."

I laugh, catching a glimpse of the playful Dad I adored, the one who teased and joked before life dimmed him. "What about you?" I ask. "Got a hottie in your sights?"

"Nurse Alexis does it for me," he says, winking. We burst out laughing, and for a moment, I have my Dad back.

As we deal the cards, the door opens, and a nurse steps in. Her name tag reads *Alexis*. I stifle a giggle, glancing at Dad, who flashes a sly smile her way.

Each laugh, each game, is a step toward healing, freeing the pain to build something new.

"Yes, Nurse Alexis, what can we do for you?" Dad asks, his voice playful.

"It's time for your CAT scan, Mr. Warren," Alexis replies, her tone light. "We've rolled out the red carpet for you." Her humor and charm explain why Dad's smitten.

"This is my daughter, Patrice," he says, gesturing to me. "She's visiting for a couple of days."

"Only a couple?" I tease, dripping with mock offense. "Trying to ditch me already?"

"I figured you'd be sick of me by day one," he shoots back, grinning.

"Could happen," I retort, and we laugh.

Alexis cuts in, her voice turning serious. "I'm glad you're here, Patrice. Nice to meet you. He needs your support. Now, Mr. Warren, into the wheelchair hospital policy."

"How long's this gonna take?" Dad grumbles, easing into the chair.

"Not too long," Alexis says. "But with other tests after, you'll be tired. A couple of hours before you're back, cheating at cards with your daughter."

"Cheating?" Dad protests, feigning shock. We all laugh, knowing it's not beyond him.

"Don't worry, Dad," I say. "I'll grab dinner and swing back later. What do you want?"

"Doesn't matter," he says. "Can't taste much anyway. See you, Pats."

"Later, Dad," I reply, watching Alexis wheel him out. A smile spreads across my face, warmed by the simple joy of the moment, a glimpse of the father I'd longed for.

Sitting in the visitor's chair, I'm pulled into memories of those hospital days. Laughter with nurses, card games on that tiny table, talks that stretched for hours. Those months were fleeting, but the richest of my life with him. He shared things I never imagined calling me beautiful, special. One day, his sadness was palpable.

"What's wrong, Dad?" I asked.

"Just thinking," he said, eyes distant.

"About what?"

"You," he admitted, tears welling. "How I failed you all those years."

I'd only seen him cry once before, during a fight with Mom before he left. "I messed up, Pats," he said. "I thought money was enough. I focused on myself, neglected you. I'm so sorry."

That moment was a gift. At *A New Me*, I'd forgiven him to heal myself, but his apology sealed it. Food lost its power over me; his love was what I'd craved. I hugged his frail frame, whispering, "I forgive you. I love you." That was our last sad day.

Now, his urn sits before me, framed by flowers and memories. A poem, found in his memory chest, rests in a frame nearby. He never shared it, but it reveals his love:

Thoughts of My Two-Year-Old
I really love my Daddy, but I didn't want to see him cry,
That's why I didn't love him when I said goodbye.

Michelle Pentifallo

He has gone away, to a very bad place,
That's why I want to cry when I see his face.
It may be a long time before he comes back home,
So I want to be a good girl, and then he may not roam.
I know he really loves me, for he's often told me so.
Why is he the way he is? No one seems to know.
He's not the bad man that some people may think.
He just does silly things when he takes a drink.
I pray that one day soon, he will learn to be
The man I know can stay at home with me.

Clients and friends will soon fill this room with tears and laughter, but these last months reshaped me. Tears stream as I stare at the urn. Does he see me? Does he know I love him? Can he feel the light I carry for the Lord of Light and His people? I wipe my eyes, stand tall, and smile as Mom enters. Life's forever changed, but I'm free. "I love you, Daddy," I whisper, heading to greet the guests.

I've redrawn my heart, committing to a life free of old designs. Each memory, each tear, is a new line of freedom, a new stroke of desire, one that runs with love and light.

Feeding Frenzy

5

OUT OF TIME

Blood pools in my mouth, its metallic burn searing my throat as I lie on the floor. What did I do this time? I don't even know anymore. Each word, each move, seems to trigger Ralph's fists. My jaw throbs; maybe a tooth's gone. Standing feels impossible. If I could just sleep here, maybe

Out of Time

I wouldn't wake up. That would be the kindest escape. There's nowhere else to go but this cold floor.

In the distance, Ralph's screams clash with Mom's. Then, a thud silences her. He's hit her, too. Maybe I can move and check if she's alive. Maybe this time she'll leave. He rarely strikes us both in one night. What set him off? I'm so tired.

"Tiana! Wake up!" Ralph's voice booms, yanking me from the haze.

God, I'm still alive? My swollen eyes barely let light in. How long was I out? "What day is it?" I croak. "Where am I?"

"Get up, you worthless garbage!" he roars. My legs tingle, numb. If I stand, will he hit me again? Where's Mom? The last sound of her body hitting the floor haunts me. Is she okay?

Ralph paces, rubbing his head. "Look what you did now," a voice sneers faintly. "You really did it this time." It's not Ralph's voice, higher, almost audible. Where's it coming from? My skin prickles.

"What are you staring at, you whore?" Ralph snaps. "Get up, or I'll knock you out."

My head pounds, legs trembling as I force myself up. "Where are you taking me?" I ask, earning a sharp slap. In the living room, the TV drones; it's still dark outside. I wasn't out long. In Mom's room, blood stains the floor more than usual. My eyes land on her, a dark pool around her head. My scream rips through me. "Ralph, what have you done?"

He lunges, then stops, clutching his head, crying with a chilling laugh. "Shut her up for good," he mutters. "Now you're gonna help me clean this up and bury her."

"What?" I scream. "Are you insane?" A voice behind me whispers, "Yeah, he is, thanks to me." I spin, hairs standing on end, but no one's there.

"You did this, you fix it," I say, defiance flaring. Mom's gone, what's left to lose? To my shock, Ralph stumbles out. I cradle Mom, sobbing until time blurs. Wandering the house, I find the front door open, his car gone. Without thinking, I grab the phone and dial 911.

Journal Entry – 1/19/15

I woke up lonely today, heavier than usual. Writing the date, it hits me: five years since Ralph killed Mom. Tears spill, unstoppable. It feels like yesterday. I wish he'd taken me instead. Living without her is hollow. At first, I was a zombie; now, I try to move forward. Next month, I turn 18, free to leave this place. I might graduate in May, but then what? Fran says I can stay with her family, but they'll tire of me. Everyone does. We'll see what today brings.

Each day is a commitment to survival, a step toward freedom from this pain.

A sharp slap to the back of my head jolts me from sleep. "Wake up, Tiana," Addie says, giggling.

"Knock it off, Adeline," I snap.

"Don't call me that," she hisses.

"Isn't it your name?" I retort, clutching my journal.

"What's in that dumb book?" she taunts, snatching it and tearing pages as she yanks it away.

"Stop it!" I yell, and we freeze, knowing someone's coming. Addie seizes the moment to twist the knife.

"So, your mom died today, huh? Boo-hoo, get over it," she sneers.

Kim, the house mom, bursts in. "You two again? Why can't you just get along?" Her face mixes regret and frustration, a woman trapped in a job corralling broken teens. "Addie, did you start this?"

"Why's it always me?" Addie whines.

"Because it usually is," Kim says flatly.

"You don't know that," Addie snaps.

"I've got cameras, Addie," Kim counters.

"Whatever. You just like Tiana better," Addie mutters, tossing my journal to the floor and storming out, flipping us off. "This place is a joke!" she screams, knocking over a lamp.

Kim sighs, picking up my journal. Her eyes catch today's entry, the bold words: *MOM DIED TODAY!* "I'm sorry, Tiana," she says softly. "I forgot it was today."

Michelle Pentifallo

"It's fine," I lie. "I didn't realize until I wrote it." The pain's still raw, Ralph stole Mom, and he's still breathing.

"Are you okay, sweetheart?" Kim asks.

"I'm alright," I say, my voice hollow.

Kim's been here since I arrived, offering love from day one. It took months for me to crack open her idea to journal, bridging the gap. Writing let me process Mom's death, though the ache lingers. Kim reads my entries during counseling, helping me find words for my grief. It's helped, but Ralph's shadow looms.

Kim's hand on my shoulder pulls me back. "If you need to talk, I'm here. You're not alone."

But I am.

"Get dressed for school," she says. "Bus comes in twenty-five minutes. Eat, brush your teeth."

I nod plenty of time. I showered last night and planned my outfit: pink sweater, light blue jeans, hair up. But my sweater's missing from the closet. I know it was there before bed. Stuff gets stolen here constantly; nothing's truly mine.

I storm to Veronica's room. "Hey, did you see my pink sweater?"

She looks up, blue eyes wide. "I think Addie had it in her back pocket earlier, heading down the hall."

That's why Addie hid her back. "She's gonna regret this," I growl, charging to her room. Last time, Veronica stopped me from swinging, but not today. I barge in, door slamming. "Give me my sweater, Addie."

"What? I don't have it," she lies.

"Someone saw it in your backpack," I say.

"Who, Veronica? I'll wreck her," Addie threatens.

"You dodged me last time, Adeline," I taunt, sarcasm sharp.

Out of Time

"You know I hate that name, you bitch!" she screams, lunging.

Rage blinds me. I tackle her, fists flying, barely feeling her hits. A voice in my head *beat her down!* Drives me. Not the PTSD whispers from therapy; this is new, primal. Security storms in, prying us apart. I'm a wild animal, swinging until I see Addie unconscious, blood pooling. My hands are red.

Kim shrieks, "What did you do?"

I collapse, sobs wrenching my chest, breath shallow. Kim wraps me in her arms, whispering, "I don't know if I can fix this, sweet love." I want to melt into her, but I'm frozen. Months of therapy gone. Why didn't I tell Kim about the sweater? That voice *Go get yours, don't back down!* Felt like a ghost, not me. It wasn't the PTSD I'd worked through; it was like a force overriding my control.

Security calls 911. Girls murmur in the hall as EMTs rush to Addie. She stirs, and relief floods me. *Thank God she's not dead.* Why did I think that? God doesn't know me. The EMT glares, his disgust mirroring mine. My bloody hands betray me.

"What happened?" he demands.

I cling to Kim, tears falling harder. She starts to speak, but he cuts her off. "I want to hear from her."

"Excuse me," Kim says firmly. "Your job is to care for Addie, not interrogate. Come on, Tiana, let's go." She guides me out, shielding me from the girls' stares, and leads me to her office.

"Sit," she says, pointing to the couch. I hesitate, glancing at my hands.

"You can't wash them," she says gently. "Police will need evidence."

"Evidence?" I whisper, fear gripping me.

"You assaulted Addie," she explains. "There'll be a report. If she presses charges, you could face juvenile detention."

"What?" My eyes widen, panic surging.

"Calm down, love," Kim soothes. "We don't know yet. If she's badly hurt, it's possible."

"I snapped," I say, voice trembling. "I'm so tired of her bullying. She stole my sweater, lied about it."

Kim steps to the door, shouting, "Girls, the bus is here in five! Get moving, or no movie night!" Grumbles echo, but they obey. Kim's love is fierce, but she follows through.

Out of Time

She sits, giving me that motherly look of pity for a lost kid. "Tiana, you can't let people like Addie trigger you. There'll always be someone like her. If you don't learn to handle it, this'll happen again, and next time could be worse."

"I'm not violent," I insist. "I just... lost it."

"I know," she says. "But you can't hit people. Yelling's one thing, there's no law against it, but hands are different."

"It was like a voice took over," I admit. "'Beat her down,' it said, and I went for it."

"Another girl?" Kim asks, concerned.

"No," I lie. "Just in my head." It was *that* voice, the one from the night Ralph killed Mom. Therapy silenced it, but it's back, like a shadow looming that I thought was gone.

"Your head needs to stay calm," Kim says. "You can't hurt people, no matter how much they hurt you."

I was triggered unknowingly yet propelled to act. *Why did I react?*

Through the glass window, I see two officers scanning the building. My stomach drops, they're here for me. Kim rises, waving them over, and opens the door.

"Hello, Officers, I'm Kim White, the house mom," she says.

"Is this Tiana Williams?" they ask, eyes on me.

"Yes," Kim replies. "She's been here five years and never done anything like this. I'm as shocked as anyone."

"Since she's a minor, you need to stay," the male officer says. "Is there a private place to talk?"

"Let's use our meeting room," Kim suggests, leading us down the hall to the space where we hold weekly group sessions.

We settle in, and the female officer speaks first. "I'm Officer Knight, and this is Officer Likowitz. Tiana, we need your statement about the incident."

"Will you arrest me?" I ask, voice trembling.

"No," Knight says. "We gather evidence first, then a caseworker decides the next steps."

"Do I have to leave?"

"We're just here for the facts," she says. "Can you describe what led to the domestic violence call?"

The term *domestic violence* sends me spiraling. Tears fall, and my voice vanishes. I bury my head in my hands, the smell of blood on them triggering flashes of Mom's blood mixed with mine that night. My breath shortens.

"Let's take a moment," Kim says, stepping out. "I'll get drinks."

Alone with the officers, the memories overwhelm me: Mom's lifeless body, Ralph's rage. Tears stream faster, my chest tight. Kim returns with lemonade and glasses, but I'm hyperventilating. "Tiana, are you okay?" she asks, rushing to me. My eyes roll back, and darkness swallows me.

I wake to the EMTs from Addie's room hovering over me, officers nearby. "Tiana, I'm here. Can you hear me?" Kim asks, her voice steady.

"She likely fainted from stress," an EMT says. "High emotions can trigger it."

"I'm okay," I say firmly, sitting up. Kim hugs me tightly.

"You scared me, girl," she says, relief in her eyes. "Officers, can we do this later?"

"We need her statement while it's fresh," Knight insists, her tone skeptical, as if I faked it.

"I'm okay," I repeat, meeting Kim's gaze, grateful for her protectiveness. It echoes Mom's kindness. I miss her. An EMT hands me water, and their footsteps fade as they leave.

"Where were we?" Knight asks, her impatience clear.

I recount the morning, Addie's taunts, the stolen sweater, and my rage. Knight scribbles notes, her brows furrowing at times. "That's all we need," she says finally. "We'll follow up in about seventy-two hours."

"Have a good day, Ms. Williams," Likowitz adds, and they leave.

Kim's composure cracks, tears welling. "What's wrong?" I ask.

"Nothing, sweet girl," she says, forcing a smile. "Days like this happen." She motions for me to follow. "Go shower. I've got something to handle in the cafeteria. We'll talk later."

Alone in my room, the door closed, and isolation engulfs me. In the bathroom, my reflection shocks me, blood matted in my hair, splattered on my face. *They think I'm a monster.* I look away, strip, and step into the shower. No soap or heat can wash away this pain. Tears flow, but a shift stirs within. *She deserved it,* I think, defiance rising. Hurt won't own me anymore.

TWO YEARS LATER

I can't believe I just hit Will. My mind flashes to that day at the group home, pummeling Addie. Months of anger management and community service should've fixed me, but here I am, swinging again. *Felt good, didn't it?* That voice, the one I buried with therapy and whiskey sneers. "Shut up," I mutter aloud.

"Tiana, what the fuck?" Will yells, clutching his face. "Why're you telling me to shut up?"

"Don't be stupid," I snap. "Why question me? I've given you no reason to doubt me."

"What's wrong with you?" he asks, stunned. "I just asked a question."

"Don't accuse me," I retort. His tone echoes Ralph's control, disguised as concern.

"I asked where you were," Will says, confused.

"I told you the store for cigarettes." I don't mention running into Steve, my ex, passed out on a couch, the last time I saw him. That fight was brutal; I don't want to relive it.

Out of Time

"You were gone a while," Will says.

"So what? I'm an adult," I snap. "I don't need you shadowing me."

"Shadowing?" he says, hurt. "I'm your boyfriend, does that mean nothing?"

"'I'm your boyfriend,'" I mimic, mocking his tone. "Whine, whine. Grow up."

"Have you been drinking?" he asks.

"What, you're my dad now?" I sneer. "Oh, wait, Ralph, the addict who killed my mom."

"He what?" Will's eyes widen.

"Ralph, my stepdad," I say, pulling out a hidden whiskey bottle and gulping. "Beat us both. Killed her years ago, nearly killed me. I went to a group home, beat up a girl there, got community service, and anger management." I laugh bitterly at the memory.

Will moves closer, trying to comfort me. "Tiana," he whispers, "I love you."

"What?" I shove him back, rage flaring. "Love me? I don't know what that looks like. Nobody stays. Maybe you should go too." I swing again, but he catches my fist.

"It's easy to love you," he says softly.

I freeze, burying my face in my hands, tears spilling. He wraps me in his arms, strong and steady. I want to pull away, but I can't. *Give me a chance,* he pleads. I have no words, only fear that trusting him is a mistake.

SIX MONTHS LATER

"I knew it!" I scream as Will storms off the porch, bags in hand. "I told you you'd leave! They all do!" He doesn't look back, tossing his bags into the car, slamming the door, and peeling out. My mind reels, and that voice taunts, *Good job. You've done it now.*

Feeling as lonely as ever, I am left with the accusatory voices I can't seem to get rid of and little hope for the future.

Out of Time

6

THE VOICE OF LUST

I spot her entering the room, and I know she's my next target. Victoria's shy eyes and downturned chin scream vulnerability. She'll believe anything I feed her. Unwittingly, she heads straight for the trap I've set: Dereck, tall, handsome, and mine. Years ago, he turned from the lord of light, and I claimed him. Physically unaware, mentally, he's my pawn, primed for my plan to unravel Victoria.

Dereck looks up from his drink. "Do I know you from somewhere?" he asks, grinning, though he's never seen her. It's a tired line, but it usually works. Victoria glances at him, giggles softly, then grabs a champagne flute from the table and drifts toward the crowd by the stage.

Dereck tracks her, replaying the moment. *What the hell? That always lands.*

He fumbled it. Maybe he's not sharp enough for her. I lean into his mind, whispering, "Hey, beautiful, maybe you didn't hear me, but I think I know you." As the words slip from his lips, Victoria shivers slightly. *Got her.*

She turns, interest flickering in her eyes, a faint grin forming, then vanishing as a tall blonde storms toward them. "Come on, darling, let's get out of here. I'm bored," the woman says, seizing Dereck's arm, ignoring Victoria.

Victoria's heart sinks, the familiar sting of rejection washing over her. "Figures," she mutters, loud enough for Dereck to hear.

"See you later," he mouths, apologetic, as his wife drags him away.

"Damn it!" I curse. "I'll do better, Lord of Darkness." My master approaches, his presence heavy.

"I was watching, Lust," he says. "Have you lost your edge?"

"No, Master!" I plead. "I didn't expect his wife back so soon. She was headed to the bar, about to chat with a friend perfect timing. I don't know what went wrong."

"Lust, you must scan the entire system," he chides. "His wife saw Dereck smile at Victoria and suspected trouble. She's convinced he's cheated before, so she's vigilant. You need to plant evidence to make her trust him, or he's useless for the next move. If she confronts him, he'll tighten his tools, thinking he's caught."

"But you said we're aiming for their divorce," I say.

Voice of Lust

"Yes," he growls. "But maximize collateral damage. The more women he seduces, the deeper the pain for Victoria and the others. Target a married woman, next, ruin multiple lives at once. Don't linger in Victoria. She's unmarried, sharp, and knows the lord of Light's rules from childhood Sunday school. That 'no adultery' nonsense could make her tricky."

"Thank you, Master," I say, bowing. "You have my full devotion."

"I'll check later, Lust," he warns. "Don't disappoint me."

"Never, Dark Lord!" I vow.

Turning, I collide with Roe, who's been waiting across the room, her patience now annoyance.

"Hey, Roe, sorry," Victoria says. "This guy was chatting me up, and I couldn't escape until his wife swooped in. Total creep."

"I know him," Roe scoffs. "New girl every month, and his wife's clueless. Let's ditch this place. My friends are at Glass, let's finish the night there."

"I just want to go home," Victoria sighs.

"Come on, Vic, it won't be long," Roe pleads.

"Go without me," Victoria says. "I'm not feeling it."

"Why not? It'll be fun," Roe insists.

"Fun for you," Victoria mutters. "I just watch everyone else enjoy themselves."

"Maybe change that, Victoria Bracton," Roe teases.

"Maybe I will, Roe Jamison," Victoria relents. "One hour, that's it."

Roe squeals, clapping wildly, forgetting they're at a formal event. "Shh!" Victoria hisses, ducking her head as the crowd stares. Roe grabs her arm, weaving through the throng, muttering, "Excuse me," as they head for their cars.

Outside, the valet eyes Roe, nudging his coworker. Victoria notices her confidence faltering. *No surprise,* she thinks. *Roe's a knockout, petite, tan, with mahogany eyes. Who'd want a redhead with hazel eyes and no curves?* She shakes off the self-doubt, forcing herself to adopt a brighter mindset.

"Vic! Victoria!" Roe calls, snapping her back. A vehicle's roar drowns her words, speeding toward them. "Watch out!" Victoria screams. The valet lunges for Roe, but the car clips them, hurling both onto the lawn.

Victoria sprints to Roe's side, blood gushing from a gash where her head struck a boulder. "Roe, stay with me!" she cries, pressing the wound. Tears stream, pooling at her dress's beaded neckline. "Someone call 911!" she screams. The crowd thickens, faces blending together. Then Harry, a woman in red, the banquet manager, comes out too. *When did I last eat? Is Roe dying? That guy was hot. Why am I thinking that now?* Victoria's thoughts spin out, disoriented and chaotic.

Voice of Lust

Sirens wail closer, lights flashing. "A towel!" Victoria yells, and the valet rushes over. She presses it to Roe's head, blood soaking through. The valet kneels, adding pressure. Paramedics arrive, but a voice is inaudible, and an eerie hums in her ears. Her heart races, vision swimming. Iron fills her nose, and darkness claims her.

"What's your name?" a voice booms. "Are you hurt?"

Hurt? No, save Roe! Victoria's eyes flutter open. She's on a gurney, rolling down a hospital corridor, a nurse peering at her.

"There she is," the nurse says.

"Victoria," she mumbles.

"Victoria, what?"

"Victoria Bracton."

"Like, from Bracton Enterprises?" the nurse asks, her tone shifting. The gurney speeds up, the nurse's voice now tinged with fear.

"Are you hurt?" she repeats.

"No!" Victoria snaps. "My friend's hurt, help her!"

"We are, Victoria," the nurse says. "We need to check you. Is this your blood?"

Victoria looks down, Roe's blood coats her hands, dress, and arms. "Oh, God, is she okay?" she cries.

"Calm down," the nurse says, patronizingly. Victoria bristles, her parents' lessons on ladylike behavior clashing with her panic. *Focus on Roe,* she tells herself, biting back a retort.

"Calm down?" I snap, voice rising. "My friend's dying, and you tell me to *calm down*?" Before I can unleash more, I meet *his* eyes, Dr. Pithers, the man from the gala whose gaze screamed desire earlier. Now, they're serious, concerned, stripped of allure.

"It's you," I whisper, his face inches from mine.

"Hi," he murmurs, avoiding my stare. "Nice to meet you, Victoria." Heat floods my cheeks, a blush I pray no one notices. I turn away as a new nurse grips my arm, asking about allergies before sliding a needle in. I shake my head, wincing at the prick.

"We need to get you fluids, Victoria," she says. "You're likely dehydrated."

"Okay," I squeak, the IV's chill creeping through my arm. I scan for Dr. Pithers, but he's gone. "Is my friend okay? She was bleeding so much. I tried to stop it, I've had training, but it was too fast."

"I don't know yet," the nurse says, unconvincingly.

"We're focused on you now," another nurse adds, rushing off to a code red call.

"I hope that's not Roe," I mutter, anxiety spiking. The first nurse ignores me, tweaking my IV drip. I grab her arm, desperate for answers, then freeze. It's *her*, the woman in the red dress from the gala. Nurse Pithers, his wife. A doctor and a nurse? Too perfect.

"Ms. Bracton, I can't answer about your friend yet," she says curtly, exiting. My parents sweep in, their faces etched with worry.

"Oh, darling, what happened?" Mom gasps.

"It's Roe, Mom," I say. "She got hit at the gala, lost so much blood." Mom's eyes drop to my blood-soaked dress.

"Oh my!"

"It's not mine," I clarify. "It's Roe's."

"Why are you here?" she asks, panicking.

"I fainted," I explain. "They think I'm dehydrated, so I'm on an IV."

"I can't believe they haven't changed these clothes," Mom frets.

"It's fine," I say, brushing it off.

"How are you, my love?" Dad asks, his gentle tone soothing me.

"I'm okay, Daddy," I say, forcing confidence.

"I'll speak with the nurse," he says.

"Can you ask about Roe?" I plead.

"Of course, Victoria." He steps out, and Mom's tears start.

"Mom, don't," I say softly. "I'm okay."

"It could've been you," she chokes. "I'd be lost without you."

"Let's focus on me getting out and helping Roe," I say, redirecting her. She wipes her eyes, sits on my bed, and smiles. Mom's always been my cheerleader, but she's fragile emotionally and physically. I draw my strength from Dad, though my social skills lag. Inside, I'm tougher than I seem, a secret only Roe and Dad know. I can't lose her. Tears well up.

"What's wrong, dear?" Mom asks.

"I'm worried about Roe," I admit, wiping my face. Dad returns, his expression grim.

"What is it?" I whisper.

"It's not looking good, darling," he says. "They're doing all they can."

"Did someone call her parents?" I ask, frantic.

"I don't know."

"My phone's in my car," I say. "Can you get it, Dad? I need to call her uncle. Roe doesn't speak to her parents—I don't know if their numbers are in her phone or who her emergency contact is. She lists me for most things."

"Don't worry, love," Dad says. "I'll get it. Your mom's here."

"I'm fine," I insist, craving a moment alone.

"I'm staying," Mom declares, unusually firm. "That's final." I roll my eyes at Dad, who winks and heads out.

Dr. Pithers reappears. "So, you're Victoria Bracton," he says, a hint of recognition.

"Yes," I reply, my tone sharp.

"Manners," Mom whispers.

He shakes Mom's hand, then offers his to me. Her glare forces me to grip it firmly. "Dr. Pithers," he says.

"Nice to meet you," I say, sarcastically. "Seems I've seen you before."

"At the gala," he confirms. "You're disoriented from earlier."

"How's Roe?" I demand, indignation flaring.

"Who?" he asks, puzzled.

"My friend," I snap, "whose blood I'm wearing!"

"Victoria!" Mom scolds. "Your manners!" Her assertiveness surprises me. What's with her?

"Sorry, Mom," I mutter. "I'm upset. Can you get a nurse to bring clothes?"

"I don't want to leave," she protests.

"Please, Mom, I need this blood off," I plead, nearly whining.

"Of course, darling," she relents, stepping out.

I glare at Dr. Pithers. "Why'd you try to hit on me at the gala, knowing you're married?"

"I didn't," he says, defensive. "You misunderstood."

Voice of Lust

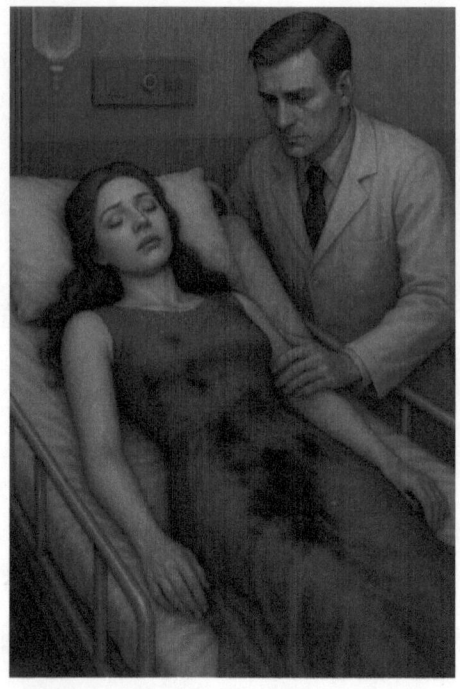

Doubt creeps in. *He's right. Why would he want me? Look at his wife.* I slump, shame replacing anger. "Sorry," I mumble. His eyes soften with pity, not desire. Before he can speak, Mom returns with Nurse Pithers. He glances at her, his tone shifting.

"Are you hurt, Ms. Bracton?"

"No," I say. "This blood's Roe's."

"We'll run tests," he says. "Fainting isn't nothing." He exits.

Nurse Pithers' blue eyes meet mine, curious but kind. *Does she know about him?* I wonder, forcing a smile. "Call me Victoria," I say.

She nods, handing me a gown. "You need to undress in front of me, Victoria. Since you fainted, I can't leave you alone."

Humiliation stings. *She'll see I'm no threat.* "Not my mom," I say quickly. "You're fine."

"Darling, I'll get coffee," Mom offers. "Want anything?"

"No, thanks," I say, grateful for her exit.

Nurse Pithers her tag reads *RN* sets the gown on the bed. "Clasps in the back. Here are socks and underwear, unless yours are okay."

"They're not," I admit. "Blood's everywhere. Can you toss my clothes? I don't want reminders of Roe bleeding."

"Of course," she says, turning for privacy. "Sorry, hospital rules."

Peeling off my dress, the metallic stench hits. I gag, swaying. Nurse Pithers steadies me. "You okay?"

"Just nauseous," I gasp. She helps with the gown, bagging my clothes. *Mortifying.* My first time exposed, and it's her, married to a flirt.

"Can I use the bathroom?" I ask.

"Let me adjust the IV," she says.

Mom's knock interrupts. "Can I come in?" Nurse Pithers opens the door. I sigh, *no escape.*

"Hi, Victoria," Mom says.

"Mom, I need sleep," I plead.

"Rest is best," Nurse Pithers agrees.

"Check on Roe, Mom, and find her uncle in my phone when Dad returns," I say.

Mom nods slowly, kissing my forehead. "I love you, Victoria."

Nurse Pithers dims the light. "If you need anything, the button's by the bed."

Voice of Lust

"Thank you," I murmur, exhaustion pulling me under as the day's chaos fades.

I wake, disoriented, feeling like I barely slept. Sunlight streams through the window, and the clock reads 9:00 a.m. *Was it only thirty minutes?* The hospital's beeping and distant intercom chatter fill the silence. Where is everyone?

Felicia's blue eyes greet me, her smile warm. "Good morning, Victoria."

"Hi, Felicia," I say, remembering her request.

"How're you feeling?" she asks, concern deepening her tone.

"Okay, really," I reply. "Any news about Roe?"

"Officers stopped by while you slept," she says, avoiding my gaze. "They'll return later."

"Officers?" I frown. "Why me?"

"Maybe they need details from last night," she offers. "I'm not sure."

"When will they be back?"

"I just started my shift," she says. "The nurses' station mentioned it. I'll get you a menu. Pick something, and I'll grab your order soon." She slips out.

Before I can process, Mom's voice cuts through. "Hi, darling!" Her face lights up as she enters.

"Hi, Mom," I say. "How are you?"

"Amazing, my love. Need anything?"

"News about Roe," I say, confused. "Someone must know something."

Mom hesitates, and panic grips me. "Mom, tell me," I plead, tears pooling.

"Victoria, my peach," she says softly, "Roe was in bad shape. Her spleen ruptured, and she was bleeding internally."

"*Was?*" I whisper, dread sinking in. I bury my face in my hands, bracing for the worst about my best friend.

"She's not with us anymore," Mom says, her voice breaking.

The room spins. I can't breathe. "No!" I gasp. "How? That driver was reckless, they took her!" Rage and grief choke me. Mom's panicked cries, "Victoria!" fade as darkness swallows me.

Felicia's voice pulls me back. "Victoria, can you hear me?" She's prying my eyes open.

"Yes," I mumble, my head throbbing.

"What happened?" she asks, alarmed.

"I don't know," I say, disoriented. "I was fine, then I couldn't breathe, the room spun, and… nothing."

"How long was she out?" Felicia asks Mom.

"A couple of minutes," Mom replies, worried.

Felicia's gaze locks on mine, her concern profound. "Are you okay now?"

"Yes," I lie, voice unsteady.

"I think you had a panic attack," she says. "We can run more tests if you want."

"No," I snap, then soften. "Sorry. I just want to go home." Tears spill as I add, "Mom told me about Roe."

"I'm so sorry, Victoria," Felicia says, her empathy genuine, like we've known each other forever.

"I don't understand," I choke out.

"I can't discuss it," she says gently, touching my shoulder. "We reached her parents. They might help."

"Thank you, Felicia," I whisper, closing my eyes, letting grief pull me under.

THREE MONTHS LATER

"Hi, Roe," I say, kneeling at her grave, the headstone reading *Roe Susanna McClaire, February 2, 1980, December 12,*

2000. "I know you might not hear me, but I miss you." I place flowers in the cement vase.

Where to start? "After you passed, I got counseling for your death and... my insecurities. I was a wreck, lost without you. That nurse, Felicia, became my best friend, not replacing you, but she's kind. She helped me heal. She introduced me to her brother, Ethan. He's amazing, Roe. Is this love? I'm clueless; you were the expert with guys. I could use your advice."

I smile through tears. "Mom and Dad are great. I'm starting a nonprofit in your name. The driver who hit you was drunk and mistook the gas for the brake. He's a mess, facing consequences. I spoke to your sister, and she misses you terribly. Your mom won't talk to me, blaming me for leaving the gala early. I told her it was an accident, but she's shut me out. I get why you cut contact."

Tears stream down. "I miss you, Roe," I whisper, touching the headstone, blowing a kiss. As I stand, a voice calls, "Victoria!"

Squinting, I see Ethan, tall and handsome, approaching. "What're you doing here?" I ask, startled.

"Visiting my grandmother's grave," he says shyly. "She passed a few years ago at eighty-five. I miss her."

"I'm sorry," I say.

"It's okay. Why're you here?"

"This is Roe," I explain. "She died three months ago. That's how I met your sister at the hospital, after the gala."

"She mentioned meeting you," he says, "but I didn't know the context."

"Yep, Felicia saw me at my worst," I laugh. "Yet she introduced us."

"I'm glad she did," he says, grinning.

"Awesome," I blurt, blushing.

"Got plans?" he asks.

"Not really."

"Coffee?"

"I'd like that," I say, smiling.

He takes my hand, his eyes locking with mine. "I'm sorry about your friend, but I'm glad it brought me to you."

My heart races. *He means it.* "I'm happy we're hanging out," I say shyly, hope stirring. Maybe this is something good, something Roe's still part of.

TWO YEARS LATER

I overslept today of all days! Panicking, I grab coffee, dress, toss my phone in my purse, and rush out. A text dings.

HEY VIC. WHAT'S UP? TODAY'S THE BIG DAY!

YEP! SLEPT THROUGH THE ALARM. UGH!

GET MOVING! MY BROTHER WAITS FOR NO ONE... LOL

HE'LL WAIT IF HE KNOWS WHAT'S GOOD FOR HIM

TRUE, BFF. SEE YOU SOON!

Today's my wedding day, and I'm marrying Ethan now, Stan to me, his middle name. I saved myself for this moment, a choice I was teased for but cherish. Stan's kindness anchors me, though his first wife's death from an aneurysm two months after their wedding haunts him. I hope I honor him today. Felicia guided me, but as his sister, there's only so much we can discuss. My parents are thrilled, and my future shines bright.

Voice of Lust

My iWatch buzzes crap, I'm late for makeup! Rushing to my car, I faintly hear a snarl: *We're done here. Can't stand this happiness.* Growls fade as I slam the door, silence settling in.

Michelle Pentifallo

7

LET'S GET DOWN TO BUSINESS

"Okay, DeShawn, you've got this," I psych myself up, stepping toward the stage. The spotlight hits, blinding me to the audience. I take a breath and dive in.

Michelle Pentifallo

Hunger claws my stomach, a beast tearing through. My ribs throb, throat parched, vision fading. Seven days without food. Can I survive an eighth? Or will I not wake up? That table over there could I snatch a piece of bread? Would they arrest me for it? Do they even see me, starving, desperate? I need food, or I'm done.

Work's not an option. My back's wrecked from that job accident. They blamed me, though it wasn't my fault. Fired, no help, no one hires a guy with a bad back. My wife left, disgusted, taking our kids. I'm alone, starving, and exhausted. Maybe if I curl up in this corner, I'll slip away painlessly. Five years ago, I had it all now, I'm at the end, my life's threads unraveled, hope gone.

As a kid, Dad said I'd never be anything. Mom called me worthless. I tried at school, but the words jumbled letters backward. Teachers treated me like a fool, so I played the class clown. A voice in my head taunted: *You'll never read. You're worthless. You shouldn't exist.* I thought it was mine, but now I know it's something darker, evil, urging me to give in. Today, it's deafening, and I can't silence it. My mind's too weak.

I could hit the liquor store, drown it in alcohol. Drinking quiets the noise, makes me feel clever, funny until I pass out. If only something could stop these voices, rattling my brain, commanding me. My life's a dead end.

The stage lights brighten, revealing a sea of eyes. I exhale, sending up a silent prayer.

"That was my life for years," I say. "Spiraling, haunted by choices I made in desperation. My goal is to take you on that journey, sharing what brought me here, speaking to you today.

"I hit rock bottom after a work injury. Hungover, I wasn't sharp, and I got hurt. My company knew about my

Let's Get Down to Business

pills, my drinking. They couldn't fire me until I messed up, and I did. They told Workers' Comp I was high, denying my claim. My wife and kids left when we faced eviction and unpaid bills. She took them to her family, somewhere safe, because I couldn't provide. Today, we talk, and I see my three kids, but I lost years with them to addiction and insecurity.

"Your story might not be as dire, but keep going down that road, and it could be you sooner than you think. Over the next two days, I'll share stories, lead group sessions, answer questions, and offer a path to a new journey. If you're ready to change, let me hear you!"

Silence. *Tough crowd.* "Come on, cheer if you're ready!" A few voices rise. "That's a start," I say, smiling. "By the end of this weekend, I want everyone cheering, ready for change. Let's head to the dining hall next door and reconvene in an hour. Thank you for being here."

The dining hall buzzes, packed with more attendees than ever. It's sobering, but I'm hopeful for breakthroughs. A young woman tugs my sleeve, her eyes bright.

"Hi, DeShawn, I'm Emily," she says. "I'm thrilled to be here and hear your stories."

"Thank you, Emily," I say, smiling, moving toward the food line.

Another voice stops me. "Mr. DeShawn, I read your book last year," a tender-faced woman says. "It changed my life."

"That's incredible," I reply. "I'd love to hear more." I nod, hurrying on, hearing her faint, "I'm sorry, I didn't mean to make you leave." I wave it off, signaling *no worries*.

Weaving through tables, I return "Hello, DeShawn" greetings with polite smiles. I need a moment alone.

Michelle Pentifallo

Slipping behind a curtain to my private room, I reach for the door when a hand grazes mine. I freeze, recognizing the touch. My head turns, meeting my father's eyes—older, less menacing. I'm taller, stronger now, but my brain struggles to process. It's been decades. I jerk my hand away, pain flooding back.

"What are you doing here?" I snap, anger unchecked. *Was that too loud?*

"Hi, son," he says softly. "How are you?"

"*How am I?* I haven't seen you in twenty-five years, and you show up at my conference? You've got nerve."

"I saw your ad online," he says, eyes dropping. "I knew you'd be here. I just wanted to see you."

"To do what talk?" I scoff. "What do you think you'll accomplish, *Dad?*" The word drips with disgust. I storm

Let's Get Down to Business

through the door, slamming it, and lock myself in my private room.

My hand trembles as I set my plate on the desk. Sinking into the chair, I bury my face in my hands. *Why now?* Does he think I'm rich, here for a handout? I barely scrape by, charging little to help people heal, not profit. A knock interrupts.

"DeShawn, you okay?" Jess, my assistant, calls gently.

Blinking back pain, I open the door. "Hey, Jess."

"You seem shaken," she says.

"That was my father," I admit, disgust lacing my voice.

"Your *dad?*" Her shock mirrors mine.

"Yeah," I say, rolling my eyes.

"I... don't know what to say."

"Nothing to say," I snap, then soften. "Sorry, Jess, I didn't mean that."

"I get it," she says. "I'd feel the same if my dad showed up."

"Thanks," I say. "I need to eat and regroup. Can you take these booklets and this box to the conference room? Grab food, and I'll meet you in forty-five minutes."

"Sure," she says. "Need anything else?"

"An aspirin?"

"Got it. I'll leave it on the podium."

"Thanks, Jess," I say. "I don't know what I'd do without you." *Was that too personal?*

"I'm not going anywhere," she teases, locking the door behind her.

I smile, grateful for her. She's a lifeline. I need to thank her properly, maybe ask my friend Jules for ideas. My thoughts drift to Dad. Grandma Ellis called him

Bobbie; Mom said Robert to spite her. I just called him Dad.

"Good evening, everyone," I say, swallowing the aspirin as I take the stage. "I trust dinner was good?" Cheers ripple through. "Scrumptious, right?" Claps and shouts fill the room. "See? It's easy to show appreciation. That's tonight's focus: gratitude."

"A 'thank you' achieves more than any complaint. Tell a kitchen worker, 'Thanks for the meal,' and you'll get smiles back. If the bread's dry, it matters less when you see their joy. Gratitude shifts your perspective; it's not about the bread but about accepting the gift. Make sense?"

"Yes," the crowd murmurs, heads nodding. I open my notes, ready to dive in, silencing the voices that once broke me, line by line, to help others rewrite their story for hope.

"Thank you all for spending these past two hours with me exploring gratitude!" I say, closing the session. The crowd cheers in unison.

"We'll dive deeper tomorrow with breakout sessions on thankfulness, forgiveness, and kindness, core steps to your journey. Get some rest; we start bright and early at 7:30 a.m. Lots to cover. Check with my staff for details, clear your tables, push in your chairs, and say 'thank you' to the crew on your way out. Good night!"

Claps and cheers erupt again. I mouth "Thank you" to the audience, slip behind the curtain, and head for my office, only to freeze. My father's face looms, just as it did this afternoon.

"What do you want, old man?" I snap, louder than intended.

Let's Get Down to Business

"DeShawn, I just want to talk," he says. "You spoke about gratitude tonight, and tomorrow it's forgiveness and kindness. Is that just for them, or does it include me?"

Guilt creeps in, but I shove it down. "You want me to feel bad? You beat me, Mom, and Desiree, then abandoned us, penniless. I was sixteen, forced to work to keep us from eviction. We barely ate. If not for the church helping us for six months, we'd have been homeless. Should I thank you for that?" My voice rises to a yell.

Jess peers around the corner. "DeShawn, please," she whispers. "People can hear."

"Mr. White, I presume?" she says, turning to him. "Follow me to a private room. Someone will join you shortly. Can I get you a drink?"

"No, ma'am," he replies.

Jess leads him down the hall to a counseling room. I steady myself, repeating, *'You are loved.' You are happy. You are healthy*. Do I believe it? I thought I did, but his presence drags me back. That voice, *You're useless. You'll never amount to anything* resurfaces, one I'd silenced after getting clean at the Rusty Bumper. "Shut up," I mutter, storming down the hall.

I thought he was dead. I told my counselors he was gone, forgiving a ghost. Now he's here, alive, and I don't know what he wants. Money? He looked cleaner, no yellowed eyes, no liquor stench. Back then, he'd stumble home drunk, yell, then pass out. Those were the good nights, no punches, no insults. On bad nights, Mom shielded me, taking hits meant for me.

"Get out of my way, Gloria," he'd slur. "The kid's a sissy," I recall the night he beat her so bad she needed a hospital. She lied, saying a mugger attacked her, but the nurse's eyes screamed disbelief. Dad, sober by then, charmed her with that "good ole charm" he bragged about.

"Charm, my ass," I mutter, passing the counseling room. Isaiah's voice drifts out, calm: "Mr. White, why are you here?" I don't linger, quickening my pace to the lobby elevator.

"Hi, DeShawn," a voice chirps.

"Oh, hi Emily, right?"

"Yes!" Her face lights up. "Your talk on thankfulness was so inspiring. Thank you for delivering it so eloquently."

"My pleasure," I say as the elevator dings. "You going up?"

"No, my room's nearby."

"See you tomorrow, Emily," I say, smiling.

"Good night," she replies, mirroring my grin. The doors close, sealing out the night's chaos.

In my room, fresh linens soothe me. I drop my bag, plug in my phone, set my wallet down, and head for the shower. Steam fills the bathroom as I start my routine, craving sleep.

I jolt awake, a dream clawing at me. Am I on the floor? Reality blurs. A figure masked, like Batman's Scarecrow, loomed in the corner, glaring: *I'm watching you.* Watching what? I'm no threat. The conference room was packed, but he hovered above, spectating, dissecting my words. Just a dream, I tell myself, shaking it off.

I splash water on my face and crawl back to bed, praying the dream doesn't resume. It felt real. He blocked my path, and I fell. Sleep pulls me under, mercifully blank.

My eyes snap open at 5:55 a.m., beating the alarm. I grab my phone, reviewing today's notes in my head. *Is the bacon crispy here?* Hunger hits hard. I need to tweak slide #3

Let's Get Down to Business

for the morning session, gentler, more nurturing. Tonight's can be bolder. Pancakes sound good, but too many carbs. I throw off the blanket, feet hitting the floor, ready to tackle the day.

"Good morning, Emily," I say, coffee in hand, returning her greeting.

"May I sit with you?" she asks shyly.

"Of course," I say. "How'd you sleep? Happy with the accommodations?"

"Beautifully," she says. "I wrote a gratitude list before bed, people, things I'm thankful for. It was long, and I didn't finish, but it helped me sleep better."

Maybe that's my issue, I think. I went to bed angry, fueling that nightmare. "Today, we'll build on gratitude and introduce steps for your journey to wellbeing," I say.

"Is that possible, Mr. White?"

"Please, call me DeShawn," I say, sharper than intended, then soften. "Mr. White's my father." My fist clenches under the table.

"Was that him last night?" she asks, hesitant.

"Yep," I say, standing. "See you in session, Emily. Thanks for sharing your time." I flash a smile, escaping to my lounge room. *Damn, someone noticed.*

Jess greets me with coffee and a grin. "Morning, DeShawn."

I grab the cup, warmth steadying me. *I love her.* The thought jolts me, *no, she's my assistant.* I can't risk ruining this. Sheila's departure scarred me; I'm not ready for love. "What do you need this morning?" Jess asks, her excitement infectious.

"Change slide #3 for the morning PowerPoint to 'When You Aren't Sure,'" I say. "For tonight, add 'Get Out of Your Own Way' to slide #5, shifting others up.

Michelle Pentifallo

This group needs gentleness now, assertiveness later. They're sensitive, craving TLC."

"Spot-on, DeShawn," Jess says. "You read the room like no one else."

"Maybe too much," I mutter.

"Just enough," she teases, winking as she leaves.

I close my eyes, meditating, praying for today's sessions. A knock shatters my focus. I open the door, half-expecting that scarecrow figure, but it's him, Dad.

"What do you want?" I snap, leaving the door ajar as I grab my things.

"Listen, Dez"

"No one calls me that," I cut him off.

"Okay, DeShawn, just a few minutes."

"Not now."

"Lunch?"

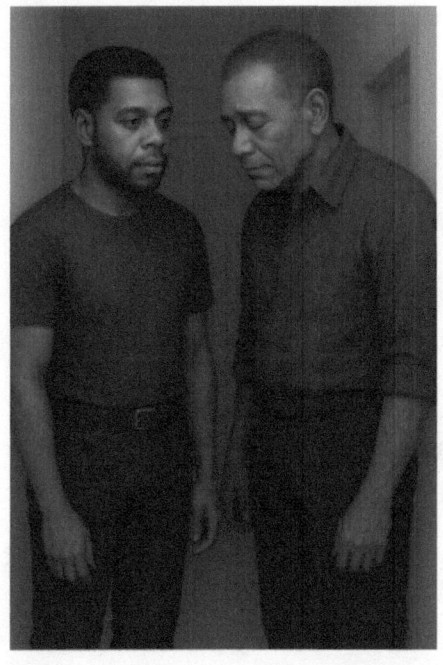

"Nope."

"How about dinner?" His voice is softer than I expect, almost pleading.

"No." My response is sharp, cutting through the air.

"So, when, DeShawn? I came all this way. I just want to talk."

"Talk about what?" I glance at my watch, impatience rising. "You've got five minutes, old man. I have morning sessions to prep for." His face fades, eyes heavy with weariness, and for a fleeting moment, guilt tugs at me.

"Never mind," he mutters, releasing the door handle. He shuffles down the hallway, shoulders slumped. The guilt lingers, sharp and unfamiliar, but I shake it off no time for this. I plaster on my stage-ready smile, let Jess adjust my headpiece, and stride out to face the crowd, ready to inspire.

TWO MONTHS LATER

"Hello?" A calm, unfamiliar voice greets me through the phone.

"Yes?" I respond, curiosity piqued.

"Is this Mr. DeShawn White?"

"That's me. How can I help you?"

"I need to confirm if you're the son of Thaddeus White."

"I am." My chest tightens slightly.

"I'm so sorry to bear this news, DeShawn, but your father passed away last night."

The words hit like a tidal wave. "What? I'm okay. Where is he?" My mind spins. I saw him just two months ago. Was that why he came to the conference? Was he trying to reach me?

"He's in hospice in Seattle. We need the next of kin to sign paperwork for cremation or funeral arrangements. Your number was found in his pocket, with instructions to call you."

My number. He must've kept it from the conference. "What do you need me to do? Can you email the forms?"

"I'm afraid we need someone to come in person with a driver's license for verification," the voice explains gently.

I bristle, my tone sharp. "Please, call me DeShawn. And you're telling me the man who abandoned me as a kid now expects me to clean up his mess? Typical Thad." My schedule is packed with conferences every month, a bestselling book, and a life I've built. I don't have time for this.

"I'm sorry, DeShawn. I'm just the messenger. We have counselors available if you'd like to talk."

"No need," I say, forcing a smile into my voice. "I'm a motivational speaker and counselor myself. I've got this. Just send me the address. I'll fly up and handle it." Pride surges as I end the call, pressing the red button with a sense of control. I'm DeShawn White, successful, booked solid, untouchable. But deep down, something stirs.

"Thank you, DeShawn, for arranging the service. We know it wasn't easy," Aunt Dee says, her kind eyes meeting mine. She was Dad's favorite sister, always his champion.

"It's okay, Aunt Dee. I know you loved him," I reply, softening my tone to match her warmth.

"I sure did. He was my sidekick growing up." Her words pull a scowl from me before I can stop it. She wraps me in a tight hug. "Don't be too hard on him, Dez. Life's too short." Her smile is wide, forgiving, and she heads out the door.

Let's Get Down to Business

Her words linger. I preach forgiveness to thousands, yet I've withheld it from the one man who shaped me for better or worse. If I'm honest, holding onto this anger is a weight I can't carry anymore. He was my dad. Despite everything, I loved him. Perhaps he came to the conference to make amends. I owe it to him and to myself to let go.

The room buzzes with anticipation, thick with unspoken questions. Family members, some of whom are strangers to me, mill about. It's been years since we've gathered like this.

"It took a death to bring us together," someone murmurs in the distance.

I scan the faces, unfamiliar after being away for years. I left Seattle at 14, when my Mom moved us to Tennessee, in search of a simpler life. But pain follows you, no matter the map. Mom never recovered from Dad's betrayal. Her next husband brought more abuse, and at 17, I fled, leaving my sister behind. That guilt still haunts me. She's not here today, and I can't blame her.

I paid for this service, so I stayed to see family and to face the past. I teach forgiveness, don't I? If I don't live it, I'm a fraud. My mind races. Maybe this could inspire new sessions, a full day on grief, on goodbyes that never happen, or ones that went wrong. I'm already building the PowerPoint in my head.

"Hey, DeShawn." Jess's familiar voice cuts through my thoughts, warm and grounding.

"Jess!" My excitement draws stares, but I don't care. I pull her into a quick hug and lead her to a quieter room. "What are you doing here?"

"I knew today would be tough, so I flew in last night," she says, her voice soft but steady.

"Last night? Why didn't you tell me?"

"It was late. I didn't want to bother you."

"You never bother me, Jess." My heart races. Does she feel what I do? I flash a smile, and hers mirrors mine, shy but warm.

"Of course," she says, almost bashfully, taking my hand. It's new, this gesture, and it steadies me as we find seats for the service.

As the pastor speaks, I struggle to reconcile his kind words with the father I knew. Did he change? Should I have met him for dinner that day? Given him a chance to explain? Jess's hand in mine keeps me grounded, her eyes holding something new, something I'm afraid to name.

As the service ends, Aunt Stacie approaches, holding a worn envelope. "Your father wanted you to have this," she says softly. "I know you two had your struggles, but he was sober for years. He made amends with us, helped me through tough times, and paid my bills when I was in desperate need. He tried reaching out to you and Desiree, but…" Her voice trails off.

I take the envelope, my fingers tracing its edges. "Thank you, Auntie. I'll read it." And I mean it. If I can change, so could he. Forgiveness isn't just a word; I preach it's a choice I need to make.

The envelope feels heavy with possibility. Part of me wants to tear it open; part of me fears what it holds. Not today, but soon.

"Come on, DeShawn, let's go," Jess says, her playful tone pulling me back.

With her at my side, I say my goodbyes, hugging family, feeling the weight of the past and the hope of what's next. As we step into the unknown, I wonder if this is the start of something new, not just for me, but for us.

Let's Get Down to Business

Michelle Pentifallo

8
WHOSE LIFE IS IT ANYWAY?

It crept in uninvited, that dark thought, while I sat alone in my room. *I want to die.* It hasn't been there before. No one ever whispered, "Hey, little girl, why not swallow some pills and never wake up again?" That wasn't part of my usual self-talk, harsh as it often was, but this was new.

The room, a somber song on repeat, each note tightening the grip of despair. The more I listened to it, the deeper I sank, convinced I was unlovable. My parents' neglect had taught me that long ago, but this felt different, sharper, self-inflicted. I'd made a mistake. I'd slept with a boy I barely knew, and he'd told everyone. His words, once seductive, now fueled my shame. The whispers followed, slicing deeper: *"What a slut!"* They didn't know me. They didn't know the promises he'd fed me, the way his gaze made me feel seen, if only for a moment. All I'd wanted was love, but instead, I found hate and disgust.

The knife in my hand trembled as their sneers echoed in my mind. Everyone at school knew. Why not end it now? Who would care? Who would show up at my funeral? If I slipped away, maybe I'd finally find peace.

Whose Life Is It Anyway?

Those thoughts felt like mine, but they weren't. Something darker, unseen yet close, urged me on: *"Just do it! Cut! Cut!"*

I remembered church as a child, singing *Jesus Loves Me*, getting baptized, and believing I'd go straight to heaven. Wouldn't I? No one wanted me here. I couldn't face school, I couldn't face their stares. I shake the memory away, trying to ground myself in the present. Why am I even revisiting this?

"Julia… Julia…" Voices pull me back. I'm in my therapy session, the room filling with sound.

"Yes, Ms. Wright?" I blink, disoriented.

"Our session's over. We'll pick this up next week." Her tone carries a hint of annoyance.

"Oh, sorry. I was… lost in thought. Next week works." I grab my things, avoiding her gaze.

Where did that memory come from? I haven't thought about that day in years. How long was I zoned out? Ms. Wright seemed irritated, but I don't even want to be here. State-mandated therapy is ridiculous. It's my life. If I want to fight someone, I should be able to. If I want to jump off a bridge, that's my choice. All this because they found me passed out in the school bathroom. I thought graduating from high school would mean freedom, a chance to escape my parents' control. But freedom's an illusion.

My parents had their own dreams for me: volleyball scholarships, college, a Christian husband, kids, and Sunday school. Ugh. That's their fantasy, not mine. I don't want kids or a husband telling me what to do. I want to travel, dance, and find my own path. It's not my fault, I'm their only child, their "miracle baby." I overheard Mom once, crying, saying she thought she'd stay pregnant "this time." I didn't even know she'd lost others. They never expected me to survive, lungs underdeveloped. Church folks prayed over me, and somehow, I lived. A miracle, they said. But what about the babies who don't make it? Where's their God? Why save me when all I want is to disappear?

"Hey, Julia!" Ralph's voice snaps me out of my thoughts.

"Yeah?"

"Wanna Netflix and chill later?" His grin implies more than a movie.

"Maybe. I've got laundry and early classes tomorrow."

"What do you care? Your parents pay for school. You only get me sometimes."

"I'll think about it. Text you later." Before I can move, Ralph's in my face, pinning me against the hallway wall.

"I'll take you right now, you slut, if you don't let me come over."

I laugh, trying to diffuse him, but his eyes darken.

"Not funny, Jules. I'll take what I want, and I won't be gentle like last time. You like it rough, don't you?"

"Alright, alright. Later. I've got stuff to do." My heart races as he backs off.

"You're stuck with me, girl," he calls after me.

Stuck? No way. Ralph's a loser, and I've got bigger dreams: dance modern, maybe ballet. I've been at it since I was three. It's the one thing I love. My parents called it a hobby, furious when I chose a New York dance program over their dreams of becoming a pediatrician. They wanted me to "pass on the gift" of my survival. What nonsense. I don't want to save babies or watch people die. I want to dance until I can no longer do so.

Whose Life Is It Anyway?

I wake with a throbbing pain, disoriented. Reaching for water, I grab a glass and spit out tequila. Memories of last night flood back: tequila shots, Ralph, Suzie, her boyfriend. They left, and Ralph...

"You want my cock, you cunt. Bend over and take it." I'd laughed, drunk, not realizing he thought I was mocking him. His rage was new, terrifying. He ripped my pants, threw me over the bed, and caused pain. That's all I remember. I didn't think he'd go that far. I deserve better, don't I? But what does "better" even look like? I've never seen it.

Limping to the bathroom, I wince as I sit. The pain is excruciating. Why did he have to be so brutal? I would've let him. What's wrong with him? In the shower, hot water stings but soothes, washing away the night. It's not new; this hurts. I'll survive. On my bed, I spot my favorite panties, shredded. Jerk. He owes me. I get dressed to head out the door to start my day.

At the corner café, Suzie's behind the counter. "Hey, what's up?"

"Nothing. You?" Her look pity? Pain?—unsettles me. As I leave, that voice in my head sneers: *She knows, you slut. Ralph told her everything, just like that boy in high school.* I push it away. What does she know?

Back at my apartment, I grab the tequila bottle. "Bottoms up, Julia," a voice taunts. I freeze. Who said that? "Join the crowd, stranger," I mutter, but I'm alone. It's like that day years ago, a presence I can't see but feel, urging me toward darkness. I shove the thought away, raise the bottle, and drink. The voices stop for now.

A ringing pierces my haze, but it's not my phone. It's the doorbell. *No way I'm getting up.*

Michelle Pentifallo

"Julia, I know you're in there. It's Mom. I'm worried about you, sweetheart. Your car's downstairs. Are you okay?"

My heart lurches. She can't see me like this, hungover, broken, a mess. She'd lose it. What day is it? My phone's at 3%, but it's Wednesday. I lost a whole day? How? Forget it. No one cares about me anyway. A missed call from Ted appears on the screen, followed by another from Mom. Ted probably wants a quick hookup, as usual. A meal, if I'm lucky, then straight to his demands. Jerk. Mom's shoes clip-clop down the brownstone stairs, fading as she leaves.

I'll call her tomorrow after classes. She'll be furious when she finds out I'm failing history. Whatever. College was their idea, not mine. It's just a roadblock to my dancing. Speaking of which, I need to pick up that new leotard from Lidia. It's going to look incredible. Maybe Ted will see me in it and want more than his usual. If we're paired up in class again, I could learn a great deal from him. He's a phenomenal dancer, even if he's selfish elsewhere.

I stumble to the kitchen, craving cereal, but all I've got is Lucky Charms. *Lucky? Charming?* What a joke. My life's a wreck. Ralph proved that, ripping my favorite underwear and leaving me sore. Oddly, he hasn't texted since that night. He's usually blowing up my phone. Maybe I pissed him off when I laughed, not at him, but he didn't get that. Or maybe he's with his mom. Whatever. I pour milk over the cereal, but the sour stench hits me. Spoiled. Figures. I grab a Lunchable from the fridge instead. As I bite into it, that voice in my head sneers: *This is as good as it gets, Julia.* I flip on *Girls Gone Wild* and let the noise drown it out.

Whose Life Is It Anyway?

A woman's yelling on TV jolts me awake. I fell asleep, and the evening sky seeps through the window. I've slept for hours. My shirt's half-off, and as I graze my breast, memories of Ralph flood back. That night on the couch, his lips on me, the fleeting pleasure before it turned ugly. My hand drifts lower, seeking escape, and I lose myself in the sensation, imagining him differently gentler. The release is sharp, violent, but it's mine. I lick my finger and head to the shower, resolved. Screw school. I'm failing anyway. I'll dance tonight. Dance is my freedom, my truth.

In the shower, I wipe steam from the mirror and spot a mark near my temple. A bruise? I don't recall hitting anything. Probably banged my head that night, too drunk to remember. Idiot.

"Okay, Ms. Leng, I'm heading out!" I call, passing my landlord on the brownstone's porch, her Lucky Strike glowing in the dusk.

"Be careful, Julia. You've only got one life," she says, exhaling smoke.

"Yeah, yeah." *One life? Thank God.* I don't even want this one.

Three blocks later, I slide into my usual spot at Charlie's Bar.

"Julia! Haven't seen you in weeks," Bernie, the bartender, calls out.

"Busy with Ralph and school. Missed you, though. What's up, favorite bartender?"

"Favorite, huh? Only 'cause I let you run a tab. You owe me forty bucks, by the way."

"I'll settle up tonight. Promise. How's Ralph?"

"Dunno. He split to help his sick mom. Haven't heard from him." Bernie's acting off, avoiding my eyes. Across the bar, I spot Suzie sipping a martini, already slurring.

"Hey, Suzie!"

"What's up, Julia?" Her words slur through her teeth. Great, she's wasted. Suzie's mouth runs wild when she drinks. I join her so she doesn't look so pathetic, but as I sit, she spills a martini on my dress.

"Watch it, bitch!" I laugh, brushing it off.

"Shut up, you're the bitch," she snaps, grinning.

"Whatever. Buy me a drink?"

"Martini, dirty, double olives?"

"You know it."

"Fancy. Don't order beer on my dime, I'm just a barista."

"You'll manage. Where's your boyfriend tonight?"

"Out with his friends." That look from the coffee shop crosses her face again, pity, or something else. "Let's dance!" She drags me to the DJ before I can protest.

A young guy with a Latin vibe looks up. "What can I play, gorgeous?"

"Got any Kanye or Eminem?"

"Got that and better. I'll spin something hot next."

As we walk away, he mutters, "I'd like to get me some of that." Seriously? DJs are a dead end. I only invest in people like Ted, my dance teacher, who can get me to Broadway. My drink's waiting at the bar. I down it, Bernie slides me another, and I hit the dance floor as the DJ spins. Dance is my escape, my joy.

A tall guy with a man bun and stark black eyes looms over me. "Want to dance?"

"Nah, I'm good."

"Come on, don't dance alone."

"I'm not. Suzie's here." I grab her arm, signaling my choice.

"Alright, your loss. I'm a great dancer."

"Sure you are." He walks off, but something about him feels familiar. Faruc? No, that's not it. The music pulls me in, and I lose myself in the rhythm.

"Another!" I shout to Bernie. A waitress delivers it fast. Then, a hand grabs mine. I look up at Ted, my dance partner, his eyes locked on mine.

"Hey, beautiful, let's tear this up."

"Let's," I purr, leaning into the heat of his gaze. We move together, his body pressed close, sparking thoughts of what's to come. We dance until my hair's soaked, and I excuse myself to the bathroom. *Ladies' room? What a joke. No ladies here.*

Inside, Suzie's snorting a line off the counter.

"What the hell, Jules? You're an incredible dancer."

"Thanks," I mutter, slipping into a stall.

"Heard from Ralph?" she calls through the door.

"No. Nothing since he left. It's weird, like he was guilty or something."

"Yeah, he was rough with you that night. I saw him slap you."

"You were there?"

"Yeah. He looked at us like we'd better leave. I was worried."

I step out, meeting her gaze. "Worried? Why?"

"He was… pulling your pants down, and you were yelling at him to stop."

"I was?" My stomach churns. I don't remember that.

"It was scary. He looked like he wanted to hurt you bad."

"Damn. I was sore the next day, but Ralph's always rough."

"Gross. I'd never do that. One-way street, babe."

"Prude," I tease, but her pitying look returns.

"Let's dance. Ted's here, and I'm going home with him tonight."

"What about Ralph?"

"Ralph's gone. Screw him."

"Wait up!"

"Catch me on the floor!" I scan for Ted, but he's gone. Then those black eyes find me again. "Hey, isn't your name Faruc?"

"Nah, it's Adeer."

"Oh, my bad."

"Adeer's far from Faruc."

"Whatever, catch you later." I sway to the music, but hands slide onto my waist—too big to be Ted's. I turn, and Adeer's eyes pin me, intense, dangerous, yet magnetic. My breath catches as he pulls me close, spinning me effortlessly. I melt into his rhythm, the heat of his gaze daring me to keep moving.

"Dance with me, pretty lady," Adeer says, his voice smooth as he guides me across the dance floor. My stomach flutters as I take his hand, and he spins me, pulling me close until my body presses against his. The music pulses, the drinks hit hard, and I lose myself in the rhythm. *I don't even know this guy,* I think, but before I can dwell on it, he dips me, brushing a kiss on the tip of my nose. Bold move. Who does he think he is? I'm not some girl who gets sweet gestures. I'm used to raw, fleeting encounters. This feels... different. He's a damn good dancer, too. *Let's see if he can kiss.*

As he pulls me up, I lean in, lips parted, but he draws back, a teasing glint in his eyes. *Not now?* Seriously? I could have any guy in this bar, and he's playing hard to get? Screw him. I storm off the dance floor to my stool, where Bernie's got a martini waiting. Reliable Bernie always gives me what I need, no strings attached. I wish more guys were like him.

A voice brushes my ear, soft and warm. "Why'd you leave me out there, beautiful? I just wanted to dance."

I sip my drink, shrugging. "Didn't like the song. Needed this."

"What song *do* you like? I'll fix it."

"Don't bother."

"No, really. I know the DJ. Name it."

"Anything but this crap." He walks off, his lean frame cutting through the crowd. Out of the corner of my eye, I spot Ted emerging from the bathroom.

"Hey! What took you so long?" I call.

"Had to take a dump. What's it to you?"

"No need to be a jerk. I was just asking."

"Saw you with bun-boy," Ted sneers. "Had to grab my drink and a condom from the machine. Ready to blow your mind tonight, Jules."

"Whoa, tell me how you *really* feel," I shoot back, half-laughing.

"You know I'm good for it. Let's go." Before I can protest, he's pulling me toward the door. I glance back, catching Adeer's eyes as he moves toward me, but the door slams shut behind us, my favorite song fading as Ted whistles for a taxi.

Before I can slide to the far side of the cab, Ted's hand is on me, invasive and quick. I pause, then lean in, whispering, "Not now," against his ear. He pulls back, settling beside me, and hands the driver a twenty. "Tenth and Central, fast. Another twenty if you make it quick."

What's the rush? His lips crash into mine, hard and hungry, before I can ask. The cab ride blurs, and soon he's carrying me up to his apartment, laying me on his bed. Then, darkness swallows me.

My eyes flutter open to dim light from the bathroom. I stumble to the toilet, piecing together the night. Adeer's eyes haunted me intense, watching as we danced. There's something about him, magnetic yet unsettling. Back in the bedroom, Ted's gone. I creep through the apartment, living room, empty; kitchen, silent. The fridge light spills across a note on the counter: *Jules had to go. Great night! Great fuck! See you in class.*

Three a.m., and he's gone? I'm just a discarded toy to him. *Don't they all just want to use you?* That voice hisses. I shove it down, collapse face-first onto the bed, and sleep claims me.

Damn it, I'm late. Dance practice starts in twenty minutes. I sprint down the street, whistling for a taxi. As it pulls over, I slide in and freeze Adeer in the back, his dark eyes locking onto mine.

"Hi," I say, bracing for a lecture about last night.

"Hi, Julia. How was your night?" His tone is calm, no judgment.

"Fine," I mumble, guilt creeping in like a slow burn.

"I went to pick a song, and when I came back, you were leaving with some guy."

"Yeah, that's Ted. My dance instructor at…" I trail off, assuming he knows.

"I know. I hired Ted. I'm one of the studio's owners."

My stomach drops. *Great, I pissed off the guy who could make or break my career.* "I had no idea."

He notices my panic and rests a hand on mine, gently. "Don't worry, Julia. You don't owe me anything. I just wanted to dance with you. I've seen you at the studio, you're incredible. I've loved dance since I was a kid, and

Whose Life Is It Anyway?

when I see talent like yours, I want to experience it. I went to Charlie's last night, hoping to see you. Been going every Thursday for a month."

"My own personal stalker, huh?" I tease, smirking. His eyes drop, and I backtrack. "Kidding, relax."

"I'd never disrespect you like that," he says earnestly. "You're a thing of beauty, Julia. This is your stop. Have a great class." He opens the door, waving off my attempt to pay. "This one's on me. See you later."

I step out, dazed, and head toward the studio's glowing windows. Ted's ahead, and I call out, "Hey, Tim!" He grabs my hand, pulling me along.

"Hey, pretty lady. Ready for class?"

I nod, caught in his confident stride, wishing he were mine. He drops my hand as we enter, heading to the front. In the locker room, I stash my bag and use the bathroom. A woman I don't recognize stands by the towels, staring. As I move to leave, she grabs my arm, her grip tight with venom, and slaps me hard. "Stay the hell away from my husband," she hisses, then walks out.

I clutch my stinging cheek, stunned. *Who's her husband? I don't even know this woman.* I swing the door open to chase her, but she's gone. Samantha, a classmate, spots me in the hall. "What happened to your face?"

"Nothing," I snap, brushing past her into class.

After our last routine, my heart hopes to talk to Ted. I wondered if he knows who that lady is, or if he knows I don't just hook up with him. Ted's surrounded, so I can't confront him about last night. Samantha catches my eye.

"Wanna grab dinner?" she asks, smiling warmly.

I'm starving. "Sure, let's hit Girrellis. I need pasta. Haven't eaten all day." As we leave, I catch Ted whispering to Amber, his hand close to her face. *Is he with her, too?* That would be too close for comfort, screwing girls from the same class? What a jerk.

"Jules!" Samantha's voice pulls me back.

"Sorry, Sam. My head's elsewhere. I'm starving."

We reach Girrellis, but a line snakes out the door. I groan. "Let's go to Panera."

She nods, and we head two blocks south. After a quiet moment, she says, "Do you think Ted's sleeping with Amber?"

My face betrays me, and she backtracks. "Oh, Jules, I'm sorry. I didn't know you liked him."

"It's not like that. We hook up sometimes, that's all. I don't love him. But sharing him with Amber? She's unhinged. I don't need her stalking me over Ted."

"I thought you were with Ralph."

"Nah, he left to help his mom. Haven't heard from him in days."

"That's weird," Sam says, frowning. "I could've sworn I saw him downtown yesterday. Must've been someone else."

We reach Panera, and I order my usual, brushing off her concerned look. The cashier, a nervous newbie, fumbles my change, dropping a quarter. "I'm such a loser," she mutters, huffing. As I turn, I feel a presence behind me, but no one's there. *Weird*. I grab my food, ready to eat.

As I finish, Ted walks in with Amber. My heart sinks. He glances at me, then quickly looks to Amber, whose eyes narrow. She knows. Her glare pins him, and she drops his hand, storming out. Through the window, I see her unleash a tirade, her lips moving furiously as Ted's eyes widen in shock.

Whose Life Is It Anyway?

Sam follows my gaze. "Oh, damn. He's in trouble now. Guess she didn't know about you."

"Ted doesn't talk about me to anyone," I say, bitterness creeping into my voice. "Says it's to avoid favoritism, but it's just another lie. I asked him about Amber, and he denied it. Liar. Good thing we're just casual, but Amber won't like that one bit." I stifle a laugh, letting out a sharp giggle, imagining her reaction. Sam catches the edge in my expression, her eyes softening with that familiar pity. *Who does she think she is?* I don't need her sympathy. I've got this under control.

She senses my tension and shifts into a different gear. "So, who's getting the lead in the fall recital?"

"Probably Amber," I slur, the subject change failing to lift my mood. "If her crazy ass comes after me, I'll send her and her stupid boyfriend packing."

"Let's get out of here," Sam says brightly, breaking the tension.

I nod, toss my tray in the trash, and refill my drink. "See you later, Sam. Thanks for dinner. Catch you tomorrow."

"Take care, Jules. Let me know if you need anything."

Need anything? Like a babysitter to walk me home or a shoulder to cry on over Ted and Amber? Please. I'm fine. I don't care about them. My thoughts argue as I trudge down the cobblestone street. That eerie presence brushes against me again. I spin around nothing. *Weird.* Turning back, I nearly slam into a lamppost, jerking away and losing my balance. I hit the ground hard, pain shooting through my wrist. It swells instantly, throbbing. *You've got to be kidding me.* Auditions for the lead start next week. How am I supposed to dance like this? Panic rises, but before I can stand, strong hands lift me. I look up into Adeer's dark eyes, filled with compassion.

"I'm fine. Put me down," I snap, my anger misplaced.

"No, Julia. Your wrist looks broken. I'm taking you to the hospital."

"Don't be ridiculous. It's not broken."

"Look at it, it's swelling fast. We're going."

"I don't have insurance."

"Don't worry. My sister's an orthopedic surgeon there. She'll help."

"Your sister?" I ask, skepticism sharp in my tone.

He smiles, unfazed. "Yeah, my sister."

"Oh," I mutter, feeling foolish. A car door opens, and he eases me inside.

"Nice car," I say, eyeing the sleek interior.

"You like it?"

"Yeah. Yours?"

"Yep. I take taxis sometimes for convenience, and my driver gets days off."

Driver? My face must betray my shock. How does he afford that? He ignores it, instructing the driver to head to War Memorial Hospital as quickly as possible. At the valet entrance, he lifts me again before I can protest, carrying me through familiar halls to a door marked *Dr. Sasha Pavlan, Orthopedic Surgeon, Room 1101*. A woman's eyes widen as she sees my wrist.

"Adeer, what are you doing here? Who's this?"

"This is Julia. She fell, and I knew you could help."

"This is unprofessional, Adeer," she snaps. "You can't just bring your lovers here for me to fix."

"Lovers?" I bristle. "I barely know him. I didn't ask to come here, he insisted."

"Sounds like him, always playing hero," she says, rolling her eyes.

"Screw you," I retort. "I'm not some damsel in distress." Pain shoots through my wrist as I try to move, and I scream, the world fading to black.

I jolt awake, shouting, "No! Stop! Get away!" My arm's heavy, pinned by a cast. The room is dim, soft lambs and clouds on the walls. I must've passed out.

Adeer's at my side in an instant. "You okay, Julia? You fainted in my sister's office. Scared me." His voice is soft, genuine. *Why does he care?* He barely knows me, but his warmth feels... safe.

"I'm fine. Why's my arm so heavy?"

"They cast it. The break was bad."

"No way," I groan. "There goes my shot at the lead."

He mirrors my disappointment. "There'll be other chances."

"Easy for you to say. You don't have parents hounding you to get a 'real job.' Dancing *is* my job." I sigh. "Thanks for helping me, though."

A nurse enters, checking my vitals. "You did well, young lady. That was a nasty break. Oh, and congratulations!"

"For what?"

Her face pales. "The baby. You didn't know you were pregnant?"

"Pregnant?" My voice cracks. "Are you insane? I'm not pregnant."

"Your blood work says otherwise. I'm so sorry, I thought you knew."

Michelle Pentifallo

Words fail me. My mind races, searching for when this could've happened. Too many possibilities. Tears stream down my face, unstoppable. I collapse into Adeer's shoulder, sobbing. He asks the nurse to leave, her apologies fading as she exits. He doesn't speak, strokes my hair, and kisses my forehead gently. I'd push him away at any other time, but I'm too weak. For the first time, I feel safe, held. His shirt soaks with my tears, but he stays steady, anchoring me as the weight of this new reality crashes in. Exhausted, I pull back, sinking into the pillow, nothingness swallowing me again.

"Ted!" I scream, chasing him in a dream. Black figures drag me back, my feet heavy, until I wake, gasping, to lambs and clouds. My mother's eyes meet mine.

Whose Life Is It Anyway?

"Julia, are you okay? You had me so worried. Adeer called, said you were hurt badly. I took the first plane here. What happened? Did someone push you?"

"No, Mom. I tripped avoiding a pole and broke my wrist."

"Figures," she says, her tone sharp. "You've had a drinking problem since high school."

"God, Mom, I was sober. Why do you always assume the worst?"

"I don't, Jules. I'm sorry. I just"

"Yeah, assume. You know what that makes you."

"Don't get smart with me. I flew here to help, and I don't need your attitude."

"Help? You mean spy on me?" Dear God!

"Don't bring God into this. No wonder you're in this mess."

"Mess? What do I do that's so wrong?"

Adeer bursts in. "What's with the yelling? This is a hospital. Show some respect."

"Yeah, Jules, show respect," Mom snaps, grabbing her purse and storming out, muttering.

"You okay?" Adeer asks, his voice calm.

"I'm fine. That's just how she is."

"Sounded like you were giving it back."

"It's none of your business. You don't know what she's done."

"You're right, but she came, didn't she?" I hate that he's right. She did fly here, even if it's to judge me. "Dr. Jones says you can go home today. I was thinking, if you want, you could stay with me for a bit. I'd help you out, so you're not alone."

As Adeer's words spill out, warm and inviting, I pause to study his face. Is he serious, or is this just another pitying glance like the ones I'm used to? But when he turns to me, his eyes hold the same steady warmth I noticed earlier. Who *is* this guy? He barely knows me, yet looks at me like we've been friends for years. "I don't want to impose," I say hesitantly. "We're practically strangers, and I… I don't sleep well at night." My voice trails off, uncertain.

"Julia," he says gently, "no need for excuses. If you'd rather not stay with me, I'll make sure you get home safely. I know your mom booked a hotel, but after what I saw today, I think you could use some peace. My place is outside the city, away from the noise. I just thought you might need rest."

His words hit a tender spot. "Well… maybe just a day or two, until I can move around better. If you're sure it's okay?"

"I wouldn't have offered if it wasn't." His eyes catch mine, and there's a flicker of excitement in them. Why would he be excited about my staying at his house? My mind spirals. *What if he's some creep? A serial killer?* I shake off the thought. *Get a grip, Jules. He runs a business. People know him. Someone would notice if I went missing.* But would they? Ted used me, discarded me like I was nothing. And Amber is probably spreading rumors at dance class. How can I face them again? Even if I do, when will I dance? My wrist is broken, my dreams shattered. And then it hits me like a tidal wave: *I'm pregnant.* My life is over. My body will never be the same. Dance is all I have, and now it's gone. What am I going to do?

Tears well up, and I look up to see my mom back in the room. "I'm sorry, darling," she says softly. "I shouldn't have snapped at you. I know you're hurting, and I don't want to make it worse. I love you."

"It's okay, Mom. Don't worry." It's my go-to line, but inside, I hear a bitter voice: *If that's love, who needs it?* I force a smile, brush it off, and flip on the TV.

As the sun sets outside, a memory flickers of a time when I was a little girl, watching my mom dance in my room as she spun a fairy tale about a queen and her princess. That was a lifetime ago. Some princess I turned out to be. Where's the knight in shining armor everyone talks about? He never showed up. Where's my fairy-tale ending? A baby? What a cruel joke.

I glance at the TV, catching my mom's gaze. Her face says it all: *What happened to my little girl?* "What, Mom?" I snap, defensive.

"Nothing, darling. Just looking at your sweet face."

"Oh." I open my mouth to respond, but the nurse interrupts, striding into the room.

"Julia, ready to go home?" she asks brightly.

"No time like the present," I reply, forcing a smile.

"Where are you staying, dear? Want to come home with me? I can take care of you until you're better," my mom offers.

Before I can answer, Adeer's voice cuts through, bold and certain. "No, Ms. Smith. I'll take her to my place. I have staff to help, and I can get her to her doctor's appointments." I blink, surprised. Is it already decided?

"I'll head to the hotel and check on you tomorrow, Jules, unless you need me sooner," my mom says.

"I'm good, Mom. Thanks. Love you."

"Love you too, dear," she sighs, leaving the room.

Adeer's gaze meets mine, unreadable disbelief? Confusion? He turns away quickly, heading to the closet. "Here are your clothes, Julia. I'll step out so you can change."

I feel oddly detached as he walks away, uncertain about this next step. The nurse helps me navigate my broken wrist through my tank top, and I wince as I slip on my shoes, the pressure shooting pain up my arm. I grab my bag and shuffle down the hall toward whatever comes next. At the end of the corridor, Adeer's on the phone, his voice low but sharp. "I'll deal with him later. Goodbye, George." *George from the dance studio?* My stomach twists. Did Adeer see me with Ted at the bar? Ted bolted for the bathroom the second Adeer appeared, and when he came back, he couldn't wait to leave. Adeer must know something. Before I can speak, he locks eyes with me. "Ready to go? I'm starving. What do you feel like eating?"

"Doesn't matter," I mumble, hoping to shift his mood. He seems unfazed, no trace of anger. As we walk side by side, he grabs my bag, his fingers brushing my skin. It's not intentional, but it feels deliberate, like a quiet promise: *I'm here.* That small gesture anchors me, holding back the flood of doubt threatening to drown me.

A sleek black Lincoln Town Car pulls up to the hospital entrance. The driver steps out, opening the door in front of me. "Miss Julia," he says with a nod.

"Thank you," I reply, confused. *How does he know my name?* The door shuts behind me, and I overhear Adeer instruct the driver to head to the house. Fear creeps in. I don't even know where he lives. Neither does my mom. What if something happens? Would anyone look for me? Samantha might, but she doesn't even know I'm hurt. I was walking away from her when I fell. *God, I'm such an idiot. What am I doing?*

Adeer slides in beside me, catching the panic on my face. "You okay? What's wrong, Julia?"

"Nothing," I lie.

Whose Life Is It Anyway?

"You looked like you saw a ghost."

"Just me and my broken wrist," I say, forcing a laugh. His face softens, that caring look returning, and my fear melts away. Why do I always spiral like this? It's all I've ever known.

As we drive down Central Ave., the city lights glow from restaurants and quirky shops selling T-shirts and trinkets. I love this city, its pulse, its chaos.

"So, Julia, do you like Indian food?" Adeer asks.

"Yes," I say softly, memories of eating with Ted flickering briefly before I shove them aside. "Let's do it," I add with more confidence. We turn toward a sign proclaiming "the best" Indian restaurant. "I've heard of this place but never been," I say quickly. "I'm not dressed for it."

Before I can protest further, Adeer hands me a bag. Inside is a long black summer dress. He meets my eyes cautiously. "I checked your size while you were resting. Thought this might work. If you don't like it, we can return it."

"No, it's great," I say, pulling it out. "Thank you."

"We'll park and step outside while you change. The windows are tinted; no one can see in."

"But I have no makeup, and my hair's a mess."

"You're beautiful, Julia." He pulls a hairband from his pocket. "Maybe this will help." He and the driver step out, facing away, giving me privacy.

This dress is adorable, I think as I slip it on. At the bottom of the bag, I find fresh panties, a thoughtful touch. The dress fits perfectly. Then I notice a smaller bag with silver flip-flops. *I could get used to this.* I tie my hair into a quick bun and step out.

"See, Julia? Perfect!" Adeer says, and the driver nods in agreement. We approach the restaurant, and the owner swings open the door before we reach it.

"Adeer!" he calls out. "It's been too long. And who's this beautiful lady?"

"Thank you, Mahesh," Adeer replies. "It's been a while. I've been craving your Tandoori chicken."

"Come in! And ma'am…"

"Call me Jules," I say with a shy smile.

"Welcome, Jules. What can I get you?"

"Butter chicken, please."

"Coming right up. Waters for both, and anything else to drink?"

"Wine would be," I start, then catch Adeer's disapproving glance. *Right. The baby.* "Actually, just water," I say, frustration bubbling up. *This baby's already controlling me.* The thoughts crash in again. *What am I going to do? I'm not ready to be a mom. I don't want to ruin another human being.*

"Water's fine for me too, Mahesh," Adeer says smoothly.

"How long have you been coming here?" I ask, trying to shift my focus.

"Since I moved here ten years ago. My brother brought me, and it's been my favorite spot ever since. Their food's amazing, not quite my mum's, but close."

"Is your mom in the States?"

"No, she's in India with my dad and sister. They won't move here, so I visit once a year. Mum's been unwell lately, and I'm heading there soon. I love seeing them, but the trip's tough. Growing up, we were poor, and my dad was distant, leaving Mum to do everything. I saw her cry too many nights. I swore I'd be different, never put a woman through that. They're happier now, but Mum's sick, and I don't know what's next. Anyway, enough about me. Where are you from?"

"Don't stop, Adeer. I want to hear more. It helps me understand you."

"Thank you, Julia, but I'd love to know more about you."

"I'm from a tiny town no one's ever heard of," I say, my voice tinged with disdain. "Two stoplights, one main street. I couldn't wait to escape. All I ever wanted was to dance, but the only shot there was taking over Mrs. Shultz's studio when she retired. That wasn't my dream. So, I came to the city to chase it. And now…" I trail off, bitterness creeping in. "Now I'm fucking stuck."

Adeer's brow furrows. "Julia, ladies don't speak like that," he says firmly, drawing gasps from nearby tables.

"What?" I snap, heat rising in my chest. "Like no one's heard that word before? Give me a break, Adeer. I'm no lady, and you don't know me." I shove my chair back and storm toward the bathroom. Swinging the door open, I find it empty. "Finally, some privacy," I mutter. The past few days have been suffocating too many people, too many questions. I crave a moment to breathe, to escape. *I need a blunt. Damn it, I can't even do that.* This baby's already rewriting my life. *An abortion's the only way out. Who'd care? No one knows except Adeer, and why would he? He barely knows me.* I stare at my reflection, unable to meet my own eyes. *Abortion, Jules? Really? Isn't that murder? A sin? Mom would say so. I don't want to burn for this.*

Pushing away from the wet granite countertop, I slip into a stall. As I adjust the silky panties, a stray thought hits me: *Did Adeer pick these out imagining me in them? They're too sexy for a stranger's gift.* I shake it off. *Adeer? I've never dated an Indian guy. What's his deal?* The thought fades as I step out and find him waiting, concern etched across his face.

"You okay, Julia?" he asks softly.

"Yeah, why?"

"I thought I upset you."

"You didn't. I just… don't get why you corrected me. You're not my dad."

"You're right. I overstepped. I'm sorry."

I nod. "I'll watch what I say in public. I don't want to embarrass you."

"You don't embarrass me, Julia. Quite the opposite." He takes my hand gently, kisses my forehead, and leads me back to the table, now laden with steaming dishes.

"Wow, this looks incredible!" I say, catching myself. "I mean… darn." I grab my fork and dig in, hunger overtaking me.

Adeer chuckles, watching me. "You were starving." Dinner seems faster than I expected, and now I can't back out.

As we approach a gated estate, a grand mansion looms in the distance, its fountain sparkling under the moonlight. A statue of a majestic black stallion comes into focus as we glide up the cobblestone drive. The driver opens my door, and we ascend a marble staircase to the entrance. A man in a crisp suit greets us. "Mr. Patel, good to see you. Adell prepared a room for Ms. Julia at the end of the hall."

"Thank you, Bruce," Adeer says as Bruce takes my bags.

"I'll have these washed, ma'am. Can I get you a drink?"

"Water, please," I reply.

"I'll have it sent to your room," Bruce says with a nod.

Whose Life Is It Anyway?

"Let me show you to your room, Julia. You must be exhausted," Adeer says, his eyes searching mine. I am tired, bone-deep.

We walk down a hallway lined with gold-framed portraits, family, I assume. Adeer opens a door to reveal a spacious room with a large bed, a vanity, and a balcony. "I had my staff pick up a few things for you," he says, gesturing to pajamas and a robe neatly laid out on the bed.

"That's so kind. Thank you."

"My pleasure." He kisses my forehead again. Why does he keep doing that? He steps out, then pops back in. "Your water." He hands me a glass and closes the door, leaving me to my thoughts.

I find the bathroom, and my jaw drops at the sight of a massive bathtub. I draw a hot bath, grab soap from under the sink, and sink into the water, playing soft music from my phone. *This is the life: a full stomach, a warm bath, good tunes.* My eyelids grow heavy, and I nearly drift off before catching myself. The water's cooled. I reach for a towel softer than anything I've ever felt and wrap myself in it.

Slipping into the silky pink pajama dress, I skip the panties and step onto the balcony. Robert Plant's voice drifts from my phone, singing *Stairway to Heaven*. *There are two paths you can go by, but in the long run, there's still time to change the road you're on.* The lyrics hit hard. *Is there time to change my path?* This baby's coming, and I can't stop it. Tears spill over, and I bury my face in my hands, sobbing.

Michelle Pentifallo

SEVEN MONTHS LATER

As they place my baby boy on my chest, I gaze into his eyes and sense something's off. Not life-threatening, but a quiet plea: *I need help*. Panic grips me. I look at the nurse. "Congratulations, you have a healthy boy," she says, but my fear doesn't fade. "Is something wrong?" I ask, offering him to her. As she reaches out, the room spins.

Beeps pierce the air. Footsteps pound toward me. "She's got internal bleeding," the doctor says. My baby's cries echo faintly. *He'll be okay,* I tell myself. The bed lurches, speeding down a hall. Lights flicker overhead.

"She's still conscious!" a nurse shouts. "Julia, can you hear me? Squeeze my hand. Tell me your name."

Bright lights flood my vision as we enter a sterile room. I squint, feeling a cold rush through my IV. Darkness creeps in, but my mind fights for clarity. My body feels distant, like I'm watching it from above. Doctors and nurses scramble, their voices a blur. In the corner, a shadowy figure looms. Its eyes lock onto mine, familiar, cruel. That voice, the one that haunts me daily, sneers, "You can't even get this right, Julia. Women have babies every day, but you're failing to come with me. The Dark Lord will deal with you. I'll take your child next."

Rage surges through me. "Get away from me!" I scream. "Stay away from my baby! You don't belong here anymore. Get OUT!" My eyes snap open, and Adeer's face hovers above me, calm and steady.

"Are you okay, Julia?" he asks. We're in our room, in our home.

"It was a dream," I gasp, trembling. "So real. I had the baby, and I was dying..." My voice breaks.

Whose Life Is It Anyway?

Adeer pulls me close, his arms strong. "It was just a dream, love. I won't let anything happen to you or our family. We'll see the doctor today to ease your mind."

"I'm fine," I whisper, unconvinced. Adeer's been incredible, attending every appointment, ensuring I eat well, taking care of me like this baby is his. But what if he changes his mind when he sees the baby's face, knowing it's not his?

"Julia," he says suddenly, "let's get married. I love you. I want to give our son my name before he's born. You know my past family means everything to me. I want to build one with you." His eyes burn with certainty.

Shock freezes me. His face falls, misreading my silence. "Wait," I stammer. "I'm just surprised. I love you too, but I don't want you to feel obligated because I'm pregnant. This baby isn't yours. It's a lot to take on."

"It'll change our lives for the better," he says. "I've always wanted a big family. He's our start."

"What if Ted wants to be involved?"

"He won't. I made sure he stays gone."

"What if the baby wants to know him?"

"He won't need to. I'll be his dad and love him like my own."

His confidence is unshakable, but doubts linger. I want to ask more, but his passion silences me. "Yes, I'll marry you," I say softly, though unease tugs at me. *Shouldn't I feel safer? Happier?*

"You will!" Adeer exclaims, joy radiating from him. He reaches into his nightstand and pulls out a ring, a stunning 3-carat princess-cut diamond set in white gold, framed by smaller stones. "I've been waiting to ask you," he says, voice thick with emotion. "I knew you were the one when I saw you dance all those months ago."

"It's perfect," I say, my heart swelling despite my fears. His lips find mine, a kiss filled with passion and promise. He gently slips off my nightgown, mindful of my swollen belly, and I feel the spark of a new beginning.

"Ms. Davis, the doctor will see you now."

Adeer and I rise, heading to the familiar exam room. As we approach, Samantha bursts through the door, her eyes widening at my pregnant belly, mirroring her own. "Jules! I had no idea. What the heck?"

"Hi, Sam," I say, flustered. "I'm heading into my appointment. I'll call you later."

Whose Life Is It Anyway?

"You better! I've been trying to reach you for months. I thought you vanished."

"Yeah… something like that," I mumble, hurrying through the door. Adeer's back is to her, but I catch Sam mouthing, *Who's this?* I look away, heart sinking. Sam won't stay quiet. Soon, everyone will know.

"Are you okay?" Adeer asks, his voice calm but laced with concern. His hand rests gently on my lower back as he guides me into the exam room.

"I'm fine," I say, though my heart's still racing. "I just wasn't ready to see someone I know." Before he can press further, the nurse opens the door and motions for me to sit so she can take my vitals. *Thank God,* I think. I'm not in a position to handle this conversation at the moment. This morning's dream shook me to my core, and I need to know our baby is okay.

Dr. Sharesh enters, his gaze steady. "What brings you in today, Julia?"

"I had a horrible dream this morning," I confess, voice trembling. "I'm scared something's wrong with the baby."

"Alright, let's take a look." I lie back as he glides the ultrasound wand over my belly. The screen lights up, and I search his face for any hint of worry, expecting confirmation of my fears. However, his expression remains focused and determined. "Hear that heartbeat?" he says confidently.

"Yes," I whisper, clinging to the sound.

"Everything looks good." He presses gently on my belly, rechecks the screen, then switches sides. Adeer and I stare at the monitor, desperate for reassurance. The doctor's calm demeanor offers none of the dread I feel. "Just a healthy baby boy," he says, shutting down the machine and wiping the gel from my skin. "Dreams like this are common at this stage. It's a time for nesting."

"Nesting?" Adeer asks, curious.

"It's when expectant mothers start preparing, organizing, cleaning, getting the baby's room ready," Dr. Sharesh explains. "Dreams often carry fears of loss because this baby is so important. It's a stressful time. Avoid heavy foods before bed and try relaxing with a good book instead of googling worst-case scenarios."

"Okay," I say softly, but the dream felt too real, too vivid. That voice, the one that's haunted me since childhood, wasn't just a nightmare. It's been with me forever, lurking, and today I *saw* it. If I say that out loud, they'll think I'm unhinged. After Sam's judgment at the clinic, I can't handle more scrutiny. I nod at Dr. Sharesh, forcing agreement. He helps me up, his hand steady. "Don't worry, Julia. You'll deliver a beautiful baby in a couple of months. Keep taking your vitamins, and we'll see you in two weeks for bloodwork." His words linger, "Don't worry," but they don't sink in.

Before Adeer can mention Sam, I pivot. "Hey, let's grab a sandwich at Patelli's. I'm craving an Italian sub." His brows furrow, a flicker of disagreement, but he softens.

"Alright," he says in that warm, loving tone I've come to cherish.

In the car, he shuts my door and slides in beside me, leaning over to kiss me. I meet his lips, hoping to sidestep the Sam conversation. "So, this nesting thing," I say lightly. "Me, cleaning and organizing? I barely do dishes, let alone wash baby clothes two months early."

He chuckles. "I know. And I love you just as you are." His acceptance wraps around me, but it's hard to believe.

Whose Life Is It Anyway?

Tears prick my eyes at the thought of losing him. I turn toward the window, hiding my face.

"I was thinking navy and white for the baby's room, with maroon accents. What do you think?" I ask, changing the subject.

"Whatever makes you happy, Julia, makes me happy," he says, kissing my hand softly. His sincerity is unshakable, but then he pauses, lowering the radio. "Why are you trying to distract me?"

"What?" I say, feigning innocence.

"I didn't know your friends were out of the loop. I thought you were meeting Samantha for lunch on Thursdays. If not her, then who?" His voice carries concern, not accusation.

I hesitate. "It's... my sister, Jane."

"Jane?" His tone sharpens. "Julia, we talked about this. She's toxic for us. She doesn't understand our relationship."

"She's not toxic, Adeer. We've had good talks lately. She hasn't pushed me to leave you in a while."

"A while? How long is that? A week?" His voice shifts, cold and cutting, echoing that inner voice that tells me I'm worthless, clueless.

Anger flares. "Fuck you!" I blurt out, instantly regretting it. His hatred for my cursing is no secret, and we haven't fought in months. Our streak is over.

"What did you say?" he asks, voice tight.

"You heard me! Back off!" I snap, my emotions spiraling.

"That's uncalled for, Julia. We agreed you wouldn't see her, and you've been sneaking around, lying to me. Are you that insecure?" His words slice deep, exposing a truth he's never voiced before.

Fury consumes me. "Let me out of the car *now*!" I scream.

"No, I'm not leaving you on the side of the road. That's ridiculous."

I grab the steering wheel, yanking it. He's too strong, holding it steady. "You'll cause an accident, Julia! Stop it!"

I fling open the door. He slams the brakes, and my head smashes the window. "I'm so sorry," he says instantly, but I'm too angry to care. I stumble out, slam the door, and march toward my old apartment, one I never gave up. My sister convinced Mom to cover the rent, just in case. My purse swings at my side, and I dig for my keys, feeling the familiar 'J' keychain.

Adeer screeches to a stop nearby and jogs to my side. "Julia, get in the car. This is foolish."

"Foolish? Like me, right?"

"No one said that."

"You called me a liar! And insecure. What's next? A worthless slut?"

"I never said that!" he protests.

"You meant it!" I yell, clutching my belly, forgetting my once-broken wrist, the spark of this whole mess. He reaches to steady me, but I shove him away. "What was I thinking?" I rip off the engagement ring, press it into his hand, and hail a cab. He freezes, pain flashing across his face. I knew that would hit hard. As I slide into the cab and give my address, regret floods me. I glance back to see Adeer walking to his car, head bowed. Can we recover from this? I don't want to lose him, but I can't be with him right now. He called me an insecure liar. It confirms what I've always known: I'm a failure. He was the one person who saw me differently, who believed in who I could be. I was wrong.

The cab driver's voice cuts through. "We're here."

I pay and step out, heading to my apartment. The landlord spots me at the entrance. "Julia! Thought you were gone for good. What happened?" Her eyes widen at my belly, just like Sam's did.

Ate a watermelon. Didn't digest well," I quip.

She cackles, her smoker's cough trailing. "Looks like it'll take a few months to work that out."

"Yep," I say curtly, climbing the stairs to my door, marked with a big 'C.' I unlock it, and everything's as I left it. At Adeer's, I wanted for nothing; every need met, every wish granted. "Guess I am foolish," I mutter aloud. "No job, no plan. How am I going to do this?" That voice sneers from the shadows: *You knew Adeer didn't love you.* I collapse onto the couch, tears streaming, desperation clawing at my heart. I've ruined the best thing I've ever had. Silence settles, heavy and cold.

I jolt awake to darkness, a chill in the air. Hours must have passed. The news warned of a colder-than-usual winter, and September's already biting. I flick on the side table lamp and check the thermostat: 65 degrees. I crank it to 74, craving warmth. If Adeer were here, his arms would chase the cold away faster. But it's too late. Tears blur my vision again. He thinks I'm with Mom, not here. I told him I'd stay with her until the baby's born. What choice do I have? I want him, but I don't deserve him. I sabotaged us. Why would he want me now?

My gaze drifts to the cabinet where I hid a bottle months ago. One drink could silence the voices. *It's too late. You messed up again,* that familiar shadow hisses. I turn on the TV, sinking into my new reality, alone.

Michelle Pentifallo

9

CONTROL CENTER

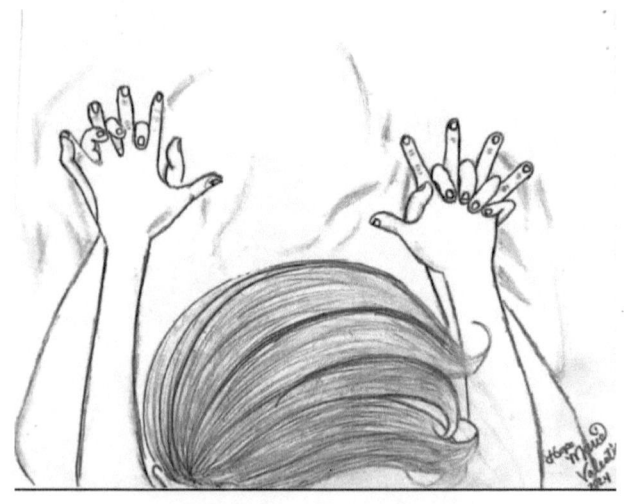

Ted's cologne hits me before I open my eyes, heavy and overwhelming. His fingers graze my shoulder, stirring me from sleep. All I want is rest, but I keep the thought silent, screaming it in my head.

"Good morning," he whispers in my ear, as if that's what I crave. My voice betrays me, weak from exhaustion. "Hi," I manage, barely audible.

"You looked so beautiful lying there, I had to wake you," he says. *Had to wake me?* I think irritation is flaring. *Five times last night wasn't enough?* His coke-and-Viagra binges mean no rest for me. I hate these nights.

"What time is it?" I ask, forcing a sweet tone to avoid setting him off.

"Six."

"No way, Ted," I say, as gently as I can. "We were up until three." *How much coke did he do?* "I have to be at work by ten," I add, slipping out of bed. His hand falls from my shoulder, his body tensing.

"What does that matter, Amber?" he snaps. "Aren't I worth it? Didn't I give you a good time? You're so ungrateful. Get out of my bed, you sorry excuse for a woman!"

And there it is. The drugs turn him into a monster. Sober, he's decent, charming, even. I should've just let him do what he wanted; I'd have gotten a couple more hours of sleep. "Ted, don't say that," I say softly. "I'm just tired. I love you, but I have a long shift today."

"I've got more blow," he says, his mood swinging. "I can hook you up."

"You know I can't. They drug test at work."

"Then quit!" Ted barks.

Control Center

I roll my eyes, hidden in the dim light, and drag myself out of bed. "So, you'll take care of me, Ted? How? You just lost your job for fooling around."

"Adeer's the jerk, not me," he mutters.

I gather my clothes, strewn across the floor from last night's chaos. As I bend down, Ted's behind me again. "Don't go, Amber. I don't want you to."

He's like a yo-yo, I think, but I seize the moment. "I have to get ready for work," I say firmly, relishing the control. I grab my bra from a chair and head to the bathroom, his hand brushing my thigh as I slip away.

"Come on, Amber, don't do this," he whines.

"No." I toss my clothes on the counter, fumbling for the light.

"I'll be good. You can sleep," he coaxes.

"I don't have time, Ted." I slip on my panties, adjust my bra, pull on jeans, and tug a tank top over my head. My shoes are by the front door, I think. Last night's a blur of shots and bad decisions.

"You don't have to go!" he yells from the bedroom. I grab my purse, find my shoes, and slam the door so hard the walls shake. I storm down the porch steps to my car in the driveway, digging for my keys. My fingers find gum instead, and I pop a piece in my mouth. It's better than the taste of last night. *He better not have done that after...* I can't remember too many shots.

My 1988 Black Ford Mustang rumbles to life, a gift from Dad. If he saw me now, he'd be heartbroken. I push the thought away and pull out. As I turn the corner, I spot Jules. *That little stalker,* I think, venom rising. *Trying to steal my man.* Thank God Ted didn't fall for her. "Pathetic," I mutter, my inner voice cheering: *She's always after what's yours.* Then I notice her belly, swollen and unmistakable. No wonder she's been absent from dance class. I thought Ted said she got in trouble for stalking him. Or was that about me? Adeer fired him for "fraternizing," but that was us, wasn't it? I slow down, catching sight of Adeer stepping out of a car. *He must be the father.* Relief washes over me. I turn my head, speed up, and head home.

"This apartment is the worst," I grumble, circling for a parking spot. There's never one near my door. As someone pulls out, another car approaches. *Don't even try it.* I flick on my blinker, claiming dominance. "Back off! I was here first!" I yell out my window. The other driver shrinks back, turning away. *That's right,* I think, smirking. The spot's mine today. I park, grab my purse, and lock the car. Passing a couple, that voice whispers, *He wants you.* I roll my eyes. *They all do.*

Inside, a rancid smell hits me. "What is that?" I gag, heading to the kitchen. Three-day-old chicken sits on the counter, forgotten in my Ted-induced haze. He never lets me leave. Sober, he's sweet, cooks dinner, opens doors, and buys me gifts. But coked up, he's clingy, insecure. I toss the chicken into a bag, throw it out the front door, and slam it shut.

In the bathroom, I pull down my jeans and panties, wincing as I sit. *Ouch.* Ted's roughness leaves its mark, especially when he's drunk or high. But the other day, he was different, gentle, asking to "make love." I almost fell over. I strip and step into the shower, letting the hot water wash away the residue from the night. Today's going to be brutal. I grab a towel, pop three Tylenol, and notice my birth control pills. My period's five days late. *Weird. Probably just off my cycle.* I shrug it off, set my alarm for 9:15, and collapse into bed, sleep claiming me instantly.

My alarm blares at 9:15, yanking me from sleep. *No way.* It feels like I just closed my eyes. I drag myself to the closet, grab my physician's assistant uniform, and pick out a bra and underwear. I do my makeup and hair, rushing to get out the door with twenty minutes to spare before work, plenty of time for a latte from Sundance Coffee Express.

At a red light, I text Ted: *Hey! How are you doing? Get any sleep?* Bubbles appear as he's typing, but no reply comes. *Asshole,* I think, irritation flaring. *He'll use me all night, but can't text back?* A honk jolts me; the light's green. I wave an apology in the rearview and pull forward.

The coffee line's short. "Is that you, Amber?" Melissa's voice crackles through the speaker.

"Yep, it's me."

"See you at the window." I hand her a five, her eyes bright with her usual cheer.

"Good morning, Amber! Hope you're having a great day!"

"So far, so good," I say, forcing a smile.

"The day is young."

"You got that right," I say, managing a grin. I pull away, latte in hand, and head to Mercy Hospital. My physician's assistant job is my lifeline, the one part of my life that feels right. Without it, I'd be lost, probably spiraling into depression. It's where I shine, where I'm more than just Ted's shadow.

I badge in at the back door. "Hey, Amber, how's your day?" Mike, the guard, calls out.

"Couldn't be better," I lie, flashing a smile. Inside the locker room, it's oddly empty. I head to my locker number 723, grab my coat and name tag, and tie my hair into a bun. *Where is everyone?* I wonder, heading to the break room. As I open the door, a roar of "SURPRISE!" erupts. Balloons and confetti fill the air.

"Happy Birthday, Amber!" my coworkers shout.

I blink, stunned. *Is it my birthday?* April 1 is April Fools' Day. Of course, I forgot. "You guys, that's so sweet," I say, touched. "I totally blanked on it."

"How do you forget your own birthday?" Eileen asks, incredulous.

"Because I'm a rock star, and you're not," I tease, winking.

"Happy Birthday, chickee!" Mike says, pulling me into a hug. Others filter out to their shifts, but a few linger to chat.

"How old are you now, Amber?" Mike asks, grinning.

"You don't ask a lady her age," I shoot back playfully, dodging the question. Today, I'll take the celebration and run with it. Maybe this year, I'll figure out how to take control of my own story.

"Girl, you're no lady," Gloria teases, her laugh warm and full as she opens her arms for a hug.

"Shut it, Gloria," I say, grinning. "I'm twenty-eight today." I lean into her embrace, soaking up her comfort. Her hugs are the best. I adore her.

"Two years 'til the big three-oh!" Mike booms.

"Not today, buddy," I reply, my voice lighter now, fueled by the festive energy.

"Grab some cake, Amber. I'll cover for you," Gloria says, heading out. "See you in surgery." Soon, it's just me and Mike, munching cake in the break room's lounge chairs.

"So, can I take you out for your birthday tonight?" Mike asks, his tone shy but earnest.

I laugh. "Have you met Ted? He'd lose it." I think he's joking, but his eyes hold a quiet strength. *Is he serious?* Mike always asks me questions, but I figured he was just being friendly with everyone.

"I don't care, Amber," he says, half-smirking. "I'd take on that dance-instructor wannabe any day." He chuckles. "Pansy."

I burst out laughing. Ted's strong from dancing, but yeah, kind of a lightweight. Mike heads for the door, then leans back. "Think about it. I'd show you a good time." He winks and disappears. I sip my latte, savoring the quiet, but the loudspeaker crackles: "Amber Ortiz, to surgery."

So much for a break, I head down the hall, wondering what's up, first, Whipple or gallbladder? I could handle a gallbladder solo if they'd trust me. Checking the schedule, I see Whipple with Dr. Madison Franklin, myself, and Gloria, a solid team. I rush to scrub in, catching Dr. Franklin's impatient stare through the glass. *The surgery's not for an hour. Why the look?* I pull on gloves, put on a mask, and step into the room, my mind locked on the task ahead.

FOUR MONTHS LATER

"Hey, Amber, you're starting to show," Gloria says casually.

"Show? What do you mean?" I ask, heart racing. *How does she know?*

"Oh, girl, I thought you were pregnant," she says, laughing. I force a smile, hiding my panic.

"Nah, just too much partying," I lie, bolting for the bathroom. I need to pee, but it's also a form of escape. Inside, Eileen's at the mirror, applying lipstick. She's the perfect greeter at the waiting room desk—always cheerful, unlike me.

"Hey, Amber! Long time no see," Eileen chirps. "Where've you been?"

"Used up some PTO for a vacation," I say, but the truth is I was puking every morning.

"Glad you're back," she says, pocketing her lipstick and flashing a smile as she leaves. I nod, then glare at my reflection. *They'd all guess if they saw me throwing up.* I can't believe this happened. I'm smarter than this. It must've been that night Ted was coked out. I drank too much, and he didn't use protection. I wasn't consistent with my pills either. My fault, too. I squeeze my eyes shut, avoiding my own gaze. *I can't be tied to Ted forever with a kid. What if it's like him?* He was just a rebound, a distraction from loneliness. A dancer? What was I thinking? My parents will freak. Ted mentioned abortion the other day. Maybe that's the answer. But killing a baby? That's not me. I'm not religious, but I'm no murderer.

Should've let Jules have him, I think bitterly. Her baby's probably his, too. When I found out he cheated with two girls, I lost it. He begged for forgiveness until I told him I was pregnant. His face pure panic. "Is it mine?" he asked, like I'm the cheater. "You're the asshole!" I screamed, storming out. Now we only text because I need his money for the abortion. I can't let anyone at the hospital, especially in pediatrics, know. I see babies fighting for life every day, parents on the edge of despair. I can't face that. If I did this, something would go wrong; my luck, the baby would have a defect. Abortion's safer. I could get my tubes tied, too. I head to a stall, relieve myself, and splash water on my face at the sink. "You're such a mess," I mutter to my reflection. A faint laugh echoes. *What?* "Anyone in here?" I check the stalls for emptiness. Must've been the hallway. But as I leave, the laugh trails behind me. I sprint out, crashing into Mike.

"What the fuck!" I blurt out.

"Whoa!" Mike says, his tone teasing but judgmental. "Didn't know you talked like that. Where have you been?"

"Sorry," I mumble. He thinks I'm some goody-two-shoes. If he knew the real me, he'd run, just like every other guy. "I've been off a couple of weeks," I add. "Visited my parents in Seattle."

"Nice. How was it?" he asks, genuine.

"Boring. Parents, you know? 'Wow, Amber, you cut your hair, gained a little weight.' 'What's new with you?' 'Finally, using that degree we paid for instead of dancing.' 'Dancing's just a hobby.'" I mimic their voices, masking my frustration.

"Got it. You look great, though. You were too skinny before," he says, winking as he heads to meet parents with that haunted look, the one that screams, *Will my kid be okay? I don't want that life.*

I pull out my phone and text Ted: *Hey, where's my money?* He's reading bubbles appear. *I'll have it tomorrow,* he replies. Relief hits me. *2:00?* I ask. *Perfect. Sundance. Don't be late,* I type, but swap it for *Thanks.* No need to stir trouble; I need his help. These hormones are brutal, and this pregnancy's draining me. I can't wait to be done.

"Hey, Ted," I say, irritation creeping in. "You said 2:00. I've been waiting fifty minutes."

"You know I'm always late, Amber. You came early? You're the fool," he sneers.

"Me? Look at me, jerk. You did this," I snap, gesturing to my belly. His eyes darken, and I back off. "Let's not fight. We both messed up. I just need the money to fix this. You won't hear from me again."

"I was hoping we could party after you, you know," he says, handing me the cash.

"Are you serious? I'm done with you!" My voice rises, drawing stares from a nearby couple. "What are you looking at?" I hiss, storming toward the door. Ted's footsteps follow.

"Come on, Amber, I love you," he pleads.

I spin around, fury boiling over. "You're delusional! You cheated with at least two girls, probably Jules, too.

That's your kid she's carrying! Get out of my life. You've done enough!" He reaches for my arm, but I dodge, sprinting to my car. The door locks between us. I start the engine and peel out, tears burning my eyes. *Don't cry over him. He never loved you.* I wipe them away, refusing to break.

At home, I collapse onto my bed, tears unstoppable now. Nothing can undo this damage. All I can do is end this pregnancy. My phone lights up Ted again: *Don't be mad. I love you. I just don't know how to be a dad. My dad was awful. Do you want to keep the baby?* I ignore him. Why would I keep it? He won't help. My parents will disown me. I'm out of PTO, and I can't do this alone. I'm terrified.

From my window, the sun sinks below the horizon. For a fleeting moment, I wonder, *could I be a good mom?* I rest my head on the pillow, staring at the ceiling, and let sleep wash the thought away.

TWO WEEKS LATER

"Ms. Worthington," a nurse calls, pushing open the clinic door. "Hi," she says, smiling. "Let's get your weight and blood pressure, sweetheart." *Sweetheart?* I think bitterly. *I'm here to end my pregnancy. That makes me heartless.* My mom would be devastated if she knew. "This way to room four."

The room is sterile white walls, a paper-covered bed with stirrups, plastic-wrapped tools, and a machine humming softly. Chairs line the wall. *Who sits there to watch this?* It's absurd.

"Okay, Amber," the nurse says gently, using my first name as requested. "Put your clothes in this bag and seal it. I'll store it in a locker down the hall for when you're done. Here's a gown opening in the back and socks if your feet get cold. It's chilly in here. Any questions?"

"No, I don't think so," I murmur, my voice barely steady.

"You'll be okay, Amber. It'll be over soon." Her words are meant to comfort, but they feel hollow.

I slip off my clothes, folding them into the bag, and hang my purse with it on the wall hook. I tie the sterile gown, my hand lingering on my belly. *Hey, little one,* I think, stroking gently. *Don't hate me. I don't know you, so I can't love you. Your dad's no good for us. I don't have a choice.* Tears stream down my cheeks. The fantasy of holding a baby in my arms flickers, but I shove it away—it's not real. I sit on the bed's edge, refusing to think about what's next, pushing back the guilt of ending an innocent life. The door swings open, startling me.

"Ms. Worthington," the doctor says briskly, "we're going to give you something to prevent pain."

Control Center

"Can you just knock me out?" I ask, desperate.

"We need you awake to push," he replies. *Push?* I scream internally, panic rising. "An instrument will guide the baby out, but you need to be conscious for the procedure."

I didn't expect this. I don't want to see the baby. I nod, swallowing my dread.

"This will numb you so that it won't be too bad," he says, smiling. "I'll check back in a few minutes to ensure it's working, then we'll begin."

Smiling? I think bitterly. *How can he smile, doing this for a living?* I work in a hospital, saving babies, watching families pray for miracles. A family would love this baby. *What's wrong with you, Amber? No one wants your messed-up kid. Let it go.*

Time drags. The doctor returns. "We're ready. Place your legs in the stirrups, Ms. Worthington. This won't take long."

That's my mom's name, dickhead, I think, but say, "Please, call me Amber."

"Alright, Amber, lie back. You'll feel pressure, but it'll be quick." *Quick?* One wild night and three months of chaos, and it's over in a moment. What a broken world.

"I'm starting the extractor," he says. The machine hums, a sickening sucking sound filling the room. A soft voice whispers in my ear: *Don't do this.*

"Are you okay, Amber? Any questions?" the doctor asks.

"No," I say, leaning back, body tense with fear.

"Open your legs wide, and when you feel pressure, push."

Don't do this, the voice urges again, clear and not the nurse's. As the machine's pull begins, I scream, "STOP! I can't do this!" The doctor looks up, startled.

"Amber, you'll be fine. Don't worry."

"No!" I shout, snapping my legs shut, struggling to sit up against the numbness. "I can't!"

"Lower your voice," he says sharply. "Other patients..." *Other patients? I don't care about them.* "If you don't calm down, we'll have to sedate you, Ms. Worthington."

"That's my mom's name!" I snap. "Call me Amber!" I see the nurse slip something into my IV. Before I can protest, my body goes limp.

"Amber," a muffled voice calls. "I need you to wake up slowly."

Where am I? My eyes flutter, frantic. I was in the clinic, and then... I search the nurse's face for answers.

"Calm down, Amber," she says gently. "You can't yell in here. Breathe slowly. Here's water—sit up and drink."

"Is my baby okay?" I ask, voice low but urgent, fearing they finished it.

"Yes, everything's fine," the doctor says. I exhale, relief flooding me. My hand finds my belly, feeling the roundness and a faint flutter, a reminder of life. I clutch the water, staring at them in disbelief. *What have I done? How will I do this alone?*

"Are you okay, Amber?" the nurse asks.

"I'm sorry," I say, tears falling. "This baby makes me so emotional. I know I might regret this, but I have to leave and never come back."

"In about thirty minutes, the numbness should wear off, and you can go," she says kindly.

I lie back, the hum of the extractor in the next room a grim reminder of what I almost did. Another woman's life is being altered nearby, but I can't save her. I'm responsible for myself—and now this baby. For the first time in forever, I realize I can't keep running from who I am.

Control Center

10

NO PLACE TO GO

She strides into the diner like she owns it, oblivious to my stare. But I'm always watching. Every time I see Julie, my stomach flips, my palms sweat, and my body reacts. She's stunning. Does she come here every day? I'm here three

No Place to Go

mornings a week for breakfast and coffee, and I spot her at least twice. "Hey, Josiah," a voice calls faintly.

"Hey!" I snap out of it, realizing Phyllis is talking to me.

"Sorry, Phyllis, just thinking about my day," I say, covering.

"Sure, man," she teases, pouring more coffee. "Looks like you're eyeing that pretty lady."

"Nah, I've got a wife at home. Don't need to look," I lie.

"Doesn't hurt to look, just don't touch," she giggles.

"She wouldn't want me anyway," I mutter. "Look at her, then look at me. We don't match." As Julie hurries out the door, my mind strips her bare, imagining her in my bed. *Damn.* Denise isn't here to distract me, so my thoughts run wild. I think her name's Julie Matt said it once when she grabbed her to-go order. She never stays. Where's she rushing off to? I want her close, showing her what a real man can do. Her guy's probably a weakling.

Michelle Pentifallo

Shit, it's 7:00. I'm late for work. George will dock my pay if I slip up again. He's itching to fire me for his nephew, but I'm union, so he needs a solid reason. As I head to my car, I see Julie in hers, crying into her phone. "What do you mean, you don't love me anymore?" she sobs. *I could love you all night if you'd let me,* I think, my body reacting again. I can't stop asking what's wrong with work calls. *Lunchtime relief, it is.*

There's George, waiting to pounce. *Asshole.* He's dying to fire me, but I won't give him an excuse.

"Morning, George. How's it going?" I say, forcing a smile.

"Cutting it close, Josiah," he grumbles.

"Yeah, spilled coffee on my shirt. Had to change," I lie.

"Good thing you did."

Idiot, I think. *I was too busy fantasizing to go home.* "Where do you want me? Crane?"

"Yeah. Bob's still out with his back, so you're it for now."

For now? What's that mean, asshole? "Happy to help," I say, heading to the elevator. On the ride to the 20th floor, my mind drifts back to Julie. The crane cabin's empty this early, no one'll know. I unzip, imagining her, and let the fantasy take over. *That's what I needed.* Now I can focus. I'll revisit her at lunch when the crew's downstairs.

"Hey, what the hell are you doing?" I yell out the crane window. "Move before I knock you off the wall!" The new guy's daydreaming again, risking his neck. This job's no place for slackers. Who hired this idiot? He's been here a month and still screws up. Probably one of George's hires. "Get out of my way, newbie!"

"Name's Jerry," he snaps. "Dick."

"Oh, I'll show you who's boss, Jerry," I retort, fuming. He mutters something—maybe "screw you"—but I let it slide. I can't risk trouble with George breathing down my neck. My thoughts shift to punching Jerry, but the lunch horn blares. As the crew heads down, I stay in the cabin. Time for Julie again. In my mind, she's with me, and I lose myself in the fantasy, tension melting away. *Good thing I'm up here,* I think, chuckling. *Drywall would've had me decking Jerry.*

"Hey, you slacker!" Tucker yells. "Gonna sit there or work?"

"Shut it, Fucker Tucker," I shoot back.

"Let's finish and hit Don's. My turn to buy."

"Damn right. You stiffed me last night, four beers for fifty bucks, fuck head. Hey, why'd they call Isaac to the office?"

"Probably to fire him. Caught him napping yesterday. George was pissed, vein popping, stuttering. Hilarious. He can't touch me, though union. Let's get this done and grab beers. My wife's driving me nuts, so I'm in no rush to go home."

"Let's do it!" I say, shutting the window. One last flash of Julie hits me, but I shake it off. *Focus, man.* This chick's messing with my head, but work comes first.

The final beam's in place, and the quitting alarm sounds. "Party time, boys!" I yell, opening the crane window. As I step out, I trip and smack my head on the bar. *Damn!* Blood trickles from a gash. I can't let George see thirty days without an incident, and the crew will roast me. I tie my bandana around my forehead and pull my CAT hat low. No one'll notice it.

At the time clock, I spot Jerry Fairy. "So, you're a slacker or what?" I taunt.

Michelle Pentifallo

"What? No!" he snaps, voice catching.

"Your hair's all perfect, shirts ironed. What's your deal?"

"Whatever, Josiah. You've got no class."

"No class? Who do you think you are?" I step closer, but Tucker shoves me toward the door.

"Come on, man, let's hit Don's. Don't mess with the kid, George will have your head."

"Why's he always on Jerry's case?" I grumble as we walk out.

"He's a neat freak, daydreaming all the time. He'll get someone hurt, and it'll fall on you. Just tell George if you see something. Chill, man. You're too wound up."

My head's throbbing as I step out of my truck. *Didn't think I hit it that hard.* I pop an Oxy from the glovebox, swallowing it dry. That'll fix it. At Don's, I duck into the bathroom to check the damage. The bandana's soaked with blood, worse than I thought. I rewrap it, reposition my hat, and head to the bar. Then I freeze. Julie's in a booth with some guy. *No way.* I blink, thinking it's another fantasy, but she's real. Is that the guy from her phone call? Tucker waves me over.

"What, Fucker Tucker?" I say, distracted.

"Getting you a shot. What's it gonna be?"

"Tequila, baby."

"Three, Don! Light it up."

"Who's the third for?" I ask, but Bob walks in. "Hey, Bob! Good to see you, man. Place isn't the same without you."

"Thanks, Josiah. Back's getting better, but I'm not young like you. Old man now."

"Whatever. Tucker got you a shot. That'll fix you."

No Place to Go

"Can't get wasted tonight. Wife's cooking something special. Don't want to miss it."

"A few won't hurt. Let's go, boys," I say, sliding into my spot at Don's. I glance at Julie, tears streaking her face, and for a split second, I feel a pang of sympathy. *What's that about?* I shake it off. *She's just like the rest.* I grab my shot, lick-suck-slam, and holler, "Another! And a Coors Light for me!" As I go down the next, I spot Julie at the bar's end, ordering. "Come here, little lady," I call out. "I'll get you a drink!"

"No, thanks," she says, tilting her head to hide her tears.

"I'm buying!"

Her guy steps up behind her, glaring at me. "No need, man. I've got her."

"Oh, yeah? Don't want to upset the pretty boy," I taunt.

"Excuse me?" he says, calm but firm. "What's that mean?"

"Nothing. Have a good night," I mutter, turning back to my beer. "Don, another Coors."

"You staying chill tonight, Josiah?" Don asks, his eyes serious.

"Yeah, I've got work tomorrow. Can't miss more days. I'm good."

Tucker laughs. "Good? You? Doubt it. I'll drag you out before you start trouble. Another shot?"

"Why not?" After a couple more, I slur, "Gotta hit the bathroom," and stumble off the stool. I catch Julie heading the same way. Around the corner, I lean close, my voice low. "You need a real man, little lady."

She spins, eyes wide with fear. "Don't get so close. If Paul sees, he'll tear you apart." She slips into the women's restroom. I pause, thinking, *That loser?* But my bladder urges me on. At the urinal, Julie's image floods my mind, spread out on my bed. *She'll be mine soon,* I think, zipping up. *Paul won't know what hit him.*

"Hey, asshole!" Tucker yells as I round the corner. "Look who's here!" I freeze. Shelly's at my spot. *What's she doing here?* I told her we're done.

"Hey, Josiah, getting wild?" she says, smirking.

"Yeah, Shelly. What's up?" I ask, wary.

She looks stunning in a short skirt and crop top, but her clinginess is too much. "Just grabbing a drink on a hot night," she says, leaning over the bar to kiss Don's cheek, her curves right in my face. *Damn, I miss that,* I admit, but she's a tease, chasing what she can't have anymore.

"Yo, Josiah!" Bob snaps me out of it.

"Here, man," I say.

"Gotta go," Bob says, sliding off his stool. "Love my wife, happy wife, happy life. Catch you later." He's out before we can argue.

Shelly claims his spot. *Great.* I don't need her drama. "Where're your friends?" I ask.

"Coming in an hour. Wanted to talk to you first," she says, leaning close. "I've got an STD. From you."

Panic hits. "What?!" I hiss, loud enough for Tucker to glance over. "Later," I whisper. She orders a vodka shot with lemon. My mind races, landing on that massage parlor visit. *That's gotta be it.* I'll deal with it tomorrow. "Don, same as her, plus a Coors." I glance at Julie's booth; she and her guy are leaving. I take one last look, slam my shot, and suck the lemon.

My alarm blares, and Shelly's parting words echo: "It's chlamydia, you cheating fucking asshole. Just get meds." I

No Place to Go

hit snooze, relieved it's not worse, and steal a few more minutes before another miserable day.

Quitting time's siren wails. "Let's grab a few," Tucker says. "It's Friday, man. Don's?"

"Bet," I say, hoping Julie's there again as I clock out.

Monday morning, sipping coffee at the diner, I see her walk in. I wasn't always like this, obsessed, crude. My mom's voice still haunts me: *You'll never amount to anything.* She was right. I'm nothing. My wife despises me, my job's a dead end, and I can't stop these thoughts. *What's wrong with me?*

"Hey, Julie, right?" I call her back.

She turns, surprised. I want to say something crude, but I catch myself. "How are you doing today?" I ask, softening my tone. "You seemed upset the other night." I fake concern, but deep down, I don't care. *Or do I?*

"Hi! Yeah, I've seen you here before," she says, almost playful. "You following me?"

She's flirting. I grin. "Just stalking you," I joke, chuckling. "So, you ditch that guy?" *Damn it, Josiah, too far.*

"Yep," she says curtly.

"Sorry, shouldn't have said that."

"It's fine. He was a jerk. It was tough."

"Sit for a bit?" I gesture to the seat.

She hesitates. "Um…"

"Come on."

"Okay, a few minutes." She sits.

Stay cool, don't scare her off, I tell myself. "I've got to head to work soon anyway."

"Where do you work?" she asks.

"Nowhere special. Cranes, building that skyscraper up the street."

"Cool! That'll be an awesome building."

"Yeah, swing by some time. I'll show you around."
"Really?"
"Sure."
"I might," she says, smiling, then stands. I touch her hand lightly.
"You sure you gotta go?"
"Yeah, but it was nice chatting..." She pauses. "Oh, I didn't catch your name."
"Josiah," I say, too eager.
"Nice to meet you, Josiah." She glances back and leaves.

Damn, I want her more now. My watch beeps late for work. *Fuck!*

"Hey, George!" I call, rushing past, but he stops me cold.

"Get in here, Josiah!" he barks. *Trouble.*

SIX MONTHS LATER

I check my phone. Julie's text lights up: *Hey, love! Can't wait for you to meet Delilah today!*

Yes! Can't wait! See you soon! I reply, heart racing.

"Hi, Delilah," I say, extending my hand. She's as beautiful as her mom. A dark thought creeps into her innocent skin. *What the hell?* I shove it away, horrified. *Why'd I think that?*

"Hi," she mumbles, clinging to Julie.

She's shy, I think. *Gotta win her over for Julie's sake.* "Great to meet you, Delilah," I say, flashing my warmest smile. It usually works. She offers a small smile back. *Progress.*

ONE YEAR LATER

"Josiah!" Julie calls from the other room.

"Yeah?"

"I've got a meeting with Ms. Francis at Delilah's school today, so I'll be late. Her grades are slipping."

"Who's that?" I ask, annoyed.

"The counselor."

"Delilah's fine. Kids go through stuff."

"I just want to be sure everything's okay."

"Whatever," I mutter. "She's fine."

A knock at the door jolts me. I know it's them. I couldn't take it anymore; I had to protect Delilah. The knocking grows louder.

"Hello?" a voice calls through the door. "Is everything okay?"

I open it, Delilah clinging to my side. "Hi, I'm Julie," I say softly.

"Are you Ms. Covington?" the officer asks.

"Yes."

"Are you safe?"

"He's gone. At work."

"Okay. Let's get you and your daughter to a safe place. We'll deal with Mr. Covington next. Where does he work?"

"He's at the construction site up the street."

"We'll get the address from you and head there. Are we arresting him?"

"Yes," I say, relief washing over me.

"No worries, ma'am. Let's get you to the safe house first."

THREE MONTHS LATER

Julie sits across from me, fear etched in her eyes. As she speaks, tears spill, her voice trembling. "I'm sorry if I cry, Ms. Francis," she says, hesitant. My heart aches for her. I step out briefly, grabbing tissues for her and likely myself.

"It's okay," I reassure her. "If you weren't crying, I'd be more worried."

Sobbing, she chokes out, "I didn't know." Those three words carry weeks of unspoken pain, shattering my assumptions. She presses a tissue to her face, wiping away raw hurt, and begins her story, a nightmare that's become her reality.

"When I met Josiah, he was so kind," she says. "I had no idea he was a monster. I never would've let him near my children. There were no signs. Delilah adored him, always sitting close, holding his hand. She'd get jealous if he sat by me. I thought it was sweet—her love for him. I didn't know he'd been abusing her." Her tears fall harder, sobs shaking her frame.

No Place to Go

"Breathe," I say gently. "Need water?" I grab a bottle from the office fridge, where cookies and drinks sit for moments like this. "Here," I offer. She takes it, sipping gratefully.

"I'm sorry," she whispers.

"Don't be. Take your time. I want to hear your story."

She inhales deeply. "Recently, my friend's daughter slept over. Delilah told her she loves Josiah and wants to marry him someday. My friend told me, and it felt… wrong. One night, when Josiah was out drinking, I asked Delilah if she said it. She denied it at first, 'No way, Mommy, why would I?' but days later, I found her crying. Her friend wasn't allowed to talk to her anymore because of it. I asked again, 'Did you say that?' She hugged me tight, tears streaming, and said, 'Yes, Mommy, because he loves me and said he'd marry me when I'm older.' My heart stopped. I didn't want to ask, but I had to. 'Does he touch you as he does me and say he loves you?' She cried harder, buried her face in my chest, and said, 'Yes.' My world spun like a movie where the walls close in. I wanted to be sick, but I had to stay strong for her."

"Need a moment, Julie?" I ask softly.

"No, I need to finish." Her voice steadies. Over the days, she told me more when he wasn't around. I convinced her to share everything that we had to tell the authorities. She was terrified, said she'd call me a liar if I told. She was so scared of him. I told Josiah she'd seen a scary movie and wanted me to sleep in her room, so he wouldn't suspect me staying with her every night. I couldn't let him near her again, but I had to plan carefully to get him arrested. One day, Delilah said he told her he missed her."

Tears overwhelm her again. "It's okay," I say. "We can pause."

"No," she gasps. "He told her, 'I miss you so much.' I knew then it wasn't just touching. I was furious, guilty wanted to end him right there. But if I went to jail, I'd leave Delilah alone. She's all I have after a hard birth. I convinced her he was wrong, that we had to tell someone. She finally agreed. There's more, but that's the short version."

"Thank you, Julia, for sharing," I say. "I knew there was more to last week's report, but I didn't want to push. Has he been arrested?"

"Yes," she says firmly. "I hope he rots in jail."

"He likely will. My focus now is on you and Delilah. Our school counselors aren't equipped for this level of trauma, but I know a program at the Rusty Bumper, odd name, I know." I hand her a business card from my desk. "It's the best place for what you're facing. We've seen great success stories. You'll need support. I'll work with Delilah's teachers to get her homework and online resources to catch up."

"I can't thank you enough, Ms. Francis," she says, eyes welling.

"It's my privilege. They offer free programs if finances are tight, no assumptions, just in case."

"Anything helps," she admits. "We lived with… him," she says, wincing at his name. "I'm staying with a friend now, hoping to move into an apartment next week for some normalcy." Tears fall again.

"This isn't your fault," I say firmly. Her eyes scream disbelief. "It's not. This evil is hard to detect, often rooted in the abuser's own trauma. Pornography can worsen it, and it's frequently generational, passed from father to son,

No Place to Go

growing stronger. Josiah may have been abused, his father, too. It persists until someone breaks the cycle. Does he have a son?"

"Yes, with his ex-wife. They were together when we met. He said he was miserable and left her. I didn't see his son much."

"Would you share their contact info? I'd like to reach out to his ex-wife and son. They may need support, too."

"Sure," she says, shrugging. As I grab a pen, my phone rings. "Answer it," she says. "I need to go."

"Just a sec, Julie," I say, picking up. "Hi, this is Ms. Francis. Oh, honey, can I call back?"

"No need," Julie says, scribbling a name and number, gathering her things, and heading out. She waves through the window, tissue to her eyes again. I dial my husband. "Hi, love, can I call you soon? I'm handling something."

"Of course," Joe says warmly. "Talk soon."

I hang up and dial the number Julie left. "Hi, is this Denise? I'm Ms. Francis. I'd like to speak with you and your son about your ex-husband."

Michelle Pentifallo

No Place to Go

11

DEATH'S DOOR

Amelia

I sit exposed in the park, yet invisible. No one seen me never have. My dad and brother are the stars of our family; I'm just a shadow, catching only a sliver of sunlight through the magnolia's shade. Beyond the tree, the river sparkles, alive with swimmers' laughter, a sound I've forgotten. When did I last laugh like that?

My thoughts drift, then snap back to the pain that brought me here. *What was I thinking?* Driving high, half a bottle of vodka in me, rushing home to clean for my brother's visit. One wrong turn, and I struck a pedestrian. The officer said I was going 100 miles an hour. My life's over. "No," my lawyer insisted, "they're investigating. Your dad will pull strings with the DA to lighten your sentence." I'm a disappointment to him, always have been. I can't go on.

The park's music and chatter fade into nothing. These people mean nothing; I'll never see them again. Today, the pain ends. No drama, just the pills in my backpack, washed down with gin and a bologna-and-cheese sandwich on stale bread. Since Dad kicked me out, I've scraped by, but that's irrelevant now. No more, "Amelia, you're such a letdown to your mother and me," or "Why aren't you using that expensive degree?" Enough.

I scan the faceless crowd. They won't notice I'm gone until I'm unresponsive, assuming I'm asleep. The ranger will find me after the park clears. I hope it's not Gomer, the kind guy from last week's recon visit. Maybe that rude woman who shooed me out two weeks ago. She deserves the shock. *So, Ms. Jones, you spoke to Jane Doe recently. Did she seem sad?* I mutter, smirking. *Disengaged?* I chuckle darkly.

Michelle Pentifallo

Suicide's close, urging me on. "Do it, and find peace," he whispers, not my voice but his, a spirit I've known since I was seven, when I first thought of ending it. After a dream revealed him, he brought friends: Depression, Grief, and others. They've haunted me ever since. *Who'll care?* Everyone's better off without me. I crave eternal sleep, hope that's what awaits.

"Ouch!" I yelp as a bee stings me. Eyes turn briefly, then back to their hot dogs and soccer. *See? They don't care.* No one asks if I'm okay. The gin's hitting hard; I need to pee. I grab a handful of pills to start this.

In the bathroom, my head swims. "It won't be long," Suicide murmurs. "Shut up," I snap, glaring at him. A woman with her kid stares like I'm unhinged. "What're you looking at? I wasn't talking to you!" I yell, storming into a stall. The wet floor, kids tracking river water, nearly trips me. "Can't someone clean this fucking mess?" I grumble. A mom in another stall huffs. *What, never heard a curse word?* I steady myself on the handicap bar, realizing I took too many pills at once. I need my blanket under the tree, not this filthy bathroom. I don't want to look like some junkie.

I stumble back, grab my "water" gin, and gulp it down. *Whoops.* I bite my sandwich, swallow more pills, and wait. Suicide's voice booms: "You're a loser, Amelia. Only cowards end it." *You said it was good!* I think. "Only if you're worthless," he sneers. *Too late.* I laugh hysterically, drawing stares. *Nothing for a bee sting, but concern for laughing? Idiots.*

Another swig, and the pills creep through me, starting at my scalp, sliding down. *Is this peace?* "Ouch!" I scream as a soccer ball hits me. "Take your ball and get lost, you brats!" I hurl it back, grab more pills, and chug gin. The world spins; I close my eyes. My body's awake inside, but my arms are lead.

A glowing path appears, a man at its end, arms open. "Choose me now or lose me forever," he says. "I died to give you life." *Who's this?* I don't know him. *Died for me? No one did.* Everyone took from me. *I don't want you.* He fades as tall, dark figures approach, fast and strong. They grab me, pulling me down into darkness, heat rising. *Wait! I know him!* A childhood memory flickers; someone told me about him. "Don't go!" I scream, but it's too late. Suicide leers. "Only losers kill themselves. Your weakness brought you here. The Deceiver's waiting." *Where are those screams coming from? It is so hot!* I scream, but no one hears. No one who matters.

Michelle Pentifallo

Sheila

Dusk falls early this time of year. I check the lawn before the bathrooms. There's that girl again, under the magnolia. "Hey! Get up! Park's closed!" I shout, then freeze. She's lifeless, a notebook beside her. *No way.* I grab my walkie-talkie. "911!" I yell, starting CPR. *Please, don't die.* My heart sinks. She is so pale, and oh, no-cold-she's gone.

What kind of world lets a girl die under a tree, unnoticed? I hear the judgment in their voices. How could I know? I patrol the whole park, not just this lawn. She was alive earlier, a bit disoriented, but that's common. People drink here, but without proof, I can't act. Will they find alcohol in her system? I could lose my job. I'm barely paying bills now. If I'm fired, Christmas is ruined. My kids will get nothing. *What'll I do?* In the distance, I can hear the sirens coming closer with each second. *I'm finished. Watch!* Within minutes, I can see them approaching. They stop to ask the maintenance guy a quick question and head my way.

"Ms. Jones, I'm Officer Peterson. How are you today? I'm here to ask some questions," a woman says.

"Of course, Officer. Call me Sheila."

"What time did you start today, Sheila?"

"Eight a.m., my usual."

"When did you first see the young lady?"

"Around 10:30, during my lawn walk. She was writing in a notebook on a blanket, seemed fine."

"Any unusual behavior later?"

"She got upset when kids hit her with a soccer ball, yelled at them to get lost, but didn't get up. The kids left, so I didn't intervene. Am I in trouble?"

"We're just gathering facts, Sheila. No one's in trouble," Peterson says.

My boss, Harold, storms over, furious. "What happened, Sheila?"

"Harold, I don't." Peterson cuts me off.

"We're investigating. Who are you?"

"Harold Lyons, park supervisor, is her boss."

"Were you here today, Mr. Lyons?"

"No, my day off."

"Please wait over there until I'm done with Ms. Jones," Peterson says sharply.

Harold glares at me, then at the girl's body in the near distance, covered with a towel, and walks off.

"When did you return to this area, Sheila?" Peterson continues.

"Around 2:00, to grab my lunch and eat on the go."

"Was she awake then?"

"Yes, heading to the bathroom, looking okay."

"Any other incidents?"

"Just the soccer ball thing."

"Anyone else working this area?"

"Landscapers trimmed trees this morning, but I'm assigned to the lawn, so no one else would've seen her."

"Have you seen her before?"

"Yes, a few times, always under this tree, writing, with food. Today, she seemed sadder than usual."

"Sadder?" Peterson asks, pen poised.

Death's Door

"Yes, she always seemed weighed down, like the world was crushing her," I say to Officer Peterson. "I don't recall her smiling, but I wasn't watching closely."

"Anything else that might help us understand why she did this?" Peterson asks.

"No, I only saw her here a few times. I didn't know her."

"Okay, Ms. Jones, I may need you for further questioning, so don't leave yet."

"I have kids at home," I say, anxious. "I don't like leaving them after dark."

"How old are they?"

"My sons are 14 and 12, my daughter's 10."

"If you provide your address and phone number, I can follow up at your home if needed," Peterson offers.

"Thank you," I say, scribbling my details. Another officer's gaze burns into me. "Officer Peterson, can you bring Ms. Jones here?" he calls, holding a bag. As we approach, he reveals a 2-liter gin bottle. *Oh no.* Harold's watching, I'm done for. Panic surges. Then he shows an empty prescription bottle, and guilt crashes over me. *I could've stopped this. I should've noticed.*

"Did you see her drinking or taking pills today?" the officer asks, disappointment in his eyes.

"No, sir, I would've removed her. Drinking and drugs are banned here."

"This is a large bottle to miss, Ms. Jones."

"I swear, I didn't see it," I insist, my voice shaking.

"We'll need you at the station for further questioning," he says.

"What about my kids?"

"Call someone to stay with them, Ms. Jones."

"Am I in trouble?"

"We're trying to understand what happened. You're our only witness right now. Her family deserves answers, and I'm sure you understand that."

"Yes, sir," I murmur.

"Let's make your calls, then head downtown for your statement," Peterson says kindly, but her eyes hint at the life-altering weight of this moment. As I walk away, I see them pull a wallet from the girl's bag. *At least they'll know her name.* I didn't. Tears well up as I wonder what drove her to this, and why here. Peterson's radio crackles: "Ask Ms. Jones if she knows what vehicle she came in."

"It's the red VW bug, dented front," I say quickly. "I noticed it one day when she sped out. I wrote down her license plate in case she returned. When she did, I asked her to drive carefully. Families are everywhere here. She was furious, told me to back off. I thought she'd been drinking that day; her words slurred, and she ignored a stop sign, nearly hitting another car. I didn't report it, no proof, just figured she was upset because I'd confronted her."

At my locker, I see three missed calls from home. *Hope the kids are okay.* I dial Charles.

"Hey, Mom," he answers.

"Hi, son. What's up?"

"When're you coming home? We're hungry."

"I had an incident at work, so I'll be late. I'll call Auntie Grace to come over. I'm sorry, but I'll be home soon."

"Okay," he says, and the line goes dead. I call Grace, bracing for her usual attitude.

"What do you want, Sheila?" she snaps.

"I need help, Grace."

"You always do."

"It's serious. A girl took her life at work today, and I have to give a statement downtown."

"Oh, I'm sorry," she softens. "I thought it was about money again."

"No," I say, defensive. "Please go to the house, make sure the kids eat and get to bed. I don't know when I'll be home."

"I'm on my way," she says, kinder than ever. "Call when you're done."

I pocket my phone, grab my backpack, my makeshift purse, and follow Peterson to her car. "Sheila, drive your own car. You're not under arrest," she says.

"Oh," I reply, relieved, and head to my rusty sedan, praying it starts. It sputters but turns over. I follow the police car, knowing this journey will test me. *I have to make it through.*

As I touch my front doorknob, I see her face and the officer raiding me at the precinct. I take a deep breath and open, taking a quick view all around and see a note from Grace. *I guess she couldn't bother to stay.* I open each room, checking on the sleeping sounds, and head to my room. The shower feels so good, but it doesn't wash away my shame. As I dry and dress, tears cascade down my cheeks, and I carefully slip into bed, pull the covers close, and drift.

Sheila stares into Josh's eyes. "Truth or dare, Connie?" he taunts again.

Her mind screams *truth*, but "Dare!" slips out. She wants to retract it, but it's too late. Josh grins wickedly. "Go upstairs, lock the bathroom door, and say 'Bloody Mary' five times."

"What?" Connie gasps.

"Yep!"

"I don't want to," she pleads.

"You have to," Josh insists. The kids chime in, "Yeah, you said dare!" Eliza pulls Connie toward the stairs.

"I don't want to!" Connie cries as the door shuts behind her.

"What's wrong with you, Sheila?" Josh sneers.

"Nothing!" I snap, but I think, *This is too far. You don't mess with evil; it messes with you.* "I'm going home."

"Don't be a baby," he mocks.

"My mom wants me home."

"Whatever. Go cry to your mommy."

"Shut up, Josh!" I retort. As I leave, I glance at Connie descending the stairs, fear in her eyes. I offer a small smile, an apology I can't voice.

Outside, Josh's laughter echoes, and I hear, "Now we can really mess with her mind." A darker voice adds, "I like this Josh kid. We can use him." I shut my apartment door, drowning out their cheers. My stairs feel safer than Connie's, my home warm with love waiting.

"Is that you, Sheila?" Mom calls.

"Yes, it's me."

"Wash up for dinner. Dad's almost home."

I head to the bathroom, noting Connie's apartment mirrors ours, but her dad's gone, and her mom's out late. *Is she okay?* She looked terrified. Maybe Mom'll let me check on her after dinner. I set the table mechanically, guilt gnawing. *I should've stopped it. I should've brought Connie here.* Josh is awful.

The door opens, and Dad's voice lifts me. "Honey, I'm home!"

"Dad!" I rush into his hug, his kiss warm on my forehead. "How was your day, sweet girl?"

"Really good," I lie, skipping the game, and join them at the table, pushing Connie's face away.

Death's Door

Suddenly, I jolt awake, sweating. *It was a dream.* I haven't thought of Connie in years. Why now? The girl's death floods back. *I didn't save her, just like I didn't save Connie.* Guilt chokes me. Connie changed after that day, spiraling into drugs, and was found dead in a dumpster at 25. *Not my fault,* I insist, shaking it off. This shame feels so heavy.

I shuffle to the bathroom, checking my phone at 3:00 a.m. I've barely slept. Officer Shultz's words echo: "How could you miss a dead person on your lawn? Were you not paying attention?" They cut deep. Connie's fearful eyes burn into me. Tears fall; I wipe them away. "It's not my fault!"

"What's not your fault, Mom?" my daughter asks, startling me.

"Nothing, sweetie. Why're you up?"

"Had to pee. I heard you yell, like you were dreaming."

"I'm sorry, honey. Back to bed," I say, guiding my daughter down the hall. I tuck her in, lingering despite her age. My kids are my world. Their dad and I split when they were young; they're all I have.

In bed, I lie awake, haunted by that girl's death. *What drove her to end it?* I pray her tragedy doesn't ruin my life. Maybe Deshawn's leaving was my fault, too. He's sobered now, thriving. If I'd held on longer, could we have made it? I'll call him tomorrow about the bills. Lying here, it feels like I've been awake for hours. I have to get some sleep, and I force myself to wash her face away and drift off again.

"Hi, Sheila. How're the kids?" Deshawn asks over the phone.

"They're good," I say, voice tight.

"You sound upset. What's wrong?"

"Rough day at work. I might lose my job," I admit.

"You've been there a while. It'll be okay," he says.

"No, you don't get it," I snap, louder than intended. That old voice whispers he hasn't changed, but I know better. He's stepped up, taking the kids, buying clothes. He can't erase the past, but he's trying.

"I didn't mean to upset you," he says softly. "I want to help. You there?"

"Yes," I choke, tears breaking through.

"Tell me."

"A girl took her life at the park yesterday," I blurt, sobbing.

"I'm so sorry, Sheila. That's awful."

"It was on my watch. I thought she was asleep." Tears stream. "Can I see you?"

"I'm free until tomorrow's conference. I'll come now."

"You don't have to."

"I want to," he says, and the line cuts off.

I cradle my head, sobs erupting. I'm glad the kids are at school; I barely held it together making breakfast, nearly burning the eggs. My mind drifts to another time I saw that girl under the magnolia, crying, her black hair messy. I meant to check on her, but a coworker's question about the canoe dock distracted me. When I looked again, she was gone.

The doorbell rings, pulling me back. Deshawn moved closer after getting clean, diving into motivational speaking. His change is remarkable. I open the door, and his arms envelop me. I collapse into his chest, lost but safe. Months ago, I couldn't have trusted this. He's earned forgiveness, proving his sincerity. I'm scared, but I believe him.

"Sheila, I'm here," he whispers, and I know he means it.

FOUR MONTHS LATER

"Hey, Deshawn!" I shout across the lawn, beaming as he loads the kids into his car. "I passed my real estate exam and joined a local brokerage this week!"

"That's incredible!" he calls, grinning and waving. "See you Monday!"

I thought losing my park job would destroy me. Group therapy at the Rusty Bumper pulled me through. I always dreamed of running my own business, being there for my kids. Real estate lets me set my hours, giving me freedom. This new path feels right. I'm still battling guilt, blaming myself for everything, but I'm less codependent, on a healthier road. Deshawn's progress steadies the kids, and his support keeps us from moving. I'm behind on bills, but I see hope ahead. I'm not who I want to be, but I'm getting there.

Some nights, as sleep nears, I see that girl lifeless, black hair framing her face, and wonder if I could've helped her. I'll never know, but I carry her with me, a reminder to stay vigilant and to care.

Michelle Pentifallo

12

CONFUSED

The dorm walls press in, suffocating me. I can't lie here anymore; I need to work on my paper. It's 7:00 a.m., campus is silent, but this deadline looms. I dress quietly, grab my backpack, and head to the open field to clear my mind. Settling under a tree, I open my laptop and begin typing.

Michelle Pentifallo

Uncle Dave haunted her life. As a teen, he'd slip into her room at midnight, calling it his way to start the day 'right.' Nothing was right about him, his lingering glances, subtle brushes, nightly violations. He'd wait until Aunt Ella, sedated by her sleeping pill, was out by 11:00, then creep into her bed.

"Angie!" a voice calls across the field. I glance up to see Tensley waving, heading my way. *Damn it.* I was in the zone. I switch to another document, frustrated. Last night, I recalled Dot's story, a perfect fit for my suspenseful short story due Monday. My English Lit professor expects me to outshine the class, but I'm stuck. Dot's tale of shooting her abuser in self-defense and walking free has potential,

Confused

but I need to fictionalize names and details to protect her. Time's tight to build the plot.

Tensley reaches me, arms open for a hug. I'm not into touchy-feely vibes, but I stand, offering a quick side hug. "Hey, Tens, what's up?"

"Not much, Ang. Rocking those new shoes from Instagram?"

"Last pair in my size, lucky grab," I say, forcing a smile.

"Wanna hit a frat party tonight?" she asks.

"Nah, I've got this paper. Professor's pushing me to nail it."

"You're the best writer I know, girl. You'll crush it in your sleep."

"I just started five minutes ago, before you showed up."

"Come on, you make killer Jell-O shots, and I promised to bring some."

"Take the recipe, it's easy."

"You know I'd burn the kitchen down," she laughs. "We won't stay late. I need my wingwoman. Plus, it's Friday, and no classes 'til Monday with the break. Plenty of time."

"Fine, but we leave by 2:00," I say firmly.

"2:30?"

"2:00, or I'm out. I need to change."

"Meet me at your dorm in an hour. We'll shop first."

"Deal." As Tensley walks off, I mutter, *She'll drag it to 3:00*. I jot a note on my laptop: *Change Uncle Dave and Aunt Ella's names*. Packing up, I head to my dorm.

Music blares as I enter Heather's in the shower. *Great, there goes 15 minutes.* I knock. "What the heck, Ang, you scared me!" she yells.

"Sorry, just letting you know I'm here. Almost done?"

"Yeah, what's up?"

"Making Jell-O shots, hitting the mall for an outfit, working on my paper, then going to a party with Tens. Need the shower."

"That frat party across town?"

"Think so."

"Cool, Brad and I are going too," she says. *Backup if Tensley gets wild.* "I've got you, but we're leaving at 1:00. Brad's working tomorrow, and I'm heading home for Thanksgiving."

"Didn't know you were going."

"Mom wouldn't let up, offered gas money. Brad's at the mall all weekend, so I figured, why not? You going home?"

The shower stops finally. Heather emerges in a towel, blue eyes sparkling. "Come home with me, gorgeous," she teases, pecking my lips before heading to her room. My pulse races. *I'm not into girls… am I?* Her closeness stirs something. *Focus, Angela.* Tensley replies with a frowning emoji. *I'll HURRY,* I type, jumping into the shower.

Post-shower, I mix Jell-O shots, planning to write while they chill. *Hope Kent's there tonight.* Where'd that thought come from?

Applying my lipstick, I hear a knock. Heather's on the couch. "Didn't hear you come in," I say.

"You were in your room, earbuds in, writing. Didn't want to bug you," she says.

"You can bug me anytime," I flirt, grinning.

"Nice curves, girl," she teases, playfully swatting me as I pass.

"I'm headed to the mall. I will be back in a while. Need anything?'

Confused

"Nah, I'm good."

"Ok. See you in a bit," and I head out to find something for the night.

After returning and working on my paper some more, I realize I am running out of time. Shit! I'd better get ready. I throw on my new stuff and touch up my looks in the mirror.

She's here I yell out as I approach the kitchen and grab my Jello shots, and Heather chimes in as I walk by. "You look hot, sista."

I giggle, opening the door to Tensley and Raquel. My smile fades; Tensley avoids my eyes. I grab my party purse, shoot a look at Heather. "See you there, gorgeous," and shut the door, butterflies fluttering for her. *I wanted to kiss her. Am I into that?* I shake it off.

"Ready for fun, girls?" Tensley chirps, grabbing our hands and singing, "It's a beautiful day in the neighborhood!" as we head to Alpha Delta Phi.

"I hope Chad's there. He's so fine," Raquel squeals, her voice grating. *Why'd Tensley bring her?*

"I'm glad you came, Raquel," Tensley says. "Angela wants to leave early, so now I can stay late."

There it is. I knew she'd pull this. I'm annoyed but relieved that Heather and Brad leave at 1:00. *Tensley always gets her way.* We're opposites: she's a jock, I'm a writer; she's carefree, I'm focused; she's coasting on her parents' money, I'm grinding to keep my scholarship.

Michelle Pentifallo

At the frat house, Mike greets us at the door, beer in hand. "Welcome, ladies," he drawls, his gaze sleazy. I feel a brush on my backside as we squeeze through the crowded hall, his hand? An accident? I can't tell. He trails us, reeking of tequila. *Gross.* He's distracted by buddies at the Jell-O shot table. *Tensley didn't need my shots; she just didn't want to come alone.* I drop mine at the table with the rest. She and Raquel head for the keg; I find a corner to observe.

"Hey, Angie!" Mike calls.

"No one calls me that, jerk. What?" I snap.

"Want a shot?"

"Nah, I'm good."

"Come on, I got you."

"I'm fine, Mike."

Confused

"Don't mess with her, man," his friend laughs. "She's got a nice figure, but she ain't into you."

"Not you, anyway!" I retort, earning laughs. Mike's stare chills me, familiar from nightmares, saying, *You're mine*. My skin crawls, but I hold his gaze, daring him to try. He backs off.

Kent walks in. *Didn't know he'd be here.* My nerves spike. I head to the drink table. Tensley appears, alone. "Sorry about Raquel. She asked to come, and I didn't want to be rude."

"It's fine," I say. "I'll leave with Heather and Brad at 1:00. You stay as long as you want. I've got my paper and Thanksgiving with Heather, so I'm good."

"Awesome!" she squeals, raising her glass. "Let's party!" The DJ cranks the music, drowning the crowd.

"Cranberry vodka, lemon," I shout to the bartender, slipping her a five and waving off change. Rounding a corner, I nearly collide with Kent, half my drink gone. He grins, amused that I didn't spill.

"Sorry!" I blurt.

"For what? You missed me."

"For almost staining your shirt with my drink."

"No harm, Angela," he says, my name rolling off his tongue. *He knows my name? How?*

"They need traffic signs in here with this crowd!" I joke, earning a chuckle. His lips are distracting. I flash a flirty glance and slip into the crowd.

"Ang, where are you going?" Heather calls, sounding annoyed. *I didn't know she was here already.* I turn, fighting through bodies, but freeze Mike's in my face, eyeing me like prey.

"Hey, Mike. Had a few, huh?" I say, uneasy.

"Why are you hiding, Angie?"

"I'm not," I reply, but his hand nears my wrist. Heather's beside me in a flash.

"Back off, Mike, you creep!" she snaps.

He glares. "Get lost, Heather."

"No, you back off, Mike," I snap, heart racing. His eyes burn, like he wants to drag Heather away to prove his dominance, but the crowd standing near me and looking his way deters him. Mike shoves through the crowd, glaring back at me. "This isn't over, Ang."

My body trembles, but Heather's hand on my shoulder steadies me, a silent show of solidarity. She meets my gaze. "Don't fear that asshole, he's a total loser." Butterflies stir in my stomach again, her closeness sparking warmth.

"I'm fine!" I shout, grabbing her hand. She leads us to the drink table. "Another, please, and one for my friend."

I smile at Heather, relief settling in. The bartender slides her drink over; she pays, and we move to the open room. "Where's Brad?" I ask.

"Work called him in. That's how I got here so fast. He called me right after you left, and I didn't waste any time since he wasn't coming to get me. I begged him to come out on our last night before I'm back Monday, but you know him, he can't say no to anyone. Except me, apparently."

"Don't say that. He adores you."

"I know, but I wanted tonight with him. At least I don't have to leave at 1:00 now." *There goes my paper tomorrow*, I think, but Heather's worth it. I finish my second drink. "You didn't answer earlier. Are you going home for Thanksgiving?"

Confused

"Why would I?" I mutter, recalling my stepdad mocking my virginity at our last family gathering. *What a creep.*

"Come with me," Heather offers. "My parents love having you."

"I don't want to intrude."

"Stop it, Ang. You're my best friend, besides Brad."

"Okay, I'll come, but we leave by 2:00. I need time for my paper."

"I'll drive tomorrow; you can write in the car."

"Deal!" I grin, the vodka loosening me up. "Another drink?"

"You know it," she says, finishing hers. Her hand lingers on mine as she hands me her cup, her shy smile hinting at curiosity. Not enough to leave Brad, but enough to fuel my dreams.

I shake it off, heading to the drink table for courage, though my heart whispers I'm right, and my head snaps, *Shut up, you fool.* Waiting for the bartender, Kent brushes my shoulder. I look up into his hazel eyes.

"Hey, Angela, heard you stood up to Mike. Nice work. He's a dick."

"Yeah, but it's his party, so I gotta play nice."

"Not too nice, save that for me," he teases.

Thankful for the drinks masking my blush, I grab our cups, glance back, and say, "I can do that." I rejoin Heather, wondering if Kent's watching, hope flickering.

"You were chatting with Kent," Heather notes. "How do you know him?"

"History class."

"Total brainiac, teacher's pet," she says.

"Really? Didn't peg him for that."

"Oh, yeah. Skipped a Harvard offer to stay near his mom, she's got cancer."

"No idea," I say, surprised.

"He's solid, but I'm jealous. I bust my butt for a C in history; he strolls in with A's."

"Bet it's not that easy."

"Never see him take notes. Like he predicts the lecture."

"Whatever," I laugh.

"Look, he's coming over," Heather whispers.

I nearly spill my drink, catching the drip with my tongue up the cup's rim. "Looks good," Kent says, smirking.

"I almost spilled!" I blurt.

"Not talking about the drink you save," he clarifies.

"Oh," I mumble, blushing hard now, no drink to hide it. Embarrassed, I turn away, but he gently lifts my chin. "Don't hide. I like your face."

My cheeks burn. *What do I do?* I'm screaming inside, saved by Raquel's nasally voice. "Hey, Kent!" My mood sours; he releases my chin.

"Hi, Raquel," he says, unenthused. I glance at Heather, who smirks, signaling he's not a fan either. Tensley stumbles beside Raquel, already unsteady. *Not babysitting her tonight, Raquel's problem.*

"Who's your friend, Ang?" Tensley slurs, eyeing Kent. "He's cute."

"Kent, this is Tensley from art class," I say. "Seems you know Raquel."

"Met Raquel in the library first day," Kent explains. "We were both lost."

"Cool," I say, flat. "Tens invited me to this… event."

Confused

Kent chuckles, catching my sarcasm. "Nice to meet you, Tensley," he says, offering a quick handshake. She leans in, flirty, but he pulls back, steadying her lightly. "Oops, sorry," she giggles, brushing his chest deliberately.

"Good to see you, Raquel," Kent says politely. "We're heading out for corn hole. Have fun." He grabs my hand, nodding for me to take Heather's, and we escape to the backyard.

"Thanks," I breathe as the noise fades.

"My pleasure," Kent says, his shy smile warming me.

"Ten!" I call in corn hole, knowing he's letting us win. *No way he's this bad.* "Don't play much?"

"Only a couple times," he claims.

"Whatever, Kent, you're a pro," Lia, a classmate, teases.

"Hey, Lia!" Kent greets, grinning.

"Don't ruin my game, girl," Lia laughs, fist-bumping him. "How's it going?"

"Great—look at my competition," Kent says, nodding at me, Heather, Tina, and Lia's friend.

"Score's 19-12, Angela and Heather's lead," Tina says.

"You're slacking, Tina," Kent jokes.

"Let us finish, Lia," she says, heading off. "Catch you inside."

I smirk at Kent. "Lying down, huh?"

"She's tipsy, ignore her," Kent deflects. I sink a three-pointer. "Nice!" he cheers. "Game!"

Heather and I squeal, jumping like kids. Tina nods, "Good game," and leaves. Kent's at my side. "Let's grab real food. You in, ladies?"

"Totally," I say. Heather nods eagerly. "But I've gotta head home after. My English Lit story's due, and my professor's counting on me."

"You write?" Kent asks, intrigued.

"She's amazing," Heather jumps in. "Her stories are so vivid, you feel like you're there."

"Gotta read one sometime," Kent says.

"Maybe if you're lucky," I tease, climbing into his car with Heather.

"Sweet ride!" Heather says. "New Lexus sport, right?"

"Yeah, graduation gift from my parents," Kent says.

"You graduated?" I ask, surprised.

"Staying for my master's in bionics."

"That's awesome," I say, impressed.

"Hope so. My dad says it's the future, and he hates being wrong." Kent shrugs. "Any food preferences?"

"Not really," Heather calls from the back.

"You up for the taco bus on 1st Street?" I suggest.

"Love that place," Kent says, eyes lighting up. We're off.

"You sure can pack away those tacos," I tease Kent as he drives us back to the dorm, just minutes from our feast.

"I hit that spot twice a week. Can't believe I haven't seen you there," he says.

"I'm on a tight budget only go once a month. Dorm food and the cafeteria meal plan save me a ton."

"Oh," he says softly, careful not to offend. He pulls into a parking spot and cuts the engine. "Let me walk you, ladies, to the door."

"That'd be nice," Heather says. She darts inside, leaving Kent and me alone. *Hope this is worth it.* He grazes my hand, his gaze warm. "I had a great night, Angela. Let's do it again, less crowded next time." His smile sparks

Confused

anticipation. He leans down, kisses my cheek softly, and steps back.

"Looking forward to it," I say, too eager. He winks and heads down the stairs. *Not worth it, Heather could've stayed.* I enter the dorm, passing the bathroom where Heather's washing her face.

"He's gone already? What happened?" she asks.

"Just a cheek kiss," I mutter, disappointed, closing my door.

She barges in, toothbrush in mouth. "Really, just the cheek?" she mumbles, and heads back to the bathroom, exposing my door, leaving it open, and spitting into the sink. "Wow!"

"Close my door!" I call from my bed. "I need sleep. Gotta write tomorrow."

"Okay," she says, returning to shut it. "He's into you, Ang, trust me." My eyes drift closed, chasing sleep.

Morning light filters through as I sip coffee at the dinette, replaying last night. *Is Heather right? Does Kent like me?* My phone buzzes with a text: *HEY BEAUTIFUL! HAD A GREAT TIME LAST NIGHT. LOOK FORWARD TO SEEING YOU SOON.*

Heather rounds the corner, catching my grin. "Kent texting? Told you he's into you!"

"Give me a sec," I tease, playing coy. She snatches my phone.

"'Hey BEAUTIFUL!' See? He's messing with you, not kissing you properly. Such a tease."

"Don't call my future boyfriend a tease," I laugh, grabbing my phone. "He's being a gentleman, giving me something to look forward to."

"Total tease," Heather smirks, tossing my phone back.

I read: *HAVE A GREAT WRITING SESSION, I CAN'T WAIT TO READ IT*. Squealing, I reply: *HAD A GREAT TIME TOO, LATER*. "That's what you get for just a cheek kiss," I mutter, smirking. "My turn to play hard-to-get." I set my phone down to write.

Before I open my laptop, my phone rings with an unfamiliar number. Fear grips me; I recognize it. *The doctor's office*. I'd hoped I was wrong, but my heart knew this call was coming. "Hello, this is Angela," I say, voice steady despite my racing pulse.

"Ms. Walters? This is Lauren from Dr. Pole's office. We had a cancellation, and we can see you sooner to discuss your results. Monday at 10:00?"

"I can do that."

"See you then."

"Thanks," I say, hanging up as her goodbye fades. *Why can't it wait?* My appointment was in two weeks. Maybe they're just filling slots? I want to believe it, but I know better. That voice whispers, *It'll be okay*. How do you know? Yet, I trust it. Whatever Monday brings, I won't let it break me.

Another text from Kent: *ARE YOU THERE?*

YES.

DO YOU HAVE TO WRITE TODAY? GOT A COUPLE HOURS BEFORE I HEAD HOME. WANNA HANG?

YES, I NEED TO WRITE, BUT STOP BY IF YOU WANT.

OK.

The doorbell rings; he must've been nearby. I open it to Kent's beaming smile. He pulls me close, kissing me fully. "Whoa!" I gasp as he steps back, already heading to his car. I lock the door, squealing.

Confused

Heather yells from her room, "What?"

"Kent kissed me and left!"

Her feet hit the floor, and she's in my face. "He kissed you and bailed? Girl, you're in deep. He's so into you."

My smile stretches wide. I sit at my laptop, ready to write.

I can't believe it is already Monday. This weekend went so fast, and I grabbed my phone to head out the door. Read: SEE YOU AFTER CLASSES TODAY. I send a quick reply. LOOK FORWARD TO IT.

"How was Thanksgiving?" I ask Kent, burger in hand, Coke in the other, sitting across from him at a dinner.

"Okay. Mom went to the hospital, but she's fine."

"What happened?"

"She fainted. Chemo makes her lightheaded sometimes."

"I'm so sorry," I say, nearly choking on my bite.

"It's not new. Heather mentioned I stayed here instead of Harvard?"

"Yeah, she wasn't gossiping, just filling me in."

"No worries, it's no secret. Mom's been sick for a couple of years. I was set for Harvard after my AA when we found out. My parents are amazing, so I couldn't leave. They pushed me to go, but I stayed. They were upset at first, but now they're glad, especially on Mom's tough days when Dad needs a break."

"That's really selfless," I say, admiring him.

"Enough about me. How was your Thanksgiving?"

Fun, went to Heather's. My stepdad's an asshole. I can't stand him, so I skipped home. He loves embarrassing me. My parents divorced when I was young; I haven't seen my dad since. Mom and my stepdad have been married for seven years. She's happy, but he gets on me. Mom didn't date much growing up, protecting me. We were tight, best friends. She worked hard, kept us stable, not rich, not poor. I needed a scholarship for school, but she's my biggest cheerleader." I take a quick bite, catching my breath.

"Sorry, that was a lot," I mumble, wiping my mouth, smiling sheepishly.

"No, I want to know," Kent says, mirroring my smile. "You and Heather are close, huh?"

"She's my girl. Day one, she was like, 'Roomie, we're in this together.' Been friends since."

"And Brad?"

"He worships her. They're disgustingly in love. 'I love you more,' 'No, I love you more.' I have to leave the room."

"What about you, Angela? Got a love of your life?"

"Nope, all about school. My scholarship's tough to keep, so I've had no time."

"None at all?" he asks, surprised.

"Not a priority," I say firmly.

"Hard to believe," he says, leaning in. "You're so beautiful, Angela Walters. How hasn't someone swept you up?"

"Swept up? Like I'm ice cream?" I tease, and he laughs.

"Not like that. You're just… different. Special."

"Well, I hope that's a good thing, Kent Ryan," I say, smiling.

"It is," he assures me.

"Any loves in your past?" I ask.

Confused

"There was a girl in high school. We dated for three years, but after graduation, we parted ways. We talk occasionally, but we've moved on."

"No competition, then?" I tease.

"None, Angela," he says sincerely, his smile warm. "You're going to change my world."

"Think so?"

"I know it."

My gaze drifts past Kent, landing on Mike's creepy stare. *Why's he watching me?* I shake it off, but Kent notices, turning as Mike looks away. Kent shrugs, and I wonder, *Doesn't he care?* I push it aside.

"Hey, Ang, want to grab dinner tomorrow?" Kent asks.

"Sure," I reply, too quickly.

"Great!" His eyes lock on mine, like I'm the only one here.

ONE MONTH LATER

"Angela! Stop! Where're you going?" Kent's voice chases me.

"What?" I snap, tears streaming, unstoppable.

"Home? Why?"

"I saw you with her," I choke out.

"With who?"

"Some blonde girl."

"Wait, please!" He grabs my arm. "It's not what you think."

I spin to face him. "How do you know what I think?"

"I know we're heading somewhere great. I'm falling for you, Angela."

"Really? Then why were you having dinner with her? If I hadn't walked by, you'd keep lying!"

"I'm here to explain. It's not what it seems."

"Stop saying that!" I yell, wrenching free. I run, his shouts fading. Years of track make me untouchable. I sprint until his voice is gone.

Panting, I realize I'm alone on a darkening campus. *Should've texted Heather.* I pull out my phone: *HEY HEATHER, ON MY WAY HOME. FOUGHT WITH KENT, SO MESSED UP.*

Turning the corner, I spot Mike. *Not now.* I pivot, but his footsteps echo behind me. "Hey, Angie," he says, voice chilling.

"Don't call me that!" I shout, quickening my pace. Trees and an alley loom ahead. I'm trapped. A shiver runs through me. I turn to confront him, but he grabs me from behind, his hand clamping my mouth. "Shh, Angie, I told you I'd take care of you," he whispers. "This won't take long."

Confused

I try to scream, but his grip muffles me. *No, don't!* I thrash, but he's too strong, pinning my hands, dragging me down. My kicks are useless as he traps my legs. Tears flood my eyes. This can't be happening! NO!!! What seems like forever, but it is only moments, he gets up and on his way up, licks my face. "See, now you won't fuck with me." I fold over and look at the ground, not wanting to get up. Scared that something could come next. After hearing his footsteps in the distance, I pull myself together.

Bruises bloom on my skin as I climb the dorm stairs. My phone's gone, dropped in the struggle. Mike's voice haunts me: "You knew I was coming, you fucking whore. No longer pure, are you?" His stench clings to my shirt. The door opens to an empty dorm where Heather's with Brad. I lock it, strip off my clothes, and toss them in the trash. Blood lingers in my mouth, my lip bitten in my silenced screams. The shower soothes, but a stinging scratch on my thigh burns. *I can't tell anyone.* It'd ruin my friends, my life. I'd be the "poor raped girl." I crouch under the water, letting it wash over my broken body, my spirit shattered.

I understand my cousin's pain now, her story of Uncle Dave. Mike's blonde curls, his liquor-soaked breath, they're all the same. *Are all men like this? Objects, not people?* Sobs rack me. *Kent won't want me now. I'm damaged.* I want to flee, never look back. The razor in my shaver gleams. It's been years since I cut. *This is Kent's fault if we hadn't fought…* The pain overwhelms me. I grab the razor, old scars staring back. I press it down, hesitate, breathe, then push, metal biting skin. I cry out.

Michelle Pentifallo

Confused

13

NO LIFE TO LIVE

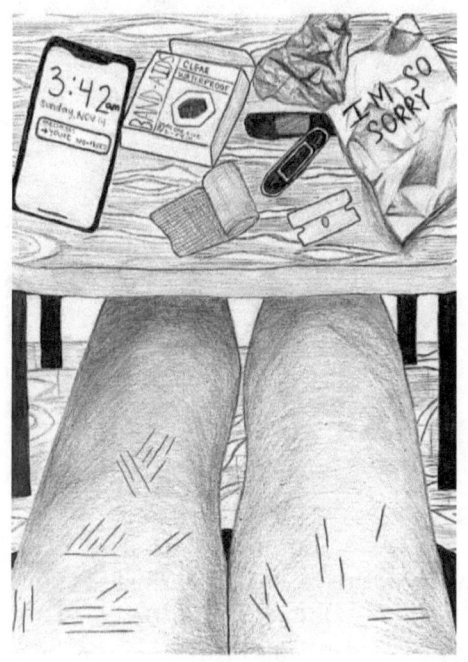

"No matter how hard I try, I fail. I'm a loser. No one could love me." The voice laughs, relentless. These humans are so weak, Ruth, the easiest target on my route. If they knew their power, I'd be jobless, rotting in hell. She has no fight left.

No Life to Live

I breeze past Lauren's office, her tears streaking as she speaks urgently on the phone. *Wonder what's wrong?* Around the corner, Stacey's familiar scowl greets me. "Ruth, my office, now," she snaps, her tone final.

I trail her, catching her frustrated sigh. "Close the door," she orders as I step inside.

I'm fuming. Fired for nothing? *Who do they think they are?* They'll never find anyone better. I'll torch them on social media, Facebook, and Twitter. They'll regret crossing me. No one will work there when I'm done. I storm out, box in hand, slamming the door.

"Hey, Ruth!" a voice calls. Doug or Justin? Their voices blur. Footsteps race toward me. It's Doug, waving my coffee cup. "Don't forget this!"

Seriously? Why chase me to humiliate me more? *Shove that cup up your ass, Doug.* I reach for it, miss the handle, and it shatters on the cement by the exit sign. *Can't even grab a cup, right?* That voice whispers, "You're useless, Ruth. What'd you expect?" I glance at Doug, but he didn't hear. Dropping my bag, I scramble to pick up the red ceramic shards, spotting the faded lips and broken "X" from "Xs and Os," a Valentine's gift from Larry, my ex. *Why would I want this?*

Doug kneels to help, his blue eyes kind. I want to lose myself in them. "Ruth? Ruth?" he says.

"Sorry, zoned out," I mumble, throat tight.

"You okay?" he asks.

No Life to Live

"Of course," I lie. *Don't I have to be?* "Thought you'd want Larry's cup," he says brightly, unaware we split two months ago. I never told him.

"He dumped me. Left it on purpose," I blurt, avoiding his gaze. I trudge to the garbage can by security, where I toss my Starbucks cup daily. *Won't be doing that anymore.* Can't afford it now. This is my third job this year, my resume's a mess. Maybe I'll work at Starbucks; my degree's useless. I could see Larry daily, grabbing his skinny caramel macchiato. *Skinny for what? He's perfect.* Another mistake, number 20 in my string of bad choices.

"Thanks, Doug, for being kind. Wish you the best," I say.

"Take care, Ruth," he replies softly.

That's it. Job gone, relationship gone, friendship gone. What's next? My car seems to drive itself, landing in a lakefront parking lot. This lake once brought joy skiing, fishing with Dad, and spotting wildlife. I miss those days. Numb, I step out, heading to my tree for a moment of peace. Shattered glass from last night's party glints on the ground. *Maybe...* A voice screams, *STOP!* I flinch. *Leave me alone!*

Icicles drip from the window as my eyes flutter open. *Where am I?* I blink rapidly, pain shooting through me as I reach up, only to hear my mother's voice. "Careful, Ruth, take it slow."

Slow? Why? My vision clears, I'm in my old bedroom at home. Panic surges; I need to leave. Mom gently lowers my hand, her eyes soft but strained. "Darling, you were in an accident. You've been out for weeks."

Accident? My last memory is leaving work, breaking that coffee cup, and saying goodbye to Doug. *What a failure.* I whisper, "What happened?"

Mom hesitates, tears brimming. "We'll talk later, dear. We're just glad you're okay. We were so worried."

"Worried? I don't remember anything," I murmur, voice weak.

"It's fine for now. Rest. Want water? Hungry?" She pauses, but I shake my head no, though my stomach growls. She steps out to the kitchen, just feet away.

I'm starving, but my jaw and neck ache, barely movable. I can't recall the accident, but last night's nightmares lingered with a dark figure chasing me, my legs sinking into mud. His eyes, black and cruel, bored into me, screaming I'm worthless, spineless, undeserving of life. I sank deeper as he cursed me, saying no one cares if I live or die. I escaped the mud, only for him to chase me to a lake, trying to drown me, hurling insults. I broke free, swam to shore, and fled to an abandoned warehouse, slipping on the icy floor, slamming my head. He pinned me, shrieking that everyone hates me, urging me to end it.

Mom returns, her smile faint, masking pity, a look I know, but never from her. As she offers water, I glimpse my bandaged wrist. My mind reels at a vague memory of cutting myself with glass surfaces, but I thought it was a dream. In it, I grabbed a shard to silence the figure's taunts. He laughed, ecstatic, as I tore my skin. "I knew you were weak, Ruthie. Finish it, death's your only escape." *How did he know my name?* He seemed to know everything about me, a stranger yet familiar. *Who is he?*

Mom's gaze feels heavy. *She must think I'm pathetic, a failure.* She's never said it, but isn't she weaker? She's been Dad's servant my whole life. I hear his voice: "Yvonne, my shoes!" "Yvonne, where's dinner?" "Yvonne, these floors are filthy!" She scrubbed daily, fearing his criticism. *How*

No Life to Live

could I admire someone so submissive? Yet she dares pity me? *Look in the mirror, Mom.*

"What's that look like?" I snap.

"Nothing, honey. I'm just relieved you're okay," she says softly.

"Why's my wrist bandaged? I dreamed I cut myself, but that's all."

"We'll discuss it later, sweetie."

"No, now!" I insist, but pain splits my head. "Ouch!" I clutch my face, feeling another bandage. Panic rises, pain surging, and I start to fade.

Darkness swallows me, but a distant light glows at the end of a hall. I walk toward it, the passage narrowing, forcing me left into a dim room. The figure sits by a bedside lamp, staring. "Think you can escape, Ruth? I've controlled you for years, and I'm not leaving."

"Who are you? What do you want?" I scream.

"Don't you know me, Ruthie?" he sneers. "I've been with you since your dad called you a loser for a messy room. He opened the door, and I've tormented you ever since. Now, stop playing games. It's time to fulfill your purpose."

"Purpose? You called me worthless, now I'm not? Make up your mind!" I shout, stepping away, but he's in my face, spewing venom. I raise my fist, but my father's voice jolts me awake.

"Why protect her, Yvonne?" he barks, entering. "She needs to grow up, not be coddled every time she messes up. She really did it this time." His chuckle echoes the figure's laugh from my dreams. *Is he in my head, too?* I can't escape him. *Why'd Mom bring me here?* I'm a disappointment, not the son he wanted for his boxing dreams. He blamed Mom for me, for her hysterectomy after miscarriages, for robbing him of a boy. His eyes scream that he wishes I were gone. *Maybe everyone does.* If I were dead, I'd stop hurting Mom. I try to say, "I'm sorry," but the words won't come.

"Mom, take me home," I croak.

"You're awake!" she gasps. "Are you okay? The doctor made us sign papers that we're going to a facility tomorrow. Your father insisted we bring you here to avoid embarrassment, or you'd still be in the hospital. He knows people from boxing."

"Yvonne, is she whining?" Dad yells from the hall.

"She just wants to go home," Mom replies.

"Home?" he roars. "You're out of your mind, girl. We signed papers, you're going away to get fixed, or I'll face jail."

Fear chokes me. I want to fight, but he always wins. I sink into the bed, voiceless. *If I don't leave this town, I'll die.* Everyone knows Dad; no one would believe his cruelty. As a kid, I dreamed of being a boy to earn his love. Before Larry, I researched transitioning, but couldn't afford it. My parents never knew I was bi in high school. Dad would've disowned me. Past, present, and future collide, overwhelming me. I claw at my bandages, desperate to tear them off, but I'm too weak.

"Ruth, stop!" Dad's footsteps thunder. I scratch my wrist, blood seeping through. "Hank!" he shouts into the phone. "Come quick!" He's beside me, needle in hand. "No!" I cry, but the world fades, despair swallowing me. The future is a blur, and I don't even know what is happening in my present. What is going on? What happened to me? Where am I going?

No Life to Live

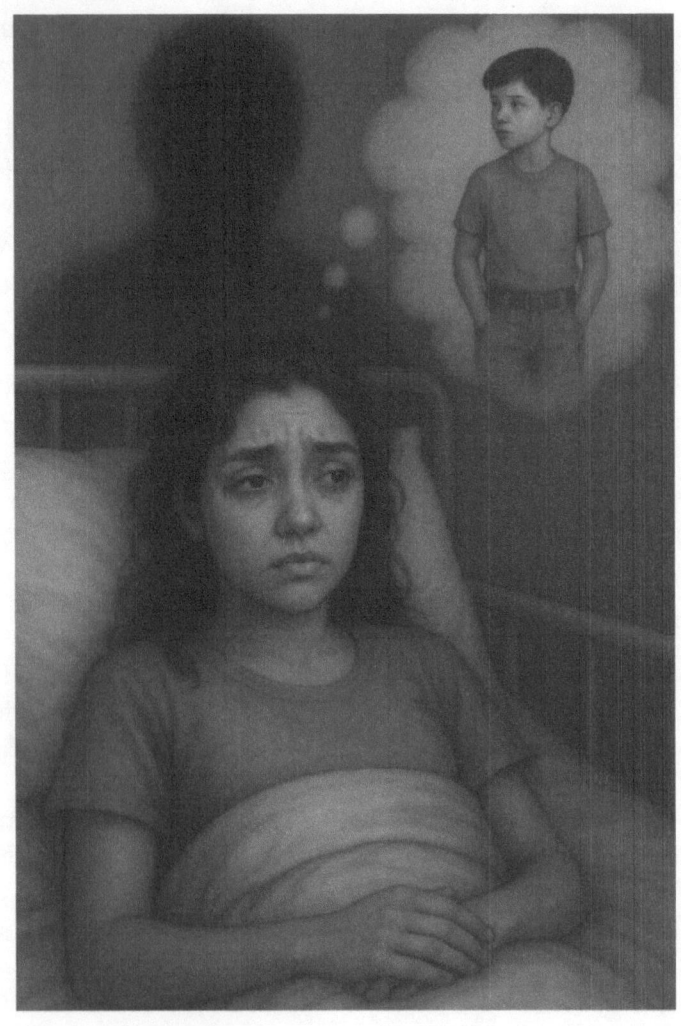

Michelle Pentifallo

14

RAY OF LIGHT

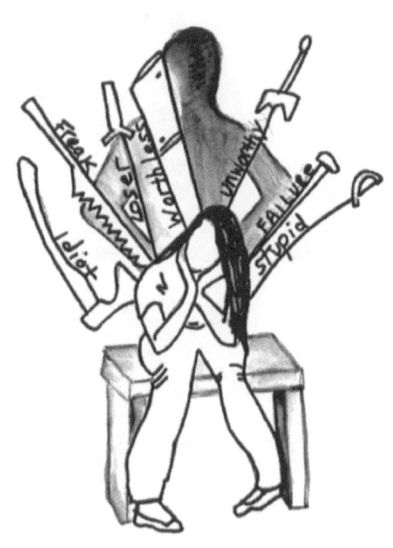

Journal Entry January 9, 2016

Today, their presence was inescapable. Eyes followed me, whispers trailed my steps, and an unseen weight pressed against my skin. The dark ones were closer than ever, their faces marked by the shadow of their master. Some call him the father of darkness, others the dark leader. Whatever his title, nothing good comes from him or his followers.

It felt like I was on a covert mission, like a spy in the 1960s slipping through enemy lines, gathering intel while being hunted. Their best soldiers shadowed me all day. Why? I'm just an ordinary woman navigating life's challenges. I'm no one special. Yet, Dan's words from weeks ago echo in my mind: "If you keep helping at the Rusty Bumper, Leslie, your life will change." I never imagined it would feel like this, watched, scrutinized, targeted. I overheard their murmurs, questions about who I am, why I matter. Why do they care?

I've seen how the dark followers operate, using humans as pawns for their schemes. Today, I witnessed a dark figure instruct a girl to tell her friend she looked ugly and should go home to change. The words crushed her spirit, and as she walked away, the dark figures cheered, reveling in her pain. It was a stark reminder: my way of life isn't the only one. As a follower of the Lord of Light, I was taught little about the lord of Darkness growing up, so my senses sharpened after that moment. Now, spotting their influence is second nature.

At lunch with a friend, I noticed them again. A group sat at the table next to ours, including a set of twins with jet-black hair and ashen skin, one with long hair, resembling a vampire, the other shorter. They seemed like foot soldiers in a larger plot, but the spirits around them cowered, unable to meet my gaze. The Light within me was too strong, and they whispered in fear: "Who is she?" "Why can't we look at her?" "The Light is too powerful." The figures around them stood motionless, heads bowed, as if movement would bring pain.

Ray of Light

The twins were unmistakable. Followers of the dark lord bear a grey hue, a mark I've recognized since childhood. Back then, I didn't understand it, but I knew to be cautious. My first encounter with a dark figure, a demon, was in high school, and it terrified me. When I tried to tell my mom about the "grey humans," she scolded me for being rude. One of them glared at me, his eyes saying, "Shut up, little girl." I'd never seen him before, yet he seemed to know me. That moment stuck with me, and ever since, I've noticed the grey people everywhere.

The day ended with another pair of young twins at a nearby table, screaming in discomfort. Too young to understand the Light, they were caught in their parents' dark allegiance, vulnerable and unaware. It's heartbreaking that they believe they're protected, but how can you be safe when surrounded by evil? I pray tomorrow is brighter. Good night.

Text Exchange

"Hey, sexy!" Henry's text lights up my phone.

"Hey, love," I reply, smiling.

"What are you doing?"

"Just writing in my journal. It was an interesting day."

"You doing okay?"

"Sure am. When are you heading home?"

"On my way. See you soon."

I don't share everything with Henry. We've only been married five months, and this world of mine, full of Light and darkness, feels too foreign for him. I've kept it secret for so long, pouring my thoughts into journals. One day, when they're read, I'll be gone, and it won't matter if people think I'm crazy. For now, I share what I can. Words carry weight. I've seen them take flight, caught by demons to be used against their speakers. Once, I heard a woman say, "I don't like fat people," and later, she was unrecognizable, having gained significant weight. Another time, a friend's mother vowed to disown her if she dated a Black man. She did, married him, and now has four children, but her mother, estranged, misses out on her grandchildren's lives. Words are powerful, and the dark lord wields them like weapons. I urge others to speak carefully, but they often laugh or dismiss me. Those who listen are spared.

Dan's warning about the Rusty Bumper lingers: "When you help others, the lord of darkness will send his messengers to try to derail you." Is that why I'm struggling to launch the recovery program? I have the names and materials ready, but direction eludes me. In my spirit, I hear, "Don't overthink it, Little Dove. Just move." Before I can ponder further, the garage door rumbles, and Henry's car pulls in. I'll revisit this tomorrow.

Henry steps inside. "Hello?"

"Hi, love!" I greet him with a smile and a kiss, my focus now entirely on him.

THE NEXT MORNING

Morning light filters through the white curtains, its rays brushing my face and stirring me from a restless sleep. A troubling dream lingers, one I'd rather forget. I reach for Henry, but the bed is empty. What time is it? My phone reads 7:30 a.m. I should be up. There's so much to do, and Dan's words echo again: "Don't overthink it, Little Dove. Just move." Move where?

I head to the bathroom, wash my hands, and start coffee. Glancing at my calendar, I see only a lunch

Ray of Light

appointment with Rachel, a new volunteer at the Rusty Bumper. She always seems sad, and I hope to learn her story today. People open up when they feel safe, and I'm grateful for that trust. I find her text to confirm our plans.

As I scroll, Henry calls. "Hi, love! How are you? I missed you this morning."

"Yeah, I had an early meeting with a builder and didn't want to wake you. You looked so peaceful."

Peaceful? Not how I felt waking up. "That's sweet, thank you."

"Just wanted to say I love you."

"Love you too. See you later, babe."

I text Rachel: "Are we still on for today?" While starting the coffee, her reply dings: "Yes, I'm looking forward to it. See you at 12:00." We'd already settled on Mexican, so I sent a smile emoji and head to the shower.

As I prepare for the day, yesterday's unease creeps back. Will I be watched again? A vivid dream from last night replays me speaking about my journals at a party. Impossible. People would think I'm unhinged. I shake off the thought and focus on getting ready. "That'll never happen," I say aloud, then catch myself. Words matter. "I take that back," I say, looking up with a smile. Never say never.

Lunch with Rachel

"Hey, Rachel, thanks for meeting me!" I say as we settle at the table.

"Of course!" she replies, her voice bright with surprise. "I was thrilled you asked."

Her warmth catches me off guard. She's so reserved at the Rusty Bumper. "I'm glad I met you," she adds shyly. I feel the same.

Her smile is radiant, a spark of Light in her eyes. She knows Him. "I keep my head down at RB, that's what I call the Rusty Bumper," she says with a grin.

"Much easier," I agree, laughing.

Ray of Light

"It gives me a chance to talk about the program without explaining the name every time," she says.

"Great idea! Mind if I steal it?"

"Go for it! I only started following the Lord of Light two years ago. Before that, I was in a dark place. I don't push my beliefs at RB. I just share my heart and let them see it."

"That's beautiful, Rachel," I say, moved by her sincerity.

"I heard you're starting a recovery program," she says, sipping her soup.

"Yes, but I'm stuck. I have the materials, but I don't know where to begin or who'd be interested."

"I have a solution, Leslie. I've been talking to people at RB, and they're excited about your program." My confusion must be obvious because she adds, "If you're okay with it, I mean."

"Of course, I'd love to! I just didn't know anyone was interested."

"Oh, absolutely. I have at least seven people ready to join."

"That's amazing!" I say, gratitude swelling, though my face betrays a flicker of fear.

"You don't have to be scared," Rachel whispers, her voice reassuring. "It'll be great."

Just then, a loud voice interrupts a man in line ordering a sandwich. His grey hue marks him as a follower of the dark lord. I snap my gaze back to Rachel, but her look of surprise mirrors my own.

"What?" Rachel's voice snapped me back, her eyes narrowing. "You look like you've seen a ghost."

I forced a smile, brushing it off. "Nothing, definitely not a ghost."

"Ghosts are real, you know," she teased, leaning forward.

"Not in my world," I replied lightly, steering us back to safer ground. The café buzzed around us, a comforting hum of life.

"So, when are you starting the group?" Rachel asked, sipping her coffee.

I hesitated. "I'm not sure. I put a signup sheet at the Rusty Bumper's front desk, but no one's bitten. I check it every shift, but it's blank."

Rachel shook her head. "Leslie, people won't do that. Signing up publicly? It's like admitting they're broken. Trust me, I'm one of them. They'll talk to me, though. They see you as... different. Putting their name on a list for all to see screams weakness. We've survived by staying strong, keeping our struggles hidden, and thinking no one cares. It took years of counseling for me even to say this."

Her words hit like a laser to my heart, revealing an error I'd missed. "I don't know their stories, Rachel, but I want to."

"They won't open up until they trust you," she said firmly. "I can help with that."

"Really?" My voice lifted with hope. "You'd do that?"

"Absolutely." Rachel's eyes softened. "I want them to heal, as I did. Someone helped me rebuild, and now I want to pay it forward. I hear your program's different real. If you'll have me, I'm in."

"Yes!" I blurted, louder than intended. Across the café, a shadowed figure at a distant table turned toward me, its ashen face framed by darker companions. One stepped forward, then froze, as if repelled by an unseen light around me. It retreated, head bowed, back to its place.

"Leslie?" Rachel's voice pulled me back. "You okay? That looks again."

"Sorry," I laughed, deflecting. "Squirrel!"

Rachel followed my gaze, her eyes locking with mine. She mouthed, *I see them, too.* My heart leapt, as I'd just found the perfect person who might just get me. Her wry expression added, *It's not fun.*

My jaw dropped, words failing. Rachel reached across, her hand steadying mine. "It's okay," she whispered. Tears welled, but I blinked them back. The café was too public for this. I took a deep breath, steadying myself.

"Later," she said, gulping her soup. I nodded, picking at my salad, my heart thrumming with certainty: we'd be friends. I'd finally found someone who understood.

Journal Entry January 10, 2016

Today was a breakthrough. Rachel shares my gift or burden. At lunch, she knew I saw the grey faces, those shadowed souls, because she sees them too. We couldn't dive deeper, but the connection sparked something in me. I'm eager to see where this leads.

I tried telling someone once, my mom, after meeting her friend. "She's a grey person, Mommy," I said. "Be careful."

"A grey person?" she scoffed. "That makes no sense, Leslie."

"They look grey," I insisted, too young to explain the shadow I saw. Mom had drifted from the Lord of Light by then, and I didn't know why. But I learned what grey meant when I saw a girl spit venom at another, her face clouded with it.

Rachel and I are starting a group at the Rusty Bumper to help others. It feels like a new build, full of potential. Maybe that dream last night, vivid and urgent, was a sign. Tomorrow's trip looms, but today, I'm hopeful for what's ahead.

The Cincinnati air brushed my face as I stepped off the plane, a crisp 55 degrees, a welcome shift from Florida's heat.

"Henry, bathroom first," I said, grinning.

"Okay, love," he replied, matching my stride.

At baggage claim, I smiled, remembering my grandmother's warm welcome here. "I'll grab the car and meet you at the entrance," Henry said.

"Thanks for this," I murmured.

"Anything for you, Leslie."

As he pulled up, I buckled in, then hesitated. "Can we stop somewhere before my sister's?"

"Sure. Where?"

"The apartments we lived in before moving. They're on the way."

We navigated the complex, familiarity tugging at me. There it was, the building where fear once claimed my nights, leaving me wondering if I'd ever be okay. I parked with Henry, gripping his arm. "I'll be quick. Stay here."

He looked ready to protest, but nodded. "Take your time, Les."

The entry door squealed, unchanged after years. Memories flooded back: playing games with friends, climbing stairs to Carl's apartment for rummy and his wife's cookies. But the weight of those lonely nights pressed in, and I muttered, "This is pointless."

Turning back, a chill followed me. Henry's voice greeted me as I slid into the car. "That was fast!"

Ray of Light

"It was a dumb idea," I said, voice tight. "That's my past. Done."

"Les, we don't have to rush off." Henry's tone was gentle. "Talk to me. I don't think you're crazy."

I tried humor, mimicking a movie line: "I see dead people!" I laughed, but his earnest look stopped me.

"Who?" he asked, genuinely curious.

I sighed, rushing the words. "Grey people, ruled by darkness." I slid on my sunglasses, hoping he'd drop it.

"Maybe a childhood dream mixed you up," he offered kindly.

"Probably," I agreed, forcing cheer. "Let's go."

"You sure?" His voice held space for me, and I loved him for it.

"Yep." I touched his arm, lowering my glasses. "Thank you, love."

As we pulled away, tears broke free, unbidden. I tried to stop them, but they flowed, a quiet release of old beliefs I thought I'd deleted.

"Is that her?" a voice hissed from the shadows.

"Can't be. It's been years," another snarled.

"She was thirteen then. Looks older now."

"Where's she headed? Terror, let's follow."

"Got nothing better to do, Fear. I'm in."

"Who's the guy?"

"Some fool. Doesn't know how we twisted her mind back then."

"Easy prey," Fear cackled. "Her and her sister, alone so often. Temptations hit hard. The lord of light marked her for something big, but the Dark Lord sent us to break her. My specialty is messing with their heads to pull them from the fight. Wonder if we won?"

"Let's hitch a ride," Terror urged.

"Outside only," Fear spat. "Their music's unbearable, Jesus this, love that. Blocks our signals."

"Idiots," Terror sneered. "If humans knew how to resist us, we'd be out of work. They fall for our traps, Anxiety, Depression, Sickness, thinking it's better than light and peace. Pathetic."

"Wait, she's crying," Fear noted, edging closer. "Maybe there's an opening."

Henry pulled over, his voice soft. "Honey, what's wrong?"

"I'm fine," I said, voice cracking. "I made bad choices there, scared all the time. But I'm not her anymore. Jesus changed me."

"Damn that name!" Terror recoiled. "No chance today. Let's tail them, see why she's here."

Henry held me awkwardly across the console. "Les, we all did dumb stuff as kids. You've grown."

"Thanks," I whispered, wiping tears, summoning a smile. He was my anchor, always.

The familiar creak of my childhood home's door welcomed me as we arrived. My sister Judith had moved in after our aunt, more a mother to us than our own, passed from cancer years ago. The air carried the faint scent of Aunt's perfume, a ghost of memory lingering in the walls.

"Judith! You here?" I called, picturing her sprawled on the couch.

"In the living room!" she shouted back.

I wanted to say she looked great, but the accident's toll was evident in lines etched deeper, movements slower. "You're looking stronger," I offered gently.

She snorted. "I look like a mess, Leslie. Let's not sugarcoat it."

Ray of Light

"Don't say that," I countered, but her bluntness was no surprise. Judith always spoke the truth, whether I liked it or not. Her behavioral science degree, earned on a scholarship, made her a master of reading people, probably me most of all. While I ran the streets as a kid, she stayed home, buried in books, keeping us out of trouble. Our young mother's rule "work together, get rewarded together; fail, and you're punished together" meant Judith often carried my slack. I'd slip out to meet friends, her warnings trailing me. That resentment, plus my leaving town as soon as I could, left our bond frayed. Both our mother and aunt succumbed to cancer, and I was barely around. Judith still saw the old me, the one who ran.

Henry caught my eye, concern flickering. I waved it off. "It's nothing."

Judith smirked. "Didn't know you were coming, Leslie Poo. I'd have cleaned up. You look fabulous, as always. Still can't believe you snagged my lazy sister."

There it was, the old jab. I swallowed a retort, heading to the kitchen for a drink to steady myself. *She only knows the old me, Leslie. Not the new me.*

"Henry, want a drink?" I called.

"Sure, love!" he replied.

Judith's voice followed me. "So, what's new with you, Leslie Poo?"

"I'm taking night classes for my PhD, working part-time at a law office, and volunteering at a rehab center." I left out the Rusty Bumper; she'd never understand my work with the Lord of Light. I could already hear her: *A higher power in the sky, Les? Stick to science. People's behavior makes sense. You're just looking for a crutch.*

"Enough about me," I said, reentering. "How about you? Nathan called me after your accident. I saw it online."

Her eyebrows lifted. "Nathan called you?"

"Yeah. He was my brother-in-law for years. Just because you two split doesn't mean we don't talk."

Judith's face softened, a rare crack in her armor. "I messed up, Leslie. After the kids left for college, I couldn't stop drinking. Ruined everything."

I winced at my earlier jab. "I'm sorry, I shouldn't have said that."

"No, you're right. Nathan's a good man." She sighed. "I was at a stoplight when a kid rear-ended me, pushing me into traffic. A truck hit the passenger side. If it had been the driver's side, I wouldn't be here. Months in the

Ray of Light

hospital, rehab, I'm walking again, but they thought I'd lose my leg."

"That's awful, Judie. I'm so sorry it took me so long to visit. Finals and my project kept me tied up. One more semester, and I'll have my degree."

Her eyes widened. "That's incredible, baby sister. I'm proud of you."

My heart soared, a rare warmth spreading through me. Judith, proud? "Thank you," I said shyly.

"You should be proud. It's tough work, I know." She'd blazed through college, meeting Nathan, marrying after graduation, and earning her PhD early. I'd always admired her brilliance.

"How are the kids?" I asked.

"They're good. Seth graduated from medical school; Christopher just returned from a business trip in Uganda. He stopped by with food, such a good kid. Seth's closer to Nathan, blames me for the divorce, but he visited me in the hospital. We'll work it out. No grandkids yet, but there's time." She paused. "You staying here tonight?"

"We got a hotel nearby for some space, but we're here to catch up."

"Don't worry about me. Pain meds knock me out, but I'm weaning off them."

"Let's settle in and bring back dinner around 5:30," I suggested. "Belice Pizza, extra garlic butter for the crust."

Judith's smile was faint but real. "You're sweet. Glad you're here."

I hugged her gently. "See you later, Judie."

"You bet, Leslie Poo."

At the hotel, Henry unpacked, glancing my way. "What's that look like, Les?"

"What look?" I deflected.

"Like you lost something precious."

I sighed. "Coming back here stirs up old memories, things I did or didn't do."

He wrapped me in a hug. "That was ages ago. You're not that person anymore."

"I know, but this place is full of negativity, old patterns I've worked to change."

"I'm here, and I'm not negative," he said, pulling back to meet my eyes.

"You're the best," I said, smiling. "I love you."

"Love you more," he teased, grinning.

"Whatever!" I laughed, the weight lifting.

"Keep your perspective clear," he said. "Judith never left; this is her world."

"You're right, as always," I said, rolling my eyes playfully.

He chuckled, heading to the shower. "Join me?"

"Nah, I'm good," I called, though his flirty tone, clumsy but endearing, made me smile.

"Your loss!" he shouted, closing the curtain.

At Belice Pizza, the door chimed as we entered. A voice cut through the hum. "Well, if it isn't Leslie Poo Nelson!"

I turned, stomach sinking. Stan, an old friend, stood with his wife, Nelly, her face shadowed with that familiar grey, a mark of something darker. I forced a smile. "Hey, Stan."

Nelly's grey aura pulsed, unsettling me. I gestured to Henry. "This is my husband, Henry. Henry, Stan, and his wife, Nelly."

"Congrats on the wedding," I said quickly, noting their rings. "Saw it on Facebook."

Ray of Light

Stan grinned, oblivious to the chill I felt. I turned to the counter, eager to escape, my heart steadying as I anchored myself in the light I'd learned to trust.

"Nice to meet you, Henry!" Stan's voice boomed, shaking Henry's hand with a vigor that grated. He gestured to his wife. "This is Nelly."

"Hi, nice to meet you," Nelly murmured, her voice faint, her face shadowed with that grey aura I'd come to recognize. She'd once sparkled with life; now, she seemed diminished, retreating to the hostess stand.

I forced myself to engage. "How are you, Nelly?" I asked, sensing her answer would skirt the truth.

"I'm good, Leslie. Great to see you," she said, but her eyes darted away, her grey aura pulsing faintly. She moved further, as if my presence unsettled her.

Stan turned to me, his condescending tone all too familiar. "What's up, Les?"

"Just finishing my PhD," I said loudly, letting the words carry. This town had written me off as a nobody; I wanted them to know I'd rewritten that script.

Stan's eyebrows shot up. "Big shot, huh? Didn't see that coming."

Before I could retort, Henry pulled me close, his voice firm. "I always knew she would." He fixed Stan with a steady look. "Nice meeting you, Stan. You too, Nelly." With pizza in hand, he guided me out, leaving Stan in the foyer.

"Nice to meet you," Stan called after us, the door swinging shut. "Her husband's a big shot, too," he muttered, drawing chuckles from a nearby table.

In the car, silence settled, heavy with unspoken tension.

"Les?" Henry's voice broke through.

"What?"

"You okay?"

"I'm fine!" I snapped, sharper than intended.

"Doesn't sound like it."

I sighed, frustration spilling over. "This is why I left! No one here supported me. They mocked me, gossiped behind my back. I hate being here!" Tears welled, and I swiped them away, pressing my tongue to the roof of my mouth to stem the flow. "I left this behind years ago. Why is it still getting to me? All I wanted was love. Mom worked constantly, Dad was gone, Aunt tried her best, but I was just a kid."

Silence returned, softer now. I reached for the radio, but Henry caught my hand, kissing it gently. "I love you, Leslie," he said quietly. "Don't let this define you. You're so much more. The past is full of things you can't erase, but you don't have to give it any attention anymore. You can let it go, forgive, and move on. It's your choice."

"I thought I had," I whispered, tears breaking free again. I let them fall, too many to fight.

"Did you notice how grey Nelly looked?" I asked hesitantly, testing the waters.

Henry frowned. "Grey? She seemed fine, just quiet. Maybe the lighting?"

"Yeah, probably," I said quickly, turning on the radio to fill the space. He didn't see it. Not yet.

"Hey, Judie!" I called, stepping into her kitchen with Henry.

"Hey, Leslie Poo, Henry!" Judith replied, stirring something at the counter. "Thought you'd be here sooner. I was about to snack."

Ray of Light

"Sorry," Henry said, setting down the pizza. "Ran into some guy, Stan, at Belice's. Took longer than planned."

Judith snorted. "That loser? What's he up to?"

"No good, probably," Henry said, winking. "Let's eat!"

Judith's eyes softened, catching mine. "You okay, Les?"

"Just chilly," I said, forcing a smile. "Not used to this weather."

"You sure? Your eyes look red," she pressed, concern in her voice.

"I'm good. Let's eat!" I flashed a grin, hoping she'd drop it.

"Was Nelly there?" she asked, taking the hint.

"Yeah, she looked rough," I said, careful. "Really grey."

Judith's tone shifted, heavy with sympathy. "She's had it tough. Lost three babies this year, miscarriages."

"Lost?" I asked, puzzled.

"Yeah," Judith said bluntly, her empathy fading. "It's been hard on her."

"Hmm," I murmured, catching Henry's curious glance. He didn't understand.

"Don't start, Les," Judith warned, misreading me.

"I'm not starting anything," I shot back, meeting her gaze. "I'm just tired of secrets, Judie. Why does everything have to be hushed up?"

"Oh, so now that you're a big shot, I can't say anything, little sister?" Her voice dripped with that old condescension, silencing my voice.

"No, big sister," I matched her tone, "I'm just done with hiding things!"

Henry's eyes widened. I rarely spoke like that. He reached for our hands, his voice gentle but firm. "Ladies, calm down. You love each other. This isn't how you want to be."

We fell silent, staring at our pizza, the TV's hum filling the void.

"Hello!" a voice sang from the front door. I knew it instantly.

"Chelly!" I leapt up, racing to the living room. Our squeals echoed through the house.

"Leslie Poo!" Chelly beamed, pulling me into a hug. "You look amazing! I'm so happy to see you!" She'd always seen the best in me, defending me when others tore me down—the first to show me unconditional love until Henry. "How are you?"

"Great!" I said loudly, for Judith's benefit, as we walked hand-in-hand to the kitchen.

"You look it," Chelly said, her voice warm. "I missed you. So did your sister," she added, projecting.

"Oh, yep, sure did," Judith said, her tone half-sarcastic. I let it slide, savoring the moment.

"Leslie Poo's getting her PhD," Judith said, pride creeping into her voice for the first time. My surprise must've shown.

"That's fabulous, Les!" Chelly hugged me tight. "I knew you'd shine." She whispered, "Judie knew it, too," holding me at arm's length, her eyes piercing. "You're full of light, dear." Chelly had always invited Judith to church, never giving up on her. Maybe she saw the grey people, too.

"Who's this?" Chelly asked, spotting Henry. He offered a handshake, but she laughed. "I give hugs, big guy!"

Ray of Light

"So do I!" Henry said, surprised, returning her embrace.

"I'm glad you brought my Leslie Poo home," Chelly said, meeting his eyes.

"Happy to," he replied, grinning.

"Belice's, huh?" Chelly noted, eyeing the pizza. "Some things never change."

"True," I said, biting into a slice. "But some do. Look at me."

"Couldn't be happier to see it," Chelly said. Her gaze shifted to me, heavy with meaning. "Nelly was there, right? She needs help." Her eyes locked with mine, that knowing look from Rachel. *She sees it, too.* "Judie, time for your show. Let's move," she said, helping Judith up.

On the plane, I buckled in, the flight attendant's instructions fading as I sent Chelly a text: *THANK YOU FOR EVERYTHING. LOVE YOU!* We'd said plenty in the past few days, but those words held it all. Knowing Chelly saw the grey people, too, was a gift. She'd prayed for me all these years, told by the Lord of Light I'd do great things. No one else had said that. Tears fell, joyful ones, and I wiped them away, smiling at Henry.

Michelle Pentifallo

"Glad to be heading home, love?" he asked softly.

"Definitely," I said, meaning it. This trip was my final step to let go. Judith and I had talked—really talked. She admitted she'd always loved me but envied my escape while she stayed, caring for Mom and aunt, her dreams sidelined. That resentment fueled her drinking, spiraling until Nathan left. Her shame kept her distant, feeling she'd failed as my role model. Her apology, raw and honest, rebuilt us. She'd started church with Chelly, and I could see her light returning. Our bond would grow stronger now.

Ray of Light

Journal Entry February 2, 2016

We're home safe from Judie's. The trip was incredible, reconnecting with her and Chelly changed everything. Sharing my gift with Chelly unlocked a memory from college I'd buried.

I worked at a bakery at the time, and this man would sometimes come in. One day, he brought a young girl, her hand tightly gripped. His face reeked of darkness, fear clinging to her. I saw his demons, knew he was hurting her, but I froze. Who'd believe me? I should've confronted him, said, "I know what you're doing. Stop." I didn't. Later, he was arrested as a predator, all over the news. I still regret it.

That memory drives me now. I'll keep leading classes at the Rusty Bumper, helping others break free from the dark lord's grip. Chelly helped Henry understand my gift as well. He's not fully there but isn't spooked, willing to learn, which means the world.

Today was good. More to come.

Michelle Pentifallo

15

NO WAY OUT

My mind races before dawn. The P&L report for Mike is due by noon. Breakfast with Kym to prep for that meeting. Dinner with Joanne and the Jenkins, when? Four o'clock to discuss the shopping center plans? Did Joanne grab my pink shirt and grey suit from the cleaners? Mike's boss is joining today; I need to nail this impression. Did I pay the mortgage? Is today the eighth?

My alarm blares, yanking me from the spiral. Did I even sleep? Dreams of buildings and reports haunted me. I silenced the alarm, reached for my anxiety meds started last month, but do they help? I'm anxious about being anxious. Classic Roger. I chuckle darkly, shaking my head.

"Morning, honey," Joanne murmurs in the dim room.

"Go back to sleep, love," I whisper, kissing her forehead, stroking her hair. She always takes care of me, my pink shirt and suit hang ready in the closet. I don't deserve her. I snap at her too often, stress spilling over before I catch it. Why does she stay? I grab my gym bag, slip into workout gear, and head to the garage.

Sliding into my car, a memory flickers of Joanne and me, young, in a beach condo. Carefree days, part-time job, no weight on my shoulders. Life felt simple, not this relentless grind of mortgages, bills, and family. I shove the nostalgia aside, start the engine, and open the garage. A pink sunrise greets me, but the knot of inadequacy in my gut tightens, same as every day. I crank the music, slam the

No Way Out

accelerator, and speed toward the chaos ahead, searching for a signal beneath the noise.

At the city exit, traffic slows. I snag a parking spot at the gym, not yet packed. The receptionist, Lauren, I think, smiles. "Good morning, Mr. Rivers."

"Morning," I mutter, heading to the locker room. I stow my suit and bag, prepping for the one place I feel in control.

"Roger!" Allen calls, standing in a towel, all grins.

"Hey, man," I say. "How's it going?"

"Great! Just closed the deal on the downtown business center. Probably fifty grand in my pocket."

"Nice work," I say, forcing enthusiasm.

"What about you?" he asks.

"Got a big meeting this afternoon," I hedge. "Could be a solid project."

"Cool, man. Catch you later off to the office." Allen strides off, confidence radiating. I envy that ease. Here, though, I shine. Taller and fitter than most, I own the gym floor. I wave at a familiar face and hit the treadmill, ready to burn off the day's weight.

"Good morning, Mr. Rivers," Lucile chirps from the office reception desk.

"Morning, Lucile. Seen Celeste?"

"She's in the conference room, setting up your PowerPoint for the four o'clock."

"Thanks." I head that way, finding Celeste and Terrance in a hushed corner discussion, leather chairs creaking.

"Morning, Celeste," I say.

"Morning, Roger," she stammers, flustered, unlike her. "W-what can I get you?"

"Need the report for Mike. I see you're on the PowerPoint. Any other appointments? Coffee would be great, too."

"On it," she says, recovering. I close the door, catching a whisper: "He has no idea, don't mention it." My stomach twists. About me? I walk away, hoping it's not.

In my office, a planter sits on my desk, a card attached: *Looking forward to your presentation. Sincerely, Tonya.* A rare gesture from a client. I should have Celeste send a thank-you tomorrow. Wait, don't I meet Silvia tomorrow morning about the housing development specs? I sigh, setting down my briefcase.

Celeste arrives with coffee. "You're a lifesaver," I say, grinning. "Keep these coming hourly till four."

No Way Out

She laughs. "No problem, Roger."

"Can you confirm tomorrow's meeting with Silvia? I think it's morning. My days are blurring."

"Want a bagel?" she offers. "Maybe some fruit, hard-boiled eggs?"

"That'd be perfect," I say. "Thanks, Celeste."

"You're meeting Silvia at eight tomorrow," she confirms, winking. "Take a break sometime, you know."

"A break?" I laugh, grabbing a file. "Nice idea."

"The Mike report's on your desk," she adds. "Review it before your meeting."

"You're the best," I say, waving her off. She giggles, heading out. My desk's organized, at least, even if I'm a mess.

"What's with the scowl?" Tom leans in my doorway.

"Just juggling tasks," I lie, hiding the mental wreck I am.

"You look sharp, man, ready as always," he says.

"Always?" I echo, skeptical. Do they see me like that? I want them to can't let them know I'm unraveling. "Thanks, Tom."

"You hide it well," he says, sauntering off, as if reading my mind.

My phone pings. Joanne's text: *GOOD MORNING LOVE. GOT YOUR SHIRTS, LEFT THEM IN THE CAR. DIDN'T FORGET. HAVE A GREAT DAY. LOVE YOU.*

APPRECIATE YOU LOVE. DINNER LATER. XOXO, I reply, refocusing.

"Roger," Celeste's voice crackles over the speaker. "Mr. Shaw on line one."

"Thanks." I pick up. "Hey, Dan! How's it going?"

"Great, Roger! Those plans you sent? Killer. Love them."

"Glad you think so. I'm presenting to the board at four, and should have final notes by seven. You free then?"

"Will be. Later, Roger. Impressive work." The line cuts off.

"That's awesome!" Celeste calls from her desk.

"Stop eavesdropping!" I shout, laughing. She's been my rock for seven years, knowing every work detail. I trust her completely.

"At least Dan's on board," I yell back. "Now for the rest of them."

"Zac's on line one," she announces, sighing. "You're the best, Rog. Everyone wants you."

I wish I believed that. The doubt lingers, a crash waiting to happen. "Thanks," I mutter, picking up. "Hey, Zac, what's up?"

"Great, Roger. Need to tweak a few things for next week's open house. Can we talk?"

"Tomorrow at ten work? In-person or phone?"

"Office, if that's okay."

"Perfect. I'll be free after a conference room meeting."

"See you then," Zac says, hanging up.

Another line blinks. Celeste peers through the window, checking. I nod, picking up. "Morning, Mrs. Downs. How are you?"

"Well, I was fine until I saw your firm's balance," she says sharply.

"I'm sorry, Mrs. Downs. Was there a misunderstanding?" I ask, keeping my tone even.

No Way Out

"No, I thought I cleared the balance last month," she snaps.

"That was the initial percentage for the mall's final section—the drywall fix due to permitting issues," I clarify.

"Why's that my problem? You handle permitting."

"Actually, we advised against it, but you insisted, saying you'd manage the permits," I say, recalling her tipsy agreement that night. I sent a follow-up email to cover myself.

"You're delusional," she retorts.

"I can resend the email if you'd like," I offer.

"Forget it. I'll pay when I'm ready." Her voice is sharp, but Tom's urgent look in my doorway pulls me away.

"Fine, we'll await your payment," I say lightly. "Someone needs me. Talk later." I put her on hold, hearing Celeste pick up. "Mrs. Downs, Roger didn't hang up; he's just on hold. I'll assist you... Okay, call him later then." I tune it out.

"What's up, Tom? I've got a lot before our eleven o'clock."

"They're here already," he says.

"What?"

"Showed up thirty minutes early to beat traffic."

"Okay, get them to the conference room. I'll be there soon." I call out, "Celeste! Offer them snacks or drinks, please."

"On it!" she shouts, hurrying down the hall. I'm prepared, but I needed that extra time. My mind's already on overload.

"Roger? Rog?" Joanne's voice cuts through the dinner table's chatter.

"Sorry," I mutter, forcing a smile as laughter ripples around me. What's that about?

"I've got a client call coming," I say, texting Celeste last-minute updates. Joanne's eyes flash with more than concern. Under her breath, she hisses, "Really? Tonight? I planned this for weeks." She turns to the Jenkins with a bright smile. "Roger's swamped lately. Clients nonstop." She sips her wine, steering the conversation. "So, Zoe, how's the new baby? Bet she's growing fast."

My phone buzzes—the call I've been waiting for. "Excuse me, I need to take this," I say, standing quickly. Joanne's disappointment stings as I step away.

"Hey, Dan!" I answer, hopeful. His voice is upbeat.

"Roger, they loved the plans. Minor tweaks for the big boss, but that's it."

"Wow, great!" I exhale, relieved.

"You sound shocked," he chuckles.

"Do I? Sorry," I say, laughing it off.

"No worries. We're pumped to start. Our CEO is impatient, though might shop around other proposals if we don't lock this down soon. Lunch tomorrow? Sign everything, then hit the front nine for drinks."

"Perfect, Dan. Thanks. See you tomorrow." I text Celeste to update my calendar, then return to the table, sinking into my seat. I grab my Merlot, inhale its aroma, and take a deep gulp, sighing. Joanne looks stunning tonight, did I tell her? Guilt twists in me. I half-smile at Zoe and Jeff, hoping they miss my self-disgust. I squeeze Joanne's hand, offering a gentle smile.

"Everything okay?" she asks.

"Yep, looks like we're sealing the deal," I say. Her smile widens, but her eyes crave more. More? She has everything: a mansion, designer clothes, top-tier SUV.

No Way Out

What am I missing? Frustration simmers as I pour another glass. Why isn't she happy?

In the driveway, I open the garage, pulling in as Joanne parks her Escalade beside me. I step out, grabbing her leftover bag for tomorrow's lunch. "Fun night," I say cautiously.

She meets my eyes, unflinching. "Fun, Roger? Really? You were barely there. Even next to me, you ignored me. I got ready, wore your favorite perfume, and you didn't notice." Her voice rises. "How hard is it? You say you love me, but you don't show it. Maybe if I were a client, I'd get your attention!"

My mind reels. She's the one person who truly knows me. I can't lose her. "Joanne, I"

She brushes past, hands raised, done listening. At the stairs, she yells, "Don't bother coming to bed!" The bedroom door slams, the lock clicking sharply. Our physical connection's always been strong. How is this happening? She must be exhausted, I tell myself, but the doubt lingers.

My body aches as I lift from the unrelenting couch, catching a glimpse of my cell reading 6:00 a.m. I'd better get going. I grab my bag and get out the door. I'll text Joanne later. She is probably still mad.

"Hey, Allen!" I force cheer as we meet for lunch. Why did I book this? He's out of my league, probably here to one-up me.

"Roger! How's it hanging?" Allen grins, leading me to a table by the bar. "How's that deal with Dan?"

I hesitate. "Going well."

"Man, I was bummed I didn't get it," he says. "I bid on it, too, but Dan ghosted me. Heard you clinched it."

"You had a bid?" My confidence wavers. Was I the right choice?

"Dude, happy for you," Allen says, but his sneer stings. "I'd have done things differently, but to each their own."

That old doubt creeps in, gnawing. I half-smile, and he knows he hit the mark. "How's Joanne?" he asks, shifting gears.

"She's great," I say. "Puts up with my chaos, but she was upset last night. Gotta make it up to her tonight."

"Good luck," he says, smirking. "Heard Dan's a tough one."

My phone rings, Dan. I give Allen a knowing look, stepping away. "Hey, Dan!" Moments later, I'm back, apologetic. "Sorry, Allen, gotta run. Issue with an elevator shaft, county's there now. Rain check?" I toss a twenty on the table, gulp my iced tea, grab my briefcase, and bolt.

"Got it, man! Catch you later," Allen calls as I rush out.

ONE YEAR LATER

"What's your problem now, Joanne?" My voice echoes through the house, mirroring the chaos inside me.

"What's my problem? What didn't you do?" she shouts. "You didn't come home last night!"

"I fell asleep at the office," I say, exhausted. It's true.

"Sure, Roger," she scoffs. "What man sleeps at his office?"

"This one," I think, stung. I'd never cheat. All I want is her happiness. Why does she doubt me?

"I called at nine-thirty," she says. "No answer. You texted at ten. A text!"

No Way Out

"I thought you were asleep. Didn't want to wake you."

"Didn't want to wake me?" Her voice cracks. "I'd rather you call than vanish! Who is she?"

"Who?" I ask, baffled.

"The woman keeping you out all night!"

"Her name's work, Joanne. Just work."

"That's impossible. You're always working gym, golf, and client dinners. You don't invite me."

"It's dull permits, site plans. Why would you want to come?"

"Because I'd be with you!" she cries. "You even skipped date night last week for Dan."

"I'm nothing without my job," I admit, the words heavy. I stare at my anxiety meds on the nightstand, grabbing the bottle, then slamming it down. "These aren't working."

"Is that what you think, Roger?" Joanne's voice breaks. "If so, we have no future." She storms to the bathroom, locking the door.

"Joanne, don't!" I plead, but my phone rings. Dan Philips. I hesitate.

"Answer it, Roger. Leave me alone," she says, muffled.

Michelle Pentifallo

"Hey, Dan," I say, forcing cheer. "How's it going?... Great... We'll finish the next phase on Friday... Ahead of schedule, as always... I'll check it in thirty minutes." I end the call, pressing my face to the bathroom door. Joanne's sobs seep through. I raise my hand to knock, but stop, defeated, my phone glares fifty emails, twenty texts, and a missed call. I can't deal with these distractions now. I slam the door, head to my car, and drive off, earbuds in, coasting without direction. Thinking to myself, I am just not equipped to deal with her right now. I will talk to her later.

Hours later, as I pull up to my home, I can't believe the scene in front of me. All of my clothes were on the front lawn, sprawled out for all to see. How embarrassing!

No Way Out

I pull in the drive, turn off the car, and put my head in my hands and scream.

Michelle Pentifallo

16

RUSTY BUMPER FINAL DEATH

The door swings open, revealing an expansive foyer that could hold a hundred souls. Beyond, vast windows frame spring flowers and towering trees, their branches tracing paths to a distant lake. Trails weave through woods and green pastures, a serene promise of peace. The Rusty Bumper's name feels too humble for this breathtaking haven, a place to reframe a broken life.

    I hesitate at the Rusty Bumper's door, skepticism gnawing. Places like this make promises they can't keep. Yet, something feels... different. I take a breath and step inside. The foyer stretches wide, easily holding a hundred people. Bow windows frame spring flowers, towering trees, and a distant lake, trails winding toward serene woods and pastures. This truly is a place to fix a fractured life.

As I turn to leave, doubting this is for me, a voice stops me. "Hi, I'm Collin. Can I help you?" A man, over six feet, with brown hair and hazel eyes, radiates strength and confidence. His gaze lacks the hurt I carry. Unburdened, that's the word.

"Hi," I murmur shyly, caught off guard.

"Can I assist you, miss?" he asks, curious.

He's kind and striking. Stop it, Tiana. Focus. "Sorry, I'm Tiana. I was told I could meet a counselor here," I say, my voice tinged with uncertainty.

"Yes!" Collin beams. "Samantha mentioned you'd stop by. Would you mind signing in? I can give you a tour if you'd like."

"Is that possible?" I ask, eagerness slipping through. "I'd love that, Connor."

"Please call me Collin," he corrects gently, handing me a sign-in sheet with a warm smile. "Feel free to sit." He gestures to a plush leather chair beside him. "Give me a moment to wrap up a call and grab my pass for the full experience." His grin is disarming, genuine. As he steps away, I peek into his office, spotting a photo of a radiant woman and two young boys, his family, I assume. Of course, he's taken. Focus, Tiana.

Rusty Bumper Final Death

He returns swiftly, offering a handshake. "Welcome to the Rusty Bumper," he says, gripping my hand firmly, his smile reassuring. He takes my clipboard. "Done with this?"

"Yes," I say, handing it over.

"Let's start down the east wing," he says, leading the way. "Please keep your voice low. Some rooms may be in use, and we host conferences. I'll show you an open meeting room, a conference space, and our dorms for the full rundown in the dorms, no photos or engaging with residents unless they approach you. Our intensive programs are rigorous, and participants remain private until they are ready. Follow me, Tiana."

"You can call me Tia," I offer quietly.

"Tia, it is," he says, smiling. We walk down a pristine hallway, white walls adorned with flower paintings. Through a glass door, I glimpse a woman speaking on stage, another beside her. Pausing, I hear, "This is our healing session for physical abuse. Please set down your workbooks; we'll share names and hometowns." A blonde woman meets my eyes, smiling as she gently closes the door. I wince, hoping I didn't intrude.

Hurrying to catch Collin, we pass a closed door with a sign: *GROUP SESSION: ADDICTIONS REVERSED, 10:00 A.M.–12:00 P.M. PLEASE DO NOT ENTER AFTER 10:00.* At the hallway's end, an open door reveals a meadow of wildflowers framed by trees. A sign above reads: *IT'S GOING TO BE OK.* Hope stirs, pulling me back to Collin's voice.

"This is a group session room," he says, gesturing to the last room on the right. "After you, Tia."

"It's beautiful," I say, stepping inside.

"Thank you," Collin replies. "We strive for a peaceful environment for our community."

"Community?" I ask, curious.

"Yes," he says. "Here, we build a family bond, redefining what connection means."

"That's amazing," I say, my eyes drifting to the meadow through a bay window.

Collin notices. "Breathtaking, right? It was my favorite when I first came here." He flashes a smile. "Let's take a closer look."

"Okay," I agree, following him outside.

"This room's class is a great starting point, Tia," he says as we exit. "You share only what you're comfortable with, but we encourage openness. It's the foundation, unless you join our intensive residential programs. We offer free classes on anger management, sex addiction, substance abuse, OCD, and more for anyone seeking healing."

"Free?" I ask, stunned.

"Yes," he says warmly. "Community supporters fund our programs. You only pay for books and commit to your chosen program. No absences or tardiness allowed, which ensures stability for members facing fears or trust issues. Make sense?"

"Yes," I whisper, my heart soaring. A place that cares? It feels unreal. "It's so peaceful here," I say, gazing at the meadow.

"That's the goal," Collin says. "Thank you for saying that."

"It's hard to believe it's free," I admit. "Nothing's free. What's the catch?"

"No catch," he assures me. "We're here to help." As we pass buildings, sitting areas, and a pool where Collin waves to a woman, likely his wife, comforting a crying girl, I see myself here. Her playful smirk confirms my guess. We return to the foyer.

"I hope this answered your questions, Tia," Collin says, handing me a folder. "Thanks for booking ahead of your 11:30 slot was a mystery without a name." He opens the folder, revealing forms and a flyer for an *OPEN HOUSE* in bold letters, featuring the Rusty Bumper. "Two weeks from today, 6:00 p.m., dinner included. Fill these out if you return."

"Thank you, Collin," I say sincerely. "I'll call next week."

He shakes my hand, his eyes steady. "Thanks for coming, Tia. I mean it."

"I appreciate it," I reply, turning away. As I open the door, warmth and peace envelop me, unlike anything I've known. Stepping into the spring air, I hope this place will change me.

Open House at the Rusty Bumper

The parking lot buzzes, packed with cars, nothing like two weeks ago. Valets dart around, a sign reading *FREE VALET*. "Sweet," I mutter, but my car's a mess. I scramble to shove trash into a McDonald's bag, tossing it in the back. Too late, a valet opens my door, grinning. I force a smile, grab my handbag, and step out, mortified.

"Good evening, ma'am," he says cheerfully. "Welcome to the Rusty Bumper."

Ma'am? Do I look that old? "Thank you," I say cautiously.

"Please, head on in," he gestures to a red carpet leading to the door.

There it is, peace, washing over me as I enter the foyer. It could hold a hundred people. But so many faces! Panic flares what now? Too late. Collin spots me, waving, standing beside that radiant woman.

"Hi, Tia!" he calls, remembering my name.

I'm committed now. "Hi, Collin," I wave back, approaching. A table displays name tags, fresh flowers, and white tablecloths. My name tag, professionally printed, catches my eye. "That's my name," I say, surprised.

"After our talk last week, I made you one," Collin says proudly. "You seemed certain you'd be here."

"That's so kind," I say, touched.

"My pleasure. Meet my wife, Alexa," he says, as she smiles warmly.

"Hello," I stammer, awed by her beauty.

"Nice to meet you," Alexa says, hugging me tightly. The embrace feels real, despite being strangers. "It's great to meet you, too," I say, stumbling back, fidgeting with my purse. If she notices, she doesn't show it.

"Let me walk you in," Alexa says, her joy infectious. We enter the large room from two weeks ago, where that kind woman closed the door. "We have a seat for you, Tia," she says, motioning to a table. "This is Lucy, who's been with us for years. She helps new members acclimate and handles onboarding interviews. I hope you'll connect tonight."

Lucy, petite and striking, all five feet of her, stands to greet me. "I'm Lucy," she says, gripping my hand with crystal-blue eyes sparkling.

"Your eyes are beautiful," I blurt, unable to hold back.

"Thank you, Tia! Great to meet you," she says, smiling. I shake her hand, returning the warmth, feeling the first threads of connection in this place of healing.

"Excuse me, I'll step to the ladies' room and be right back," Lucy says kindly. "I was waiting for you, Tia."

"Sorry," I murmur, embarrassed.

"No worries," she assures me. "I just didn't want to miss you. Be right back."

I settle at the round table, set for ten, adorned with a white tablecloth and fresh flowers like the entry. Silverware nestles in linen napkins, and water glasses drip condensation onto the cloth. This open house feels grand, belying the humble *Rusty Bumper* sign, a name that conjures a rundown shack, not this haven. Who named it that?

People pass, smiling and introducing themselves. Lucy returns, her warmth easing my nerves. "Thanks for waiting, Tia," she says.

Michelle Pentifallo

"No problem," I reply, louder than intended, my cheeks flushing. Lucy's smile softens, but she pauses as the event begins, touching my forearm and mouthing, *I'll tell you later*. We're in VIP seats, amazing!

Music swells, and a voice booms over the microphone. "Welcome to our annual Open House!" The room erupts in claps and whistles.

"I'm DeShawn, and I'm thrilled you're here!" the speaker says, his joyful confidence infectious. Applause continues. "Thank you! Please, take a seat." He gestures gracefully. "You're too generous! I'm DeShawn, clean for 17 years, and your speaker tonight." Cheers flare briefly. "Before joining the Rusty Bumper three years ago, I was a global motivational speaker, wrote books, and earned a degree in social therapy. Now, I'm Vice President of Community Group Awareness. I'm blessed to be here and excited for tonight. Servers will bring food soon—enjoy! We'll resume in 40 minutes, and I'll share more about our team and the lives we touch." He exits to roaring praise.

Conversations bloom around me. Lucy turns my way. "So, Tia, how'd you find us?"

"My friend Samantha," I say. "She's changed so much since coming here. I thought it might help me, too."

"That's phenomenal!" Lucy beams. "I know Samantha well; she's so sweet. I was in one of her classes, and we got close. It's special to meet someone who's walked with her, since she's lost touch with many from her past."

Before I can reply, a server in black appears. "Ma'am, steak or chicken?"

"Chicken, please," I say, wincing at "ma'am" again. He sets the plate down gently. Lucy's chatting with someone else now. Did she think I was rude? I glance her way; her smile reassures me. All's well.

"Tia, meet Amber," Lucy says, turning back. "She's our resident nurse and a former member of our sex addiction group."

I freeze. Did she just say that out loud? Mortified, I force a smile as Amber waves brightly. "Nice to meet you, Tia!" she calls over the noise.

I wave back, stunned. No secrets here, I guess. Strange, but... freeing?

Music cues DeShawn's return. "Hello, guests, family, and Rusty Bumper community," he says. "Enjoy your meal and keep eating as we dive in. More about me: I've been here three years with my wife, Jessica, and our two children. We've been happily married for seven years. I have three older kids from a prior marriage, ruined by my addictions to alcohol, drugs, and anything for a fix. I followed my father's path, and his father's, a generational mess I had to break. Thanks to the Lord of Light and the Rusty Bumper, I'm here." Cheers erupt.

"Thank you," DeShawn continues. "Losing my father eight years ago hit hard. His letter showed me I hadn't forgiven him, and it tore at my heart. I couldn't love myself or others. I spent a year speaking globally on forgiveness and grief, writing books, but not living it. I nearly drank again unacceptable. Collin and Alexa, who founded the Rusty Bumper, got me into their program. I'm a changed man, ready to pay it forward. We all have stories here, none perfect, none unscathed. This isn't rehab, it's a new beginning!" He gestures to a woman across the room.

A spotlight finds her, dimming the room. "I'm Sheila," she says calmly, her voice drawing us in. "DeShawn's ex-wife and the mother of his three older children. Nine years ago, I came here after losing my job when someone took their life. It shattered me. Through group therapy, I faced my codependency, marrying an addict, and playing the victim after our divorce. I relied on everyone but the Lord of Light. I hit rock bottom financially, emotionally, and spiritually before walking through these doors. Now, I run a successful business, my adult kids thrive, and I mentor others here on freedom from codependency. Visit my table tonight." Gentle applause follows as she steps down.

The spotlight shifts to a tall, striking woman with dark highlights against a crimson backdrop. "I'm Victoria, grief counselor and group therapist," she says. "I came here after losing my best friend in a tragic accident. I blamed myself for years until a friend, here for marriage counseling, introduced me to the Rusty Bumper and my husband, Ethan." The light swings to a man in the VIP section, waving. "We start with shame, guilt, insecurities, and loss—issues you can't outrun. Hiding them builds walls. Visit my table for death and grief recovery." She

Rusty Bumper Final Death

gestures to a corner. "Now, welcome Dr. Sanchez!" The crowd roars louder than ever.

Dr. Sanchez, mid-height in a stunning gold gown, steps forward. "I've been here since day one," she says. "I dreamed of helping people, wondering if anyone would walk through our doors. Tonight marks our 20th anniversary, made possible by your support." She waves, and the crowd stands, applauding endlessly. "Thank you! Please, sit. Meet Ruth, who's been with us a year."

A young woman, unnoticed until now, stands beside her. Dr. Sanchez hugs her. "Ruth, how has the Rusty Bumper helped you?"

Ruth's face reddens. Dr. Sanchez whispers, *You got this*, hugging her tighter. Ruth smiles, taking the microphone. "I'm Ruth Mendoza," she says softly. "I've lived here a year. I arrived in crisis, my wrists and half my face bandaged from cutting myself with glass." She pauses, clearing her throat, a tear glinting. Dr. Sanchez steps closer, but Ruth signals she's okay. "I don't recall it all—dreamlike. My parents were done with me. My father controlled everything; my mother enabled him. With nowhere to turn, they called the Rusty Bumper. Days later, I moved in for intensive counseling, recovery, and physical therapy. Eight months in, my parents joined me. We're repairing our relationship through family recovery groups." Dr. Sanchez gently takes the mic.

"This is one of our success stories," she says. Visit my table to learn about family therapy. Now, welcome Alex and Nadia Rutherford, our biggest donors." The spotlight shifts to a couple on stage. Nadia, with radiant red hair and a slight pregnancy bump, smiles as Alex, blond and tall, kisses her forehead. They approach the podium hand-in-hand.

What a stunning pair, I think, assuming they've had an easy life. Alex speaks. "Nadia and I welcome you to a place my wife envisioned after we met. She grew up in foster homes, facing a difficult life, and dreamed of creating a haven for others like her. I won't tell her story, let's hear from Nadia, the Rusty Bumper's dreamer." The room leaps to its feet, the sound deafening. Smiles, whistles, and cheers fill every corner, joy pulsing through the crowd. I stand, swept up in the energy. Who is this woman?

"Oh my!" Nadia exclaims into the microphone, nearly shouting over the roaring crowd. "Thank you! Wow, thank you!" She wipes a tear from her eye, smiling and waving. "Wow," she says softer, "thank you." Reaching for a tissue, she dabs her cheeks. Clearing her throat, she continues, "Wow, thank you. I didn't expect that." The audience quiets, settling back into their seats, murmurs fading.

"Let me gather myself," Nadia says. "I'm Nadia Rutherford, and I'm so blessed to be here tonight to share about the Rusty Bumper. When we dreamed this up, we had no idea it would grow this big. We're grateful for each of you. I was a young woman, unloved and insecure, working my last show at a strip club to fund a move to New York for modeling. As you see, that didn't happen." A man shouts, "You look like a model!" Laughter ripples through the room.

"That's my friend Dr. Pithers, who flirted with me once, long ago," Nadia teases, giggling. "Another story for another day. Many ask, 'Why the Rusty Bumper?' It came from my old car that night, worn with a rusty bumper. I looked at it and thought, we're all like that bumper battered, needing a fresh start. It stuck when we planned this place. It's more inviting than 'Rutherford Treatment Center,' don't you think?" Light laughter spreads.

"We invite you to visit our tables on suicide prevention, unwanted pregnancies, family trauma, grief relief, and intensive therapy groups. The grounds are open, except the dorms, to protect resident privacy. We hope you'll see our staff's impact and open your checkbooks. We'll provide the pen!" She winks, and the crowd stands, applauding her journey. I was wrong about her easy life. I'd love to talk, but she's probably too busy. I clap loudly, joining the praise.

DeShawn returns to the podium. "A few notes before we mingle. Dessert's in the back-right group therapy room, with coffee, tea, and water. Please take your belongings as we clear this space. I'll see you at our table. Thank you and farewell." The lights brighten, and conversations spark anew.

"Hey, Tia!" I turn to see Collin as I head into the hall. He's accepting a check from a man. "Thank you, Roger," Collin says excitedly. "Your donation makes this possible."

"Thanks to you, my business and marriage didn't collapse," Roger replies, flashing me a smile before heading to the dessert room.

"Hi, Collin," I say. "Thanks for inviting me. The stories of changed lives were incredible."

"I'm so glad you came," he says, his warm smile returning. "Stay and meet our staff, you'll love them." He seems ready to hug, but offers a handshake instead. "See you in class, I hope." He joins Alexa, guiding her out with a hand on her back.

I want a love like that, I think wistfully.

"Tia!" Lucy's familiar voice calls. "Thanks for coming. It was great meeting you." She hugs me, then gestures to a woman nearby. "Meet Patrice, who leads our eating disorder and OCD classes. She's amazing."

"Hello, Tia," Patrice says, shaking my hand. "Nice to meet you."

"You too," I reply.

"Wish I had more time, but I need to get to my table," Patrice says, hurrying off. "Hope to see you around."

"Thanks, Lucy, for making me feel welcome," I say. "I'm heading out."

"Sure? We've got great dessert," she offers.

"I appreciate it, but I need to get home," I say.

"Okay, I hope to see you soon," Lucy says, hugging me again.

"I think you will," I reply, half-smiling, and head to the parking lot. I hand my valet ticket 622 to the attendant, who fetches my car. As it pulls up, I notice its rusty bumper. Laughing softly, I slide behind the wheel and drive away.

MONTHS LATER

"Hi, everyone. I'm Leslie, your group leader today," the woman says warmly. "This starter class at the Rusty Bumper can feel overwhelming. No one knows your struggles yet, as you haven't chosen a specific program. That comes after about a month, when we'll find the best path for you. Let's go around the circle, sharing your name and why you're here, if you're comfortable. We'll start there." She points to me.

My stomach drops. "Um, I didn't think I'd have to talk if I didn't want to," I say shyly.

"Absolutely, you don't have to," Leslie assures me. "This is a safe space, and we want you to be comfortable. If you're ready, just share your name and anything else you're okay with. Sound good?"

"Okay," I say hesitantly. "I'm Denise, and I'm here because my husband died."

"I'm sorry, Denise," Leslie says gently. "It's nice to meet you. We're glad you're here." Smiles surround me. Why are they smiling? I just said my husband died. What's that about?

Leslie moves to the next person, and I'm off the hook. Across the room, a sign above a window framed by spring flowers reads: *THIS IS THE FIRST DAY TO*

Michelle Pentifallo

BEGIN A NEW DAY. Sunlight streams in, illuminating a woman outside, her face tilted to the sun, arms raised in joy. I want that freedom again, I think somberly.

Applause jolts me back. I clap for someone I don't know, feeling obliged. "Hi, I'm Julia," a woman says. "I've been here a few months. Today's my last day in this class, and I'm moving to Healing from Addictions."

"That's amazing, Julia," Leslie says sincerely, turning to the next person.

"I'm Angela," another says. "I'm staying in the dorms. I came a month ago to face the fear of being raped in college. I never dealt with it. My friend Heather invited me. She was helped here. I hope it helps me."

That's heavy, I think. Maybe we could talk. She might understand my shame about Josiah. I didn't know he was a pedophile when we married. I was furious at Julie, but it was Josiah's fault. He got help but died in prison. What a mess.

I tune out the next person, staring at the woman outside, raising her face to the sun. Who is she? The light wraps her like a shield, untouchable. I smile faintly, then glance at the person opposite me, sharing their story.

Rusty Bumper Final Death

Samantha, you did it! I raise my face to the sun. As the sun shines through the trees onto my face, I can feel a sense of relief. I feel the victory of so many years with my hands held high to the sky. *Wow! This feels safe.* So many generations before me struggled with the same demons. The same demons that followed them had followed me, but not anymore. They are gone. It took years of focus and hard work, and trust. Trust that the Lord of Light would take me to a new place. A place where I could be at peace in the world. A place where I would no longer be looking over my shoulder or feeling the presence of darkness behind me, staring at me. This is a new place, with trees and limbs and moss and vines all around me. I'm no longer afraid that the vines will entangle me and take me down. *Victory is mine!! I have won, and the lord of darkness is defeated!*

Who's that?" I hear a voice in the distance coming toward me.

Hey Sam! My head turns to see. *Tia! What?* And I run to her.

We all have a story, we all have a past, we've all been in a place where we felt just like a *rusty bumper*. And we all have a choice to make. Are we going to stay in that place, or are we going to rise, seek the Lord of Light, and shine our brightest?

You can take back your driver's seat and truly enjoy the ride.

THE END

www.ingramcontent.com/pod-product-compliance
Lightning Source LLC
LaVergne TN
LVHW041745060526
838201LV00046B/913